Praise for *Lady Night*

"I love it when a sequel not only matches the first book but surpasses it! It's such a pleasure to see and with how much I loved Amulet of Wishes, I didn't know if this one could. But it did. Oh, it did!"

> — Cat Bowser, author of Mirrors and Ashes: A Snow White Retelling.

"Simultaneously a mystery and adventure, Lady Night will keep you guessing until the end. This is an edge-of-the-seat sequel that has me begging for the next book."

> —Talli L. Morgan, author of The Windermere Tales.

"Chronicles of the Guardians is a lovely, entertaining series and I was excited to pick up this second installment."

> — A. E. Bennett, author of the Serrulata Saga.

Chronicles of the Guardians

Lady Night

Rita A. Rubin

Chronicles of the Guardians, Lady Night.

Cover design by Emily's World of Design.

ISBN: 978-0-6450928-3-7

Also by Rita A. Rubin

Chronicles of the Guardians

Amulet of Wishes

Content Warnings

- Violence
- Blood and mild gore
- Sexual references
- Depiction of panic attacks
- Mentions of parental death
- Implied childhood sexual abuse

PROLOGUE

The red-eyed man stood on the footpath outside, a shard of glass wrapped in cloth and string, tucked under one arm, watching as the fire consumed *Blackwood's Spells, Potions and Magical Objects*, with a detached sort of fascination. Seeing the fire and the smoke climb into the night sky reminded him of another night, many years ago. Another building—a cottage—set alight.

Even fighting the Elf woman, Blackwood, just now had brought back memories of a fight with another Wood Elf. She'd even had the same black hair, although she hadn't been a mage like this one.

"Who are you?! Answer me!" she had screamed at him right after he had cut her husband's throat.

"No one," he had replied.

Only that wasn't really true. He wasn't no one, had never been no one—no matter how much he might have wished to be at times.

Being no one meant that you were inconsequential, just another face in the crowd. No one special. No one to be remembered.

Draken had never been that. Whether it was *"abomination"* or *"cursed"* or *"kin slayer"*, from the moment he had been born—no, even before that—he had always been someone.

The blaze had started to garner attention. All around him, people were beginning to emerge from the surrounding buildings. Lights were being lit and there were shouts of alarm, calls for the Town Guards, and help to put the fire out.

Draken took this as his cue to leave. He turned on his heel, away from the burning shop and mid-step, he burst into red flame until there was nothing left.

He reappeared, moments later in another burst of red fire, completely unharmed, in a cold and dark corridor. The old fort had been abandoned for many years now. It had been built during a time when blood-thirsty creatures known as daemons roamed the lands. The royal family back then had often used this fort as a refuge from the daemons. High up on the mountains, it was a perfectly defensible structure.

However, no one had set foot in this fort since the daemons had been banished by Aryanna Vir Fortis more than a hundred years ago.

Which made it the perfect place for Draken's hideout.

His footsteps echoed against the stone floor as he made his way down the long corridor. With each step he took, the torch sconces on the walls lit up, casting a flickering glow and long shadows.

The great doors of the second floor's study were flung open as Draken entered. The chandelier that hung in the middle of the ceiling lit itself, making the room more visible.

Draken seldom used any of the rooms in this fort, only this study and the bedroom across the hall. It was spacious, with a circular floor and floor-to-ceiling window. Two identical oak desks occupied the east and west walls. The brass handles on the drawers had been carved to look like the snarling face of a bear. On one of the desks sat a miniature pencil portrait of a smiling woman holding a small boy.

Draken stepped over to the desk by the west wall and set down the item he had taken from Aurelia Blackwood. He unwrapped the cloth to reveal a jagged glass shard, almost as long as his forearm. His reflection was clear in the glass.

Draken had been searching for this shard for close to a year now. Looking for the one he knew would be hiding it, but they had proven to be surprisingly elusive. When he finally tracked down the young woman who had been in possession of the shard, it had been to find out that she no longer had it. The woman refused to tell him where the shard was and Draken had been forced to resort to some admittedly unsavoury methods of persuasion. Soon enough, she told him that the shard was at a shop called *Blackwood's Spells, Potions and Magical Objects* in Florintsone

Lifting the glass shard from the desk, Draken carried it over to a tall object by the window concealed by a purple cloth. Gripping the cloth with one hand, he pulled it away to reveal a mirror.

It was large and oval in shape, with a black, metallic frame. By all means, it looked like any ordinary mirror. Only the glass was marred with cracks. Jagged lines splintered across the reflective surface, and in some places, the glass was even missing.

Draken looked down at the shard he was holding and then scanned the mirror until—*ah*—there it was. A missing piece that was exactly the same size and shape as the shard he held in his hand.

He fitted the shard into the gap. It went in easily, like fitting a jigsaw piece into its correct place. Draken watched as the mirror lit up with a pale, red glow and for the briefest of moments, he caught a glimpse of something in the glass: reddish skies, a dead, grey landscape. Hunched shapes skulked around in the shadows, before it all disappeared and Draken was left gazing at his own reflection in the cracked glass.

There were now only two pieces missing.

"Excellent work", came the voice in Draken's head, a hissing amalgamation of many different voices, men's and women's . . . even children's. The first time Draken had ever heard it, he had wanted to tear his ears off and beat his head against a wall. Anything so that he wouldn't have to hear that disturbing voice anymore.

"My, my, was that actually a compliment?" He responded.

"Your job is almost finished," the voice continued, as if Draken hadn't just spoken. *"Find the next two shards."* The voice went

quiet and Draken knew that he wouldn't be hearing from it again anytime soon.

"Hmph. What was even the point of dropping in just to tell me that?" He muttered to himself.

He knew full well what it was he needed to do, he didn't need to be reminded like a forgetful youth.

With a careless gesture of his hand, the purple cloth picked itself up off the floor to cover the mirror once again.

Draken stepped over to the window. With his hands clasped behind his back, he surveyed the view of the night sky, growing lighter with the impending dawn. The mountains, the forests below and the specks of light from the hamlet by the river.

Draken couldn't wait to see it all destroyed.

But first, he thought. *I need the remaining shards. And then, the boy.*

1

Four Months Later

It was sometime around midnight when Derek Draco yawned.

"Oi," said Jared Regalias, shoving him playfully. "No dozing on the job."

Derek shot him a glare. "I wasn't dozing."

"You were yawning. Dozing was imminent."

"It was not."

"Yes, it was."

"You two sound like my brothers arguing," said Arabelle Aloria, Jared's cousin. She was sitting across from them on her own bedroll, her arms wrapped around her knees. The icy breeze ruffled the fur lining of her cloak and blew the golden-blonde strands of hair that had come loose from her braid into her face.

"I doubt we could ever pass for brothers," Jared said with a dismissive wave of his hand. "I'm much more handsome, after all."

Derek shoved his elbow into his friend's stomach. Although he wasn't wrong about the two of them looking nothing alike. Where Jared was all soft brown skin, warm brown eyes, brown curls and dimpled grins, Derek was fair with raven black hair that looked like it needed a good brush, and sky-blue eyes.

The three of them sat together on the snowy hilltop not too far from Serpent's Cove, and close enough that they could smell the salty tang of the ocean on the wind and hear the distant sounds of waves breaking against the shores.

It had been four months since the death of Durbash, one of the most notorious slave traders in all of the four lands. With his death had come the assumption that the dregs of his crew and slave trading business would simply wither away into nothing.

That assumption had been proven wrong.

Rall—one of Durbash's cronies and his self-appointed successor—had also proven to be just as elusive as Durbash had been. It was only thanks to an inside tip-off that the Guardians—Aloseria's sworn protectors—had learned that Rall and his crew would be making a private trade tonight at Serpent's Cove.

All they had to do now was wait for the right time to act.

Soon enough, Derek heard the familiar sound of wing beats in the air. They looked up in time to see a pale yellow dragon, no bigger than a horse, land in the snow in front of them. A moment later, the dragon Changed into a tall, young man with long, golden-brown hair pulled into a ponytail. The man was Darus Flynn,

Derek's adoptive father.

Another dragon landed next to Darus, this one with red skin, and Changed into Lila Delron, a petite-looking young woman with auburn hair.

For Derek, seeing a dragon Change into a human was not an uncommon sight. It was something that Derek himself could do, as could Jared and Arabelle and many of the people from their home city of Ember. It was what made them Guardians; the ability to Change into dragons through the use of enchanted rings that had been passed down to them from the very first Guardians hundreds of years ago.

Darus and Lila strode towards them, snow crunching under their boots. They were both dressed in the uniform of the Guardians—a brown leather vest over a gold shirt and armguards, with the addition of cloaks to keep them warm. Derek, Arabelle and Jared were dressed similarly—only they wore the blue shirts of rookie Guardians instead of gold.

"All right, kids," Darus announced happily. "It's time to go to work."

Rall and a few of his men met the buyers by the road just outside of their Serpent's Cove hideout. The buyers were two men, the golden brown tone of their skin gave them away as Ishlavan and the make of their clothes suggested they were merchants. Although one of the men looked more like a bodyguard than a merchant, with his tall and imposing stature. His head was bare with the tattoo of some kind of bird etched onto the side of his skull. They stood huddled by a closed cart hitched to two piebald horses.

So far, neither party had noticed the Guardians hidden in the shadows of the treetops.

"You're lucky hardly anyone ever comes by this road," Rall said upon greeting. "It's risky, us leavin' our hideout like this."

The shortest of the two men, wearing rings on all ten of his fingers, smiled diplomatically. "Forgive us for the inconvenience," he said in heavily accented Aloserian. "We would have made the journey to you, but it is likely our cart would have gotten stuck in the snow."

Rall shrugged. His expression unconcerned. "Here's the four slaves ya wanted."

He stepped aside to allow one of his men to bring forward four individuals—three women and one man. All human and all Aloserian. They all wore the same tattered, rough spun clothing that provided them with little protection from the cold. They had their hands and feet shackled and attached to a single length of chain that one bandit used to usher them along like dogs on a leash.

The man with the ringed fingers stepped forward to consider them. He even took the chin of the one closest between his fingers and turned her face from side to side as if he were inspecting the quality of a fruit.

Finally, the merchant took a step back and said, "Yes, I think they will do." He gestured to his companion. "*Bahmir, poystik yiv shet volzt,*" he ordered. "Bahmir, put them in the back of the cart."

Wordlessly, the larger man, Bahmir, took the chain and keys from the bandit and walked the prisoners over to the back of the cart where they were loaded inside.

"Thank you. They will make fine workers back home," said the merchant with a pleasant smile.

"Glad to hear it." Rall held out an expectant hand. "Now, the payment?"

"Of course." The merchant reached inside his cloak and produced a coin purse, bulging at the seams, and tossed it at Rall.

Something sliced through the air, catching the purse midair and pinning it to the trunk of a tree. The fabric tore and dozens of gold coins spilled out onto the snow.

"I think this has gone on long enough."

Like spectres materialising out of the darkness, the Guardians moved to surround the bandits and the merchants, Derek and Darus, Lila, Jared and Arabelle among them.

Rall and his bandits drew their weapons while the merchants looked around at the new arrivals in panic.

Derek saw Rall take in the appearance of Derek, Jared, and Arabelle in particular. His eyes narrowed. "Not you bloody brats again," he growled.

Derek waved the sword in his hand. "Nice to see you again, too."

"Lay down your arms," Lila demanded in a clear, hard voice. "And give yourselves up. This doesn't have to end in a fight."

"Ha! Ya think we're gonna give ourselves up just like that 'cause

10

you ask all nice?" Rall sneered. "Well, you're dead wrong. Get 'em!"

The bandits rushed the Guardians, and the quiet woods were quickly filled with shouts and the sounds of ringing steel.

One bandit charged at Derek. He raised his own sword—the shortsword of blue steel that had once belonged to his father—to meet the bandit's blade.

Derek managed to push the bandit back, parrying a few more strikes before he could get under the bandit's guard and aim a kick to his gut.

The bandit doubled over, and Derek slammed the hilt of his sword against the bandit's temple with enough force to knock him unconscious. Their orders had been not to kill anyone if they could help it.

As the bandit fell face first into the snow, Derek heard the pounding of hooves against the snow and spun around to see that the Ishalvan merchants had taken the opportunity to escape, their cart clattering down the road at high speed.

Sheathing his sword, Derek took off after them. Of course, he knew there was no chance of him catching up to them on foot, so as he raced down the road, he reached beneath his shirt collar and unclipped his ring from the chain around his neck. He slipped the black band onto one of his fingers and Changed, turning from a boy to a black and blue dragon in the blink of an eye.

He spread his great blue wings and launched himself into the air. He was able to gain ground that he never would have on foot, and it wasn't long before he had caught up with the merchant's cart.

Bahmir hung onto the side of the cart while the man with the ringed fingers sat up front, flicking the reins and urging the horses on. It didn't take long for Bahmir to spot Derek and climb onto the roof of the cart. He drew a crossbow from beneath his cloak and took aim.

Derek rolled to the side in midair as the crossbow's bolt shot past him. He didn't even give the man time to load another bolt, before diving towards him and digging his claws into the front of Bahmir's cloak, Derek lifted him off of the cart and threw him over the side.

He didn't bother to see where or how the man landed before he turned his attention to the one in the driver's seat. Changing, he sat himself down next to the merchant, who could do no more than let out a startled shout when Derek appeared next to him, and knocked him out with a strike to the back of the neck.

As soon as the merchant went limp, Derek took up the reins, pulling on them until the horses came to a halt.

Everything seemed to fall quiet, only the horses' huffing breaths breaking the silence. Derek slumped against the seat to catch his breath.

A low creak from behind him was the only warning he had to move out of the way in time to avoid being split in half by an axe.

It buried itself in the wood of the cart with a loud *crack*. The horses whinnied, startled by the noise, but thankfully, didn't bolt.

Derek looked up to see Bahmir standing on the roof of the cart.

How the hell did he catch up so quickly?

As Bahmir dislodged his axe, Derek leapt from the cart, landing on the snow packed ground. He unsheathed his sword, spinning around to face his attacker at the same time Bahmir jumped from the roof of the cart and landed with a heavy thud.

"Is there any chance you'll drop your weapon and let me arrest you if I ask nicely?"

The man lunged towards him.

"Didn't think so," Derek muttered to himself just before their weapons clashed.

Such a heavy battleaxe should have at least cracked Derek's shortsword. But his sword had been enchanted long ago to withstand even the harshest of attacks from the toughest of weapons without even receiving so much as a dent.

They disengaged. Almost straight away, Derek lashed out with his sword, only managing to open up a red gash along Bahmir's cheekbone when the older man moved out of the way.

Bahmir responded with a well-aimed kick to Derek's ribs, knocking him off his feet and sending him skidding across the ground.

Derek regained himself in time to duck out of the way of Bahmir's axe. The blade sunk into the snow instead and in that split second before Bahmir lifted his axe from the ground, Derek raised his sword in an arc that sheered straight through Bahmir's extended arm, just below the wrist.

Blood gushed and Bahmir loosed an agonised cry, the first

sound Derek had heard from him. He fell to his knees, clutching the stump where his hand used to be to his chest, staining the front of his clothes red.

Derek pushed himself to his feet and Bahmir turned to look at him with amber eyes swirling with fury. He started to speak in Ishlavan, "*Tik kebat—*"

Derek didn't let him finish. He struck the man hard across the temple and sent him sprawling into the snow.

His arm continued to bleed profusely, but he would live, so long as Derek brought him back to the others in time.

"Derek!"

He looked up to see that Jared and Arabelle had joined him.

"You two certainly took your time," he said.

"Sorry, but we had our own mess to clean up," Arabelle said. "Darus is really pissed at you for running off on your own like that, by the way."

"Would he have rather I let them get away with the prisoners?" He gestured to the cart behind him.

Jared came up to where Bahmir was lying unconscious, his blood staining the snow beneath him. "Derek . . . you didn't . . .?"

"He'll live." *Probably.*

Arabelle walked over to the back of the cart, trying the door only to find it was locked.

"Maybe there's a key—" Jared began, but Arabelle had already proceeded to kick the rickety door down. It fell from its hinges with a loud clatter.

"Or just knock it down with brute force? Whatever works."

Inside, the fear-stricken faces of Rall's captives peered up at them from where they were all huddled in a corner.

"It's all right," Arabelle said to them. "You're all safe now."

They regrouped near the entrance to Serpent's Cove. Rall and his bandits and the Ishlavan merchants had all been rounded up and loaded into the wagon the captives had previously occupied. They would be on the way to Black Rock prison the next day to face trial for their crimes.

Only one bandit had still been left standing free, the informant who had told them all about tonight's trade. In exchange for helping them capture Rall and his crew, he would be allowed to go free and return to his homeland in Tybenia.

After Derek was finished being scolded by Darus for taking off on his own, he went to join Arabelle and Jared, who were busy freeing the captives from their chains, and not only those they had rescued from the wagon, but others who had been held at the slavers' hideout. While Jared worked on unlocking them with the key that had been taken off one of the bandits, Arabelle handed them thick blankets to wrap themselves in.

"What's going to happen to us now?" asked a young man, with unruly dark hair and a scruff of a beard. The left side of his face was mottled with bruises.

"You'll be taken to Rosewold, which is the closest town from here," Arabelle explained as she handed Derek a blanket to give to the trembling Dark Elf girl.

"You'll be given food, water and accommodation there while they work to get you all home," added Jared, freeing the last of the prisoners from their shackles.

At the mention of the word home, the Dark Elf girl started trembling harder, tears streaking down the grey skin of her cheeks.

"What's the matter?" Derek asked her, keeping his voice soft.

"M-My family," the girl stammered through her tears. "It's been—I-I have not seen them in three years. I wonder . . . if they will even remember me."

He noticed that both of the girl's skinny wrists were adorned with silver cuffs with odd markings that Derek knew to be Magic Mufflers, instruments that inhibited the powers of mages, making it impossible for them to use magic unless commanded to.

"They'll remember you," he said with conviction. "Your family would have thought of you every day since the moment you were taken from them. Because you never forget the ones you love. No matter how long they've been gone."

Fresh tears welled in the girl's eyes. She bowed her head, a lock of tangled, red hair fell into her face. "Thank you," she whispered.

They were startled by a woman making a sound somewhere between a squeak and a scream. Derek looked over and saw that she was staring at Jared with wide eyes.

"You—aren't you the Prince?" she asked almost reverently.

"Um . . . Yes?"

A few of them gasped and the man with the scruffy beard even dropped to his knees in front of Jared.

There were whispers of, "The Prince saved us!" and "He held my wrist. *The Prince* actually *held my wrist.*"

Jared was beginning to look more and more pleased with all of the attention.

At least until Arabelle flicked him in the ear. "Careful now, wouldn't want your head to get too big for that tiara you like to wear sometimes."

"It is not a *tiara,*" Jared protested, indignant. "It's a *circlet.*"

Later, Derek, Arabelle and Jared stood off to the side, watching as Lila and other Guardians prepared to escort the now freed men and women to the town of Rosewold while Darus and another Guardian discussed something by the wagon now holding the merchants and Rall and his bandits.

"What day is it?" Jared asked after a while.

"The sixth, I think," said Derek. "Why?"

With a smile, he said to Arabelle. "We should make it home just in time."

"*Shh,*" Arabelle hissed.

Derek looked at the two of them curiously. "In time for what?"

"Nothing!" they said in unison.

Derek frowned, but they had both become suddenly very interested in the tree canopy above their heads. He knew they were hiding something from him and he would have pressed further on the matter if it wasn't for the arrival of Darus.

"Excellent work out there tonight." He sounded more than a

little pleased. And why not? Their assignment was a success. No one had been killed or seriously injured—not including Bahmir—they had captured Rall and freed his prisoners.

"Now, who's ready to head home?"

2

The air was like ice that morning, but wrapped up in his cocoon of blankets, Derek was pleasantly warm. So warm, in fact, that he felt as if he would never get out of bed for as long as he lived.

There was a knocking at his door. "Derek, you lazy bugger, it's almost ten o'clock."

Groaning, Derek pulled the blankets over his head in an attempt to drown out Darus's voice. Sadly, it didn't work.

"Breakfast is ready and if you don't get up before it gets cold, I'll give it all to Daisy." As if to enforce the point, he could hear the aforementioned dog making snuffling sounds outside of his door.

Once Darus appeared to have left, Derek sat up, disturbing his blanket cocoon to face the onslaught of frigid air. It was the middle of winter and a permanent chill now clung to the air, even indoors.

Finn, the grey tabby cat, blinked blearily at Derek from where he was curled up at the foot of the bed, his sleep disturbed by Derek's movement.

"At least he didn't threaten to give your food to the dog, so you get to stay in bed," he grumbled.

Finn's response to that was to roll onto his back, stick his paws in the air, and go straight back to sleep.

Once he was dressed, Derek made his way down the stairs and into the kitchen, where the scent of freshly cooked food was heavy in the air. He had expected to find a simple meal of perhaps eggs and toast set out on the table, instead, Derek found the table was laden with all different kinds of dishes. There were fried eggs and crisp, brown toast, as well as strips of bacon glistening with butter, a plate of succulent sausages and even a stack of pancakes drizzled with honey. A carafe of freshly squeezed orange juice stood in the middle of it all.

Darus stood at the stove, brewing himself a pot of coffee and feeding Daisy bits of leftover sausage.

When Darus spotted him standing in the doorway, a broad smile spread across his face, and he opened his arms wide and said, "Happy Birthday!"

It took Derek a moment to register the words before realisation dawned on him. *Ah, that's right.* Today was the ninth of July. His sixteenth birthday.

"That explains the feast then," he said, eyeing the crowded table.

"You can at least try to sound grateful. I spent hours making all of this and waged a valiant battle against Daisy to keep her from eating it all."

"I am grateful. I just . . ."

The look on Darus's face gentled. "I know." He came up to Derek and pulled him in for a hug. Derek let him.

Over the past nine years, birthdays had always been more of a melancholy occasion for Derek, rather than a happy one.

When he was a child, living in the Valley outside of Windfell, his mother and father, Erica and Alexander Draco, always went to great lengths to make his birthday a special day. It was the one day of the year he could have just about anything he wanted. If he wanted to stay up past his bedtime, then he certainly could. His father would even stay up and have pretend sword fights with him. If he wanted sweets for dinner, his mother would go into town to buy him a whole bag full.

Derek had never been starved for affection with his parents, but on his birthday, they would spoil him rotten.

And then they were gone. Killed by a red-eyed stranger on a rainy night nine years ago.

Now, the ninth of July filled him with an ache of loneliness for his father and mother, despite Darus's attempts each year to make it a pleasant day for him.

"I'm speaking at a lecture at the Academy today," Darus explained while they ate. "So it looks like I won't be able to spend the day with you. Sorry."

"It's fine," said Derek. The Academy was where aspiring Guardians were taught everything they needed to know in order to become one of Aloseria's famed heroes. Derek himself had graduated from the Academy at the beginning of the year.

"So, do you have any plans for today?"

"Not really." He thought back to last night, sitting with Jared and Arabelle in the billiard room of the Aloria household. They had both mentioned that they would be busy today. Arabelle said she had to spend the day watching her youngest brother while her parents were both at work and Jared would be helping his Queen mother with redesigning part of the palace gardens.

Neither of them had said a word about Derek's birthday, and he wondered if they even remembered it.

Once they finished their breakfast, Derek cleaned up while Darus disappeared upstairs to get ready for his lecture.

"I'll be home by seven o'clock," he said before leaving. "Make sure you're home by then, too."

"Why?" Derek asked.

Darus winked. "Just make sure."

The day passed by rather uneventfully. Derek spent the rest of the morning tidying up his bedroom, reorganising his books and his wardrobe. After lunch, he did some training in the backyard while Daisy played around in the snow and Finn watched them from the window.

By the time night fell, Derek was curled up by the fire in the lounge, his nose in a book, a cat in his lap, and a dog at his feet.

Darus returned home as soon as the clock struck seven.

"Put that book away and go upstairs and get changed," he announced. "We're going out."

"Where are we going?"

"I can't tell you. You'll just have to wait and see. And make sure to wear something nice."

After changing into his nicest black coat and pale blue button-up shirt, Derek returned downstairs to find Darus already dressed in a startlingly red coat and plum-coloured waistcoat that matched his cravat.

"Really, Derek?" Darus looked him up and down. "Black? Why don't you wear something with a bit more colour?"

"I think you're wearing enough colour for the both of us," he pointed out.

Together, they stepped out into the cold; the snow was beginning to fall again.

"Are you going to tell me where we're going now?" asked Derek as they stepped onto the cobblestone path, bathed in the light from the flaming lamp posts.

"Absolutely not. It's a surprise until we get there."

They walked through the streets of Ember. Aloseria's capital city was not only the largest, but the most colourful. Each house and shop was built with brick and mortar of vibrant shades of reds and blues and pinks and any other colour one could think of.

Now the colourful rooftops were blanketed in white snow, as well as gardens and trees had been stripped of their leaves.

New decorations had also sprung up around the city; wreaths made of pine and bramble adorned front doors. Ribbons and tinsel of green and silver wrapped around lamp posts and fences, the sorts of decorations that came out every year to celebrate the festive season of Nativitas. A time of year where friends and families came together to exchange gifts and eat crackling pork and cinnamon cakes and drink eggnog together.

They passed through the city centre—normally bustling with people and vendors selling their wares, but on a frosty night like tonight, many chose to stay indoors. Derek had thought Darus was bringing him to a diner, but as they crossed into the upper part of the city, walking through the streets lined with lavish, noble households, Derek felt that assumption dwindle.

Just where are we going?

His unspoken question was answered when Derek found them drawing up to the wrought-iron gates of the royal palace. Two Crown Guards stood on either side in their golden armour and blue, capes. Swords were sheathed at their sides, ready to be drawn at any moment to defend the royal family, if necessary.

But when he and Darus approached, one of the Guards wordlessly moved to open the gate, allowing them to pass through onto the palace grounds.

"Why are we at the palace?" he asked.

"Like I told you," Darus answered. "You'll just have to—"

"Wait and see. I know, I know."

When they arrived at the top of the palace's front steps, they were met by Aldred, the elderly footman who had worked in the palace for longer than Derek had been alive.

"Good evening, Master Flynn," Aldred greeted them genially. "Master Draco. And if I might add, Happy Birthday."

"Good evening, Aldred," said Darus. "Is everything in order?"

The look on the footman's face turned slightly mischievous. "Indeed. If you'll follow me, please."

Following Aldred, they were led through the huge foyer with its spotless marble floors and towering ceilings, and up the grand staircase that had banisters so well polished they seemed to shine. They travelled through hallways that had grown familiar to Derek after years of being friends with Jared and being invited to the palace on countless occasions. Despite its sheer size, Derek knew the royal palace almost as well as he knew his own home.

Which was why he knew that Aldred was taking them towards one of the palace's two ballrooms before they even arrived at the white double doors that stretched all the way up to the ceiling.

"We have arrived," Aldred announced rather loudly as he placed a hand upon one of the ornate door handles. As the door eased open and Darus ushered Derek through, they were greeted by a chorus of, *"Surprise!"*

Standing in the middle of the ballroom with its amber painted walls and round tables draped in white cloth, was a gathering of familiar faces.

Jared and Arabelle were the first ones Derek noticed, and he saw that they were joined by Julianna, Jared's older sister, and their parents, the King and Queen. Arabelle's parents, Victor and Amara Aloria, and her brothers, Callum and Amias. There was Lila and Charles Decorus and Veter, the blind mage who crafted the Guardians' rings, and his ferret Familiar, Cornelius. Abigail Perril, the Academy Headmistress and quite a few who Derek had attended the Academy with, such as Rosalie Decorus and William Frain.

Four illuminae crystal chandeliers hung from the high ceilings, bathing the room in a bright, white light. A fire burned in the large, ornate hearth on the other side of the ballroom, warming the air.

"What is this?" Derek asked, and he knew his voice came out sounding just as stunned as he felt.

"It's your birthday celebration," Darus explained cheerfully. "We've all been planning it for a while now, but we thought it would be fun to make it a surprise this year."

A thought occurred to Derek. "Did you really have to give a lecture at the Academy today?"

"I did, but only for an hour. I spent the rest of the day helping Jared and Arabelle get everything ready." Darus put an arm around Derek's shoulders. "Now, come and enjoy the party we so painstakingly put together for you."

The Queen caught him up in a tight embrace and, true to motherly form, lamented on how quickly he was growing up.

"Yes, it seems like just yesterday that Darus first brought you into the palace," said Jared's father, Jonathan. He was smiling, but Derek glimpsed a forlorn look in his eyes and he knew the King was thinking of Derek's father. Jonathan and Alexander had been close friends before Alexander went into his self-imposed exile.

Servants came in soon after, carrying plates of food: flatbreads topped with melted cheese and slices of dried tomato, crisp chips and roast chicken, corn cobs and salads, pastry rolls slathered in cream and cinnamon, raspberry pies and sticky caramel tarts.

Musicians arrived as well and when their music took on more of an upbeat tempo, some of the guests gathered round to dance. Derek spotted Jared dancing with a brunette girl from the Academy—who looked quite ecstatic to be dancing with the Prince—just as Arabelle's parents came over to wish him a happy birthday.

"Your father hates me," he said to Arabelle once they were alone again, near the back of the ballroom.

"He doesn't *hate* you," said Arabelle. "He just . . . probably still thinks of you as a delinquent who dragged Jared and I off on some misadventure that could have gotten us all killed."

Earlier that year, Derek, Jared and Arabelle had snuck away from Ember on a quest to find the three pieces of an amulet created by one of the legendary daemon lords, Milrath. The amulet was said to be able to grant wishes once all the pieces were brought together. Derek had wanted to use it to change his past and bring his parents back to life, and Arabelle had wanted to use it to help

27

her find her birth mother, but in the end, neither of them had gotten their wishes. When the Ogre, Durbash, had tried to use it, he had ended up dead, and they had known for certain that the amulet would not grant them any wishes.

"He looks at me like he'd rather lock you away in a tower than have you near me."

Arabelle laughed. "Now you're just over exaggerating."

"I'm not. It's slightly unnerving, actually."

"Maybe you should make an offer of marriage?" She joked.

Derek made a face. "No, thank you. Your father's not really my type."

That startled more laughter out of Arabelle.

"Don't laugh," said Derek, pretending to sound affronted. "I'm sure your father would look positively radiant in a wedding gown."

Arabelle laughed harder, even wiping a tear from the corner of her eye. Derek found himself smiling at the sight. He liked it when Arabelle laughed, and he liked it even better knowing that he was the one who made her laugh.

She looked at him with her deep violet eyes. "What?" she asked, still smiling.

"What do you mean?"

"Why are you looking at me like that?"

"How am I looking at you?" Derek asked, confused.

Arabelle's brows furrowed slightly. There was a thin scar that sat horizontally above her left eyebrow, a token from their fight with Durbash and his bandits in the Bone Swamp back in

February. "You're looking at me like—never mind." She shook her head.

That was when little Amias Aloria came wandering up to them.

"Arabelle," he said, rubbing his eyes. "I'm sleepy."

"Well, it is getting pretty late." Arabelle bent to scoop her little brother up into her arms. "Do you want to go home to bed?"

"Nooo," Amias mumbled even as he rested his head on his sister's shoulder and closed his eyes. "I wanna stay."

"Sure you do." To Derek, she said, "I'm going to take him to Amara."

He watched as Arabelle disappeared into the crowd of partygoers. He spotted Darus and Lila talking with Julianna and one of her friends. The King and Queen were dancing together at the other end of the ballroom. Callum Aloria was sitting with a group of other children in front of Veter, who was conjuring dazzling lights out of thin air.

Derek was just wondering where Jared was when he spotted his friend making a rather hasty exit to the gardens outside.

* * *

The cold air was a shock as Jared stepped outside onto the terrace that overlooked the gardens. Sona and Garrett, two Crown Guards, stood at attention on either side of the door he had just walked through.

"Your Highness," they greeted him.

"Um, do the two of you mind guarding somewhere else?" he asked. "I'd like to be alone for a bit."

The Guards looked perplexed by the request and at first Jared thought they were about to refuse, but they silently moved off of the terrace, taking up new positions somewhere out of sight.

Jared moved to lean against the stone railing and looked out at the gardens, at the trees with their bare branches, the white snow that hid the lush green grass below, and the pond that had now completely frozen over.

This is so unlike you, Jared, he thought. He was never one to sneak away from parties—at least not alone. He liked parties, liked being surrounded by people and their laughter and their attention. Normally, Jared would never choose to be alone out in the freezing cold when he could be in a room full of people he could strike up some banter with.

But Jared wasn't feeling quite himself at the moment. He thought of the way Derek and Arabelle had looked standing together in the ballroom, laughing and smiling at one another, and he felt something inside of him curdle.

He knew that Arabelle had feelings for Derek and that she'd had them for some time. It was obvious—to Jared, at least—in that look in her eyes whenever they were focused on Derek. That had never bothered him, but over these past few months, Jared had noticed something similar in Derek's eyes start to emerge whenever he was looking at Arabelle.

And it made him realise that Derek had never looked at him like that.

Would probably never look at him like that.

"By the Goddess, it's cold out here."

Jared startled at the new voice and spun around to find William Frain striding towards him, one hand tucked away in the pocket of his green coat and the other clutching a beaten up flask.

"Will," said Jared as the other boy came to stand next to him by the railing. "What are you doing out here?"

"I could ask you the same question." He was looking at Jared with a sly grin on his face. The gentle breeze ruffled his short, tawny brown hair. "Aren't you the host of this party? It seems like poor manners to hide out here, Your Highness."

"It's my parents' palace, so that really makes them the hosts. And this is Derek's birthday celebration. It doesn't matter if I want to hide away or not."

"But aren't you Derek's best friend?" Will asked. There was something off about his voice. It sounded almost . . . slurred? "Why wouldn't you want to be in there with him on his special day? Or perhaps it isn't all smooth sailing between the Prince and his best of friends?"

"Of course that's not it," Jared snapped. "The sailing is perfectly smooth between us."

"Is that why there was such a sad look on your face while you were watching Derek and Arabelle earlier?"

"I . . . I have no idea what you're talking about."

Will laughed. "Oh, you're an awful liar, Your Highness." There was a mischievous gleam in his moss green eyes now. "If I didn't know any better, I'd say that maybe you were in love with him."

Jared fought to keep his face straight. Was he that obvious? "Well, you *don't* know any better, do you?" he said.

"Unrequited love," Will murmured, taking a large swig from his flask. "How fun."

"What are you drinking?"

"Not too sure, really," Will admitted. "I nicked this from my da. It tastes like cherries, though."

"I see. So, did you come out here just to mock me?"

"Of course not. I simply wanted to have a nice chat."

"Well, I'm not really interested in having a *'nice chat'* at the moment. So if you don't mind, I'd like to be alone for a bit."

"All right. But one last thing, before I go."

"What is—" Jared didn't have the chance to finish before Will sealed his lips with his own.

He jolted in surprise at the unexpected move. At the feel of Will's cold fingers at the back of his neck. *He tastes like cherries,* was the only thought that flitted through Jared's mind just before Will stepped back.

"Enjoy your solitude, Your Highness," Will said to him as he headed back to the ballroom.

Jared was left standing there, feeling dazed, and with the lingering taste of cherries on his lips.

3

Arabelle found that the best way to fend off the cold was with some training. She'd spent the past three hours in the Academy's training hall—which was empty, thanks to a day off for students and professors—working through sword manoeuvres, sit-ups, push-ups and the like, until every muscle in her body felt like it was on fire. When she finally returned home, it was to the warmth of a fire burning in one of the many fireplaces throughout the house.

She was on her way to her bedroom on the second floor when she heard her father call out to her. She found him in the parlour, sitting in one of the wingback chairs by the window, drinking tea.

"Arabelle," he said in his deep, gruff voice when he saw her standing in the doorway. "You're home, good. There's something I wanted to talk to you about."

"What is it?"

"It can wait until after you've had a wash. Meet me in my study once you are ready."

Despite being filled with a burgeoning curiosity, Arabelle did as her father suggested and made her way upstairs. She arrived in her bedroom, with its lavender painted walls and four-poster bed. Her desk was the only untidy thing about her room, covered with sheets of paper, an open notebook filled with pencil sketches—and a fluffy white kitten.

"Annabeth, what are you doing up there?" she said to the kitten, walking over to pick it up from on top of her notebook. It let out a squeaking mewl as she did so. Annabeth was a new addition to their household, given as a gift to her brother Amias for his seventh birthday last month.

Arabelle placed the kitten on the soft white coverlet on her bed. "That's a more comfortable sleeping spot, don't you think? Much better than getting your fur and paw prints all over my drawings."

Annabeth curled up into a tiny, fluffy ball and close her eyes.

It didn't take long for Arabelle to shower and change into clothes that didn't reek of sweat. Once that was done, she headed for the third floor where her father's study was. The door was open, and he was already seated at his desk, studying a bunch of papers that were laid out before him.

In one corner of the study was her father's golden Crown Guard armour, held up on a stand like one might see in a clothing store.

"You wanted to speak to me, Da?" she said by way of announcing herself.

Victor gestured to one of the seats opposite him. "Come sit."

"The house is unusually quiet," she noted as she took a seat at the desk. "Where is everyone?"

"The boys went sledding with some of their friends and Amara's at work in the Healing House."

There was an unmistakable note of tenderness in Victor's voice when he uttered his wife's name. One Arabelle suspected was reserved only for couples who had pledged to love and devote themselves to each other until the end of their days. Arabelle wondered if her father had ever spoken like that about her real mother. Had there ever been love between her father and mysterious mother? Or had the affair that had borne Arabelle only been about lust?

Arabelle studied her father as he busied himself with putting away his papers. He was a thickset man, with burnished brown skin and a balding head of red-brown hair. Arabelle looked very little like her father, with her yellow hair and violet eyes that she must have inherited from her birth mother, she could not have looked more like the odd one out in her family. Both of her brothers had inherited their dark brown complexions and black curls from *their* mother.

He also had the first two buttons of his shirt undone, so that she could see the red wedding gem that hung from a gold chain around his neck. She knew Amara wore the same gem on a matching chain, as all married couples did.

"Now," her father began. "You know of the tradition, particularly amongst noble families such as ours, of arranging marriages once one turns seventeen or eighteen years of age?"

"Yes," said Arabelle even as she felt a sinking feeling in the pit of her stomach.

"Well, I have done just that for you."

"You . . . What?"

Victor didn't seem to take any notice of the barely concealed distress in his daughter's voice. Instead, he pulled out something from a drawer in his desk and passed it to Arabelle. It was a miniature portrait done in pencil of a young man with a strong chin, fair curls and an arrogant tilt to his mouth. The sinking feeling in Arabelle's stomach intensified.

"I made the arrangements between the Hargrades and their eldest son, Alistair. You know him, don't you?"

Oh, Arabelle knew Alistair Hargrade all right. He had been in the year above her at the Academy and he had spent most of their time there bullying her relentlessly. Tripping her in the corridors and taking every opportunity he could to remind her that she was an illegitimate child. There had even been one memorable occasion where she'd gotten into a fist fight with him in the Academy courtyard because of it.

Now she was supposed to *marry* him?

"I—you want me to marry Alistair Hargrade? I don't—"

"The wedding won't take place until next year," her father continued practically, as if he were discussing some new business

36

venture. "After your eighteenth birthday, preferably. But the engagement will be made official as soon as we've organised a time where both families can get together to make the—"

"Wait, *stop*," she said. Her head was spinning from all this talk of marriage and engagements. And to Alistair Hargrade of all people. "Da, I . . . I don't want to get married. Not so soon, and certainly not to Alistair."

"Then to whom?"

"I—someone of my own choosing. But not *now*. Not for a while."

Truth be told, Arabelle already knew exactly who she would choose to marry one day if she could. But even if her father had presented him as an option instead of Alistair, she would still refuse. Marriage was not something she was ready for, whether it was in one day or one year.

Victor sat back in his chair, rubbing at the bridge of his nose with a look of vexation. Through the window behind him, Arabelle could see that it had started to snow.

"I have already spoken to Lady Hargrade about this," he said. "And you expect me to cancel everything just like that?"

Well, perhaps you shouldn't have gone and planned this engagement without telling me about it first! A part of her felt like screaming. Instead, she blurted out. "Da, I want to join the Crown Guard."

Now Victor was the one to look surprised. "Why, all of a sudden?"

"It's really not all of a sudden. I've been thinking about it for a while now and next year I'll be old enough to start the training for new recruits."

"Arabelle," her father sighed. "I don't know."

"What do you mean you don't know?" she demanded. "I'm a good fighter. I'm hardworking, I'm loyal to the royal family and I'm . . . I'm your daughter." She added that last part a little hesitantly, as if afraid that he would deny it.

Victor nodded. "You are all of those things and then some," he agreed. "But being a Crown Guard isn't like being a Guardian. As a Crown Guard, your sole purpose is to defend and protect the royal family, and every decision you make reflects on them."

Arabelle frowned. "I understand that."

"And as Captain, I'm responsible for who I allow to join the Crown Guard. So I must be *very* selective in who I choose to guard the King and his family."

"What are you trying to say?"

Victor watched her with unwavering brown eyes. So much like his sister's, but unlike the Queen's, there was a hardened glint in her father's.

"Arabelle, listen to me. You *do* have the qualities to make a fine Crown Guard, but you can also be too rash and too impulsive, and there's no room for someone like that in the Crown Guard."

"You're just saying this because of what happened back in February," Arabelle said accusingly. "Because I ran away with Jared and Derek."

"You're right," Victor admitted without hesitation.

Arabelle flinched, her fingers curling into fists where they rested on her knees. She had half a mind to tell her father that maybe she wouldn't have run off with Jared and Derek like that in the first place if he would only talk to her about who her mother was. If he would just answer her questions and stop making her feel as if he were keeping something from her, then she wouldn't have felt like a daemonic amulet was her only option to find out the answers she had a right to know.

But she didn't dare. As she never dared to speak out against her father. Fearful that one wrong word was all it would take to shatter this tentative relationship she had with him.

"Now, about this engagement—"

A knocking at the door interrupted them and Tirshi, their housemaid, stepped in. She was a short woman, well into her thirties and, like Amara, she was Samweanese, her black hair mostly hidden beneath her white cap.

"Excuse me," she said, "But this just came in for Miss Arabelle." She held up a golden envelope stamped with a red seal.

Even before Arabelle opened it up to see what was inside, she knew what the golden envelope meant.

She had been selected for a new assignment.

The Mandatrum was the tallest building in Ember, made of white brick and over five storeys high, even taller than the highest towers in the royal palace. Just a little further down the street from the

Academy, the Mandatrum acted as a sort of headquarters for the Guardians, where they reported to receive their assignments and submit reports once those assignments were completed.

Arabelle was made to walk all the way up to the fifth floor, which was nothing more than a wide corridor lined with huge oak doors on either side. She entered through the second to last door on the left, as she had been instructed to, and found herself in a circular room with black marble floors. A man with a bare head and a sour look on his face sat behind a tall wooden bench that looked like something a judge at a trial would sit behind.

Two others stood in the centre of the room. One was Rosalie Decorus, adopted granddaughter of Elias Decorus, one of the King's Advisors. She had coppery skin and a head of black hair that fell around her shoulders in thick waves. Beside her was an older woman that Arabelle recognised as Cassandra Luteus.

"Sorry," said Arabelle as she approached the pair. "I didn't keep you all waiting, did I?"

Rosalie shook her head. "It's all right. We're still waiting on one more."

"Who?"

Arabelle's question was answered barely a moment later when the door opened once again and in stepped Derek Draco.

His hair was in its usual untidy state and bits of snow clung to the black strands and dusted the shoulders of his coat. His nose and cheeks were pinked from the cold and Arabelle felt her heart flutter at the sight of him.

"How nice of you to finally decide to join us, Master Draco," the man at the bench drawled unpleasantly.

Arabelle glared at him. Derek hadn't even arrived that much later than she had. It seemed unfair to call him out on tardiness. Then again, it was normally with unfairness that others treated one with Wood Elf blood. Derek's mother had been a Wood Elf, which made him half Elf—noticeable in the delicate points at the tips of his ears—and ever since the war between humans and Wood Elves that only came to an end seventeen years ago, there were many who harboured bitter feelings.

The man cleared his throat; the sound echoing throughout the room. "There have been two murders that have gone unsolved in a town up north. A request was put in for Guardians to provide assistance in apprehending the killer. Cassandra Luteus, Arabelle Aloria, Derek Draco and Rosalie Decorus, you have been selected for this assignment. Do you accept it?"

All four of them gave their assent.

"You are to depart by tomorrow evening at five o'clock. Your earnings for the completion of this assignment are forty coins each. Are there any questions?"

It was Cassandra who spoke up. "You forgot to tell us where exactly we are going?"

Arabelle had the pleasure of seeing the man flush with embarrassment at the blunder. "Ah, yes, your destination is . . ." he scanned the papers in his hand. "Windfell."

Windfell. Arabelle knew that name.

It was the name of the town that Derek had grown up in.

Looking over at him, Arabelle was stunned to see his face drained of colour, leaving him white as a sheet.

He looked as if he had just been handed a death sentence.

* * *

Derek had been sitting outside on the rooftop of his house for the past hour—that's how long it felt to him, at least. He hadn't exactly been keeping track of the time.

Windfell. The name echoed through Derek's head over and over again. He was being sent on an assignment to Windfell. The place where his parents had been murdered. The town that was home to some of the darkest moments in his life.

Derek didn't quite remember much after they had been dismissed from the Mandatrum, only that he had begun to feel light-headed and like he couldn't breathe in enough air, no matter how hard he tried. He remembered Arabelle calling out to him as he sped out of the room, only coming to a halt once he was out on the street and found a tight little alleyway to duck into. He'd fallen to his knees, his breath coming out in frantic gasps while he pressed his forehead to the cold brick wall.

Darus had been livid when Derek had told him of his new assignment once he finally managed to stumble home. He had since stormed out with the intention of yelling the ears off all the staff at the Mandatrum.

The sky was growing darker as the day drew to a close. The air turning colder too, but Derek couldn't bring himself to move from his perch on the roof and go back inside.

A bronze dragon flew over Derek's head and he immediately recognised it as Jared.

Changing once he touched down on the roof, Jared carefully took a seat beside Derek. "Mind if I sit here?"

"What are you doing here?" said Derek

"I spoke to Arabelle earlier. She told me about the assignment and that you left the Mandatrum looking as if you were going to be sick. So, I thought I would come around and see how you were doing."

"I'm fine."

"Really? Because you look pretty awful to me."

"Thank you, Jared," Derek deadpanned.

Jared chuckled, and his cheeks dimpled. He was handsome, Derek thought absently. Not that this was a new revelation. He had always thought that Jared fit the description of a typical story-book prince: kind, charming, and handsome. At the Academy, there had been no shortage of boys—and even some girls—fawning over him. There had also been a time when Derek had wondered if he himself had more than just friendly feelings for his best friend.

They sat in silence for some time before Jared spoke up again. "Do you want to talk about it?"

Derek sighed. "You probably won't leave unless I do."

Jared frowned at him. There was concern there and maybe even a hint of hurt. "If you want me to leave, I will."

But Derek found he didn't want that. He wanted Jared to stay here with him because having Jared by his side steadied him. His presence was like a soothing balm. "No. Stay. I want you to stay."

"All right." Jared visibly brightened. "And we don't have to talk about it, if you really don't want to. But I just want you to know that you can. You can talk to me about anything. I'm here for you."

"I know," Derek said softly. "I don't . . . have the fondest of memories of Windfell."

"Because of your parents?"

Among other things, he left unsaid. "I don't know if I can do it. I don't know if I can go back there."

He felt ridiculous saying it, but Jared only looked at him with earnest eyes. Not a trace of judgement, or even pity, was on his face. Jared didn't know the full story of Derek's life after his parents died and before he came to Ember. No one did. The only ones who knew the full story were Darus and probably the King and Queen as well. It wasn't that Derek didn't trust Jared to know; it was just that he couldn't bear the thought of Jared knowing. Didn't want to see the look on Jared's face if he told him. Nor did he want to have to speak of those memories.

Derek put his head in his hands. "No, I *know* I can't. I can't go back to that place with all of those bad memories. I'm not strong enough."

"Are you joking?" Jared said, incredulous. "You don't think you're *strong enough*? Of course you are."

The derisive snort that escaped Derek was automatic. Someone strong enough wouldn't have collapsed in an alleyway, struggling to breathe. Someone strong enough wouldn't have allowed the things that happened to him happen in the first place.

"I'm serious," Jared's voice was adamant. "You, Derek Alexander Draco, are the strongest person I know and I won't hear anyone say otherwise. Including you."

"Is that so? And what are you going to do about it?"

"Beat some sense into you, that's what," said Jared, shoving him in the shoulder. Then, more seriously, he added, "I know that Windfell must hold a lot of painful memories for you, and I'm sure going back there won't be easy. But there are people there who need your help. Any one of those people who were killed could have been someone's mother or father. Maybe there are children there who are just like you were when your parents died. If that's so, then don't you think it would feel good to give them what you couldn't have and bring the killer to justice?"

Give them what you couldn't have. It was true they'd never found the man who had slain Derek's parents. Mayor Goldridge hadn't seemed too concerned about it at the time, hadn't made any real effort to try and catch him, and a search attempt by the Guardians three years later had been quickly quashed. Derek hadn't gotten the vindication of knowing his parents' killer was rotting in prison, but perhaps he could give it to someone else?

I'm not that scared little boy anymore, he told himself. *I am a Guardian. I'm sworn to protect and help people and there are people in Windfell who need help right now. I can't let childhood fears get in the way of that.*

He had to be as strong as Jared seemed to believe he was.

Feeling suddenly bone weary, Derek slumped to the side and rested his head against Jared's shoulder, closing his eyes. He felt Jared stiffen momentarily before the tension slowly bled out.

"Thank you," Derek murmured.

"O-Oh, you're welcome."

They stayed like that for a while longer, with Derek's head on Jared's shoulder. The sounds of Ember coming to a halt for another day washed over them.

"Derek," Jared said. "I—There's . . ." His voice sounded hesitant, shaky even.

Derek lifted his head to peer up at the other boy. "What's wrong?"

Jared wasn't looking at him, instead he had his gaze firmly fixed on his gloved hands in his lap. His throat bobbed as he swallowed.

"Spit it out," Derek prompted.

"I was just—" he sighed. "No. Never mind, it doesn't matter."

Derek frowned. Whatever Jared had been about to say was obviously weighing on him. And after lending an ear to Derek's problems, it seemed only fair that he should return the favour. "Are you sure about that?"

"I'm sure," Jared said with a poor attempt at a cheerful smile. "I should really get going, actually. But I'll see you before you leave tomorrow."

"It goes both ways, you know."

Jared looked at him quizzically."What does?"

Derek pointed to himself and to Jared. "You and me. If you say that I can talk to you about anything, then you can do the same to me. You know that, right?"

Jared smiled again and this time Derek believed that he wasn't faking it. "I know."

* * *

The tavern door swung open, and a woman stepped inside. It had begun to pour rain outside and water from her sodden cloak and boots dripped onto the wooden floorboards. She didn't take it off though and kept her hood up as she made her way to the bar.

The tavern was empty apart from the barkeep cleaning glasses behind the counter and two men nursing their drinks by the burning hearth at the other end of the room.

The barkeep raised his eyebrows as the woman walked up to the bar. "You look like something the cat dragged in."

"One beer please," was all the woman said as she took a seat on one of the barstools.

The barkeep nodded and moved off to prepare her drink, and when he finally set the mug with its frothy top down in front of her, she drank in long gulps, caring little for decorum.

"You a traveller or something?" the barkeep said conversationally.

"Something like that, I suppose."

"So, where you from?"

"I would rather not say."

"Well, what brings you to these parts, then?"

"I'm looking for someone."

"What kind of someone?" asked the barkeep. "A lover?"

The woman shot him a withering look from beneath her hood and the barkeep chuckled.

"All right, all right," he said. "I see you're one of those private types."

The woman took another sip from her drink.

The next time the barkeep spoke to her, it was to say he had to go take care of something out back.

Not long after he had slipped out the back door did the two men that had been sitting at the back of the room approach her.

"Hello, darlin'," the first man leered at her drunkenly. "What's your name?"

The woman stayed silent.

"What's wrong? Don't feel like speaking?" said the second man. He had a gap in his front teeth. "That's all right." He reached for her. "I can think of a better way for you to use your—"

The woman's left hand shot out from beneath her cloak to wrap around the man's wrist in an iron-like grip.

"Do not *ever* think about touching me," she hissed.

The man's expression quickly morphed into one of pain and he screamed as the skin under her grip began to burn and blister.

"What the hell are you doing?!" the other man shouted. He lunged for the woman, but she had already released her grip on the first, pulled out the knife at her belt, and rammed the hilt in between his legs.

The man howled pitifully and crumpled to the floor.

The gap-toothed man seemed to have regained himself. "You stupid bitch—" He grabbed for her right arm, only to find there was nothing there to grab beneath her cloak.

The woman flicked her hand, as if she were brushing away a fly, and he went sailing across the room, slamming into the back wall and falling still on the ground, taking a few of the hanging picture frames with him.

It was at that moment that the barkeep chose to return. He was brought up short by the sight of two of his customers on the ground, one unconscious and the other writhing with his bloods between his legs and muttering curses while she stood unscathed in the middle of it.

Then she saw the way his eyes widened further when he saw her hood had fallen down. "You're a—"

"I will be leaving now." She pulled her hood back up and made four gold coins from her purse appear on the bar top, neatly stacked on top of each other, with the same magic she'd used to fling the man across the tavern. "That's my compensation," she said before striding out the door.

Outside, the rain had lightened to a drizzle. The streets were empty and lamp lit. It seemed the woman was the only one foolish enough to brave the outdoors in this bitter cold.

As she started off down one of the stone paths, wet from rain and snow, she noticed something land on a sign post above her. The woman paused to look up at a black raven, its feathers wet and ruffled from the downpour.

"There you are, Cora."

The raven made a clucking sound.

"What? Are you upset that I left you out here in the rain?"

Another cluck.

"I am sorry, but I did not want to draw too much attention. Entering that tavern with you on my shoulder would have either gotten me kicked out or had everyone figuring out I was a mage." *Although they might have already figured that out when I burned a man with my bare hands, sent him flying into a wall and made coins appear on that counter.*

And then, of course, that barkeep had seen her ears. Her distinctively pointed ears.

"You're a Wood Elf," he had no doubt been about to say.

Aurelia Blackwood had not done an outstanding job of appearing inconspicuous tonight.

"Come along." She extended her arm to the bird.

Cora alighted onto her shoulder, tugging on a short strand of black hair with her beak. It was as if she were saying, "I'm still cross with you."

A small smile tugged at the corner of Aurelia's mouth.

With Cora on her shoulder, Aurelia made her way through the quiet streets. At one point, stopping so that she could pull something out of the inside pocket of her cloak. What she held in the palm of her hand was an old scrap of metal, barely longer than her index finger. She considered it as one might consider a map or a compass and she supposed it was. Of a sort.

Only a map or a compass would be more reliable, she thought, when she felt nothing from it. With a sigh, she pocketed the scrap metal once more.

Perhaps she would have better luck with it the next time she tried using it to track down her would-be killer.

4

One of the most heavily guarded buildings in Aloseria and home to many of its most dangerous criminals, Black Rock prison was an imposing structure of towers with sharply pointed rooftops and black, granite walls. It stood alone on an island of rock. An old bridge that looked barely stable enough for a single person to cross was the only point of access.

Draken stood on the edge of a cliff overlooking the prison.

The winds were blustering tonight, and it whipped the ends of his coat about his legs. The hiss of unfrozen ocean water crashing against the rocks was audible even over the howl of the wind.

However, Draken wasn't here for the scenic view. Instead, what brought him here was the promise of finding the second to last mirror shard. Inside that maze of prison cells was a man, Nile Fera, sentenced to life in prison for the murder of his own wife. Thanks to his gift with somniamancy—the ability to walk through the dreams and memories of others—Draken had good cause to believe he would find the shard with this Nile fellow.

All he had to do was find his way inside.

For as long as Black Rock had stood, no one had ever managed to break in or out. Not only was it defended by some of the strongest and most disciplined men and women Aloseria had to offer, it was also protected by powerful magical wards.

In all the years that Black Rock had stood, its defences had never been penetrated.

Except by one person.

And he was about to do it again.

The last of the prison guards stumbled back against the wall.

"No . . . Wait! Please—"

A flash of metallic red cut off the man's pleas as Draken's scythe sheered through his neck. The helmeted head toppled, clanking against the flagstones, blood already beginning to pool around it.

The inner courtyard of the castle was littered with the bodies of prison guards. As well as cracked stone and scorch marks, fallen swords, and splatters of blood—all evidence of the violence that had befallen this place.

Now only Draken was standing in the middle of it. He lifted a hand to wipe a smear of blood—not his own—from his cheek. Once he was certain that anyone who would oppose him was dead, Draken let the scythe in his hand vanish in a burst of red sparks and picked his way across the ruined courtyard. The step of his boots echoed in the eerie silence, towards the open gate of the west tower.

As he walked up the narrow, torch-lit stairwells, he was pleased to find that he encountered no more resistance. While Draken had no problems with dismantling the wards around the prison, he had not been able to stop it from alerting whoever had constructed the wards in the first place. He'd felt it, right when the wards had come down, like seeing a messenger bird take flight, and knew that it would not be long before word reached the Guardians. He'd already wasted enough time dealing with all of those guards.

He found Fera's cell on the fourth floor of the tower. Ignoring the other prisoners calling out to him, he focused all of his attention instead on the rangy man in prisoner's rags, huddled in the corner of his cell. He looked up at Draken with dark, hooded eyes.

Draken smiled pleasantly. "Nile Fera?"

A muscle in the man's jaw twitched and Draken took that as all the answer he needed. He lifted a finger to the lock on the door and a red spark was all it took for the door to swing open and Draken to step through.

"You him?" Nile Fera spoke in a deep rasp.

Draken cocked an eyebrow. "Am I who?"

"The man my pa always told me to watch out for. The man who would come and kill us all in our sleep to steal our family treasure. *"But we can't let him, Nile,"* he'd tell me. We have to protect it.

Keep it safe and keep it hidden, just like my father and his father before him. And I did. I kept it hidden and safe for all those years, even when the nightmares came and even when I saw the monsters while I was awake and playing with my boy. And when I caught my wife trying to make off with it in secret, I put a knife in her back."

Draken studied the man—his sallow skin and wide, unfocused eyes. He knelt down so the two of them were eye to eye. "Where is it?"

"I told them they couldn't take me away. But they wouldn't listen. I fought as hard as I could, but there were too many. At first they were people and then they were monsters with sharp teeth and wicked voices."

"The shard, Nile," said Draken. "Where is the shard now?"

"The boy was there. He called the monsters. I took his ma, so he had the monsters take me."

So his son has the shard now? "Where is your boy now?"

"My boy . . . My boy. I had to keep it safe. I had to keep it hidden."

"Nile."

"How could he do that to me? *How?*" The man blabbered on as if he had completely forgotten about Draken's presence—had he ever been truly aware of it in the first place? "Safe. I must keep it safe and hidden. I must. *I must keep it—*"

A knife materialised in Draken's palm and in the next second, he thrust it through Nile Fera's throat.

Fera made a wet sound, his eyes going wide, the manic glint fading. Draken withdrew the knife and Fera's body slumped back against the wall, the front of his rags growing red with the blood spilling from the wound in his neck.

"I suppose you were helpful," Draken muttered while looking down on the body. "To a certain degree, at least."

He stepped out of the cell and spotted a man in one of the cells opposite him, with a wild mass of red hair and a beard. As Draken approached, the red-headed man stumbled backwards until he was huddled against the back wall of his cramped cell, watching Draken with wary eyes.

There would be no hiding what had happened here tonight. The dozens of dead prison guards, the destroyed wards. Even now, Guardians could be making their way to this place and while Draken didn't doubt his capabilities to be gone within a matter of seconds, any one of these prisoners could say to the Guardians that they had seen him. Seen what he had done and seen his face.

He supposed that he could kill them. It wouldn't be hard.

But Draken had a much more entertaining idea.

Smiling down at the prisoner, he said, "How would you like to get out of here?"

5

Jared wandered about the halls of the palace aimlessly. It was one of those days where there seemed to be absolutely nothing to do. Jared hated those days.

It didn't help that he'd also woken up feeling a bit melancholy that morning, and he wasn't sure why. Perhaps he was already missing Derek and Arabelle, although it had only been a day since he'd had to say goodbye to them, and it wasn't as if they were Jared's *only* friends.

Maybe I should pay a visit to the Gold Rose after, he thought to himself. There was never a shortage of young people at the tavern who wanted to spend their time fawning over their prince.

It wasn't until he heard a pair of familiar voices that Jared realised he was approaching his father's study. The door was open and sure enough, when Jared peered inside, he saw his father and sister standing around the desk, both with serious looks on their faces.

It wasn't unusual to find his father and Julianna like this. Since Julianna was to be Queen someday, Jonathan had taken her under his wing these last few years, showing her the ropes of running a kingdom—or queendom, as it would be under Julianna's reign—and making sure she understood the demands of being a queen.

In another time, that might have been Jared standing there with his father, learning all the lessons he needed to be King. Julianna was the first princess to inherit the throne before a prince, thanks to their father changing the rules of inheritance once he became King. Not that Jared minded, it suited him just fine to never have to bear the burden of Kingship.

He slipped past the doorway before either of them could notice he was even there.

He found his mother in the gardens. The Queen had a fiendish green thumb—something she'd passed down to her son—and even a cool July day couldn't keep her out of her beloved gardens.

She was in the eastern part of the gardens, pruning one of the rose bushes herself while one of her ladies-in-waiting stood to the side, ready to lend any assistance at a moment's notice. His mother's three small spaniels—Beth, Lucie, and Spot—also loitered around, snuffling through the nearby bushes.

"Do you need any help?" Jared asked as he drew nearer.

"If you'd like," said Charlotte Regalias, and then to her lady-in-waiting, "Could you fetch Jared a pair of gloves please?"

"Of course, Your Majesty."

It wasn't long before she returned with a pair of thick, brown gardening gloves for Jared and bypass shears.

"Thank you," he said, pulling on the gloves and kneeling down in the snowy garden bed beside his mother.

Once upon a time, royals working in the garden like this was unheard of. It was a job for the servants, not members of the monarchy. Then his mother had married into the family and she had made a servant faint when she walked into the mud and began pulling out weeds with her bare hands—or so Jared had been told.

"It's been a while since you and I did some gardening together," Charlotte said, stripping a couple of leaves from a thorny branch.

"Has it?"

"We used to do this all the time when you were little. Now, you usually don't offer to help me in the garden unless you have something on your mind."

Jared stayed silent. His mother was far too good at reading him.

"So," she prompted. "Are you going to talk to me, or should we continue our pruning in silence?"

Jared shrugged, snipping away some dead wood from a rose stem. "It's nothing really, I just—I thought that I *might* have been in love with someone, but I've realised that they might be interested in someone else."

"Oh, dear. Has my little boy had his heart broken?"

Jared huffed. "Of course not. The Prince of Aloseria allows no man to break his heart."

His mother smiled fondly. "Well, call it whatever you like. I know all too well what that feels like."

"You do?"

"Oh, yes. I've told you that your father was my first love, but I wasn't his."

"I thought you and Father had an arranged marriage?"

"That didn't happen until we were seventeen. Before that, I remember feeling as if my whole world would end when I found out he was walking out with Carvilla Hargrade."

Jared nearly dropped his shears. "Pa walked out with Carvilla Hargrade?" Carvilla Hargrade was the mother of one of Jared's old classmates at the Academy, Elijah Hargrade.

"And after that, he walked out with another girl, Jemma . . . oh, I can't remember. But both times I felt as if I would never be lucky in love. But here I am now, married to the man of my dreams," she reached out to pinch Jared's cheek, "with two darling children."

"So, are you saying that I shouldn't give up on D—on this person?"

"That's up to you, dear," said his mother. "I only want to reassure you that hurt like this is temporary. Perhaps everything will work out with you and this boy, like it did for your father and I, or maybe, someone new will come along and you'll be happier with them than you ever could have been with this other person."

Jared nodded, feeling oddly reassured by his mother's words. "Thank you, Mum."

They went back to quietly pruning for a little while longer before they were approached by Aldred carrying a golden envelope with a red seal for Jared.

Looks like I might not make it to the Gold Rose after all.

When Jared arrived at the Mandatrum, his Guard, Beatrice, said to him, "I'll wait for you outside, Your Highness."

Despite not being first in line to the throne, and being a Guardian who faced danger with every assignment, Jared still had to be accompanied by a Crown Guard whenever he ventured out of the palace grounds.

Inside, he was instructed to head to the top floor and when he entered through the wide doors of the first room to his left, he was surprised to find it was already quite full with Guardians, their quiet chatter echoing across the chamber.

He spotted a few familiar faces, Eliza Qui and Amelia Caritas, who were good friends with his parents, Charles Decorus and the Hargrade brothers, Alistair and Elijah, standing with their mother, Carvilla Hargrade, all three of them looking very blonde and very muscular. He also caught sight of Darus standing near the back window, conversing with two others.

Jared was just about to make his way over to him when a voice from behind him said, "Fancy meeting you here."

He spun around and found himself face to face with green eyes and tawny hair.

"Will," he said.

"Your Highness," Will said with a mock little bow. "Long time no see."

"The party was only a few nights ago."

"Was it? It seems so much longer." Then, his demeanour turned more serious. "Also, I should . . . apologise about that night. I might have had a bit too much cider to drink."

"Really? I hadn't noticed." Truth be told, Will's kiss that night hadn't bothered Jared exactly. It had certainly been unexpected, but he did not think he could honestly say that he had disliked it. In fact, Jared found himself now watching Will's mouth, thinking about the taste of cherry cider and—

Looking over Will's shoulder, Jared locked eyes with Elijah Hargrade. The other boy was watching them with an intense, almost furious, glare.

What's his problem? Jared thought just as the door opened once more and a woman of middle years in black robes entered. The talking died down and everyone's attention was drawn to the woman as she crossed the chamber towards the wooden bench.

Taking her seat, the woman looked at them all from over the rim of her spectacles. "Guardians, thank you all for coming. I'm sure that many, if not all of you, have yet to hear of this. But in the early hours of this morning, word reached Ember about an attack on Black Rock prison that took place sometime last night. We do not know why or by whom, but we do know that all of the guards on duty at the time were killed and all of the prisoners were set free."

"But . . . how?" said Adolphus Solum, a barrel-chested man who stood beside Darus, giving voice to the shock that rippled through the room. "The wards. I thought they were impenetrable?"

"It appears someone did find a way to penetrate them."

"Do we at least know who could have done this?" Carvilla Hargrade demanded.

"No. As I said, everyone who could have witnessed the attack is either dead or on the run." The woman adjusted her spectacles as she looked down at the papers before her. "All of you gathered here are to round up the escaped convicts of Black Rock. As this is a matter of utmost urgency, you will be given only ten hours to make any necessary preparations. You will then gather at the Patched Cloak where Veter will open a portal that will take you directly to Black Rock, and you will receive further instructions there. Do any of you have any more questions about the assignment?"

No one spoke.

The woman nodded. "You are all dismissed."

6

After three days of travel, they finally arrived at Windfell, a town built into the side of a snow-capped mountain, overlooking the valley and the forests below. All Arabelle could think as she took in the scenery was that it looked rather dreary. It was a landscape of white and grey. Even the sky looked miserable with low-hanging clouds. Not a speck of blue sky or sunshine to be seen.

Oddly enough, she felt a stirring of nerves as they approached. Before Arabelle had left Ember, her father had come to speak to her. "If you do well on this assignment," he had said, "I'll consider enrolling you into Crown Guard training next year."

This assignment was her chance at proving to her father that she was worthy of being a Crown Guard, and perhaps at making him take her word more seriously when she refused to marry Alistair Hargrade.

I have *to do well on this assignment,* she thought determinedly. *No time for screw-ups.*

As they were about to pass over the Valley, Derek broke their V formation to fly on ahead of them. Arabelle watched as he made a descent into the Valley and she remembered. *Derek used to live in the Valley outside of Windfell.*

Breaking formation as well, she took off after him.

She landed on the hillside at the Valley's edge. The Valley was an enormous expanse of snow, with houses with smoke rising from their chimneys, and gardens dotted here and there. She even spotted a cow grazing in a small paddock.

It didn't take long before she spotted Derek's familiar, dark-haired figure, crouched in front of a cherry blossom tree, close to the Valley's edge. Its branches still dotted with the closed, pink buds despite the cold.

She came to stand behind him with enough distance between them that he could ignore her if he really wanted to, but close enough that he'd know she was there—there for him.

Because at the base of the tree was a stone plaque with words carved into it.

In the Goddess's embrace

Alexander Draco
9-12-390 — 21-5-419

Erica Draco
14-6-393 — 21-5-419

"They made this after my parents died," Derek said. He didn't turn to look at Arabelle and he didn't take his eyes off of the plaque where his mother and father's names were written. "And they planted this tree in honour of them. This was where our house used to be. The first and last time I was here was six years ago, on the day that Darus took me away."

"The first time?" she asked with a frown and then immediately snapped her mouth shut. She wondered how the last time he had been here could've also been the first time? Hadn't Derek lived in Windfell for three years after his parents' passing? But she realised that now may not be the time to ply him with such questions.

"The Mayor would never let me go beyond the town walls. I tried, but he'd always have the Guards drag me right back. I think he was too worried that once I left, I'd never come back." There was a bitter edge to Derek's voice.

Arabelle felt her chest tighten. "I—" She began but stopped. What could she possibly say that might bring him some comfort? 'I'm sorry', seemed woefully inadequate. Actually, she wasn't sure there was anything she *could* say. She had never lost a parent—not the way Derek had—and she didn't think that there were any words alone that could ease that pain.

Arabelle heard the footsteps approaching from behind and turned to see Cassandra and Rosalie had joined them. They stood in silence, allowing Derek to take this moment in front of the memorial for his family.

And as Arabelle watched his sorrowful, hunched form, she wished more than anything that she knew of a way to rid him of this pain.

* * *

Later, they climbed the rocky slope at the base of the mountain and led a winding path up to the town gates. When Derek and his companions passed through, they were met by two Town Guards, in silver armour and blue capes. One of them was a Dark Elf with red hair shaved at the sides and a beard.

Cassandra introduced them as Guardians and the Guards led them through the town, headed for the Mayor's Manor.

Derek found Windfell was just as he remembered. It was a town entirely devoid of colour. Where Ember was a riot of it, Windfell was made entirely out of grey. Grey stone pathways and steps, grey stone buildings, grey smoke filtering up through chimneys into the grey sky. Windfell also had no gardens or greenery to speak of, either. They passed a couple of boys, relieving themselves in the snow outside of someone's home, until a woman armed with a frying pan burst out of the front door, shouting and sending the snickering boys scurrying off down the street.

"What a charming place," Rosalie muttered sardonically.

But it wasn't only Windfell's structure that was so different to Ember, it was the people as well. In Ember, everyone seemed to walk around with a bounce in their step. They smiled at one another as they passed by, calling out cheerful greetings and pausing in the streets to talk about how beautiful their neighbour's roses were looking or to ask a friend for the recipe to their carrot cake. In Windfell, everyone was much more sombre, looking either sad or irritable as they shuffled up and down the streets, grumbling about the cold or trading insults and gossip like it was coin.

They passed through the town square where vendors selling their wares had set up stalls. There were more townsfolk gathered here than along the rest of the streets. Some stopped to stare at Derek and the others, and he could hear the word, "Guardians," whispered through the square.

He heard other whispers, too.

"Isn't that him? That boy who ran off to be a Guardian?"

"The old Mayor's son?"

"I heard it was him who—"

Thankfully, they departed the square before he could listen to anymore.

The Mayor's Manor was the home of acting Mayors of Windfell and while it was built from the same grey stone as the rest of the town, it had been built with greater care and properly maintained than the rest of the buildings. Even the pathway that cut across the front yard from the gates to the front door was devoid of any visible cracks. It was also the only house in town with a garden, with red roses lining the stone fences.

They were brought up to the heavy, oak front doors where one of the Guards knocked using the brass door knocker. A few moments later, it was opened by a short, elderly maidservant with thin white hair and a cross look on her gaunt face.

"Yes?" she spoke in a raspy voice with a squinty-eyed glare.

"The Guardians have arrived," said Rolven, the Dark Elf Guard.

The woman grumbled about something under her breath, but stepped aside to allow them in.

Inside was pleasantly warm, yet Derek felt himself growing overly warm in his cloak. But maybe that was not the only reason why he felt pinpricks of perspiration breaking out on the back of his neck.

The wide, open entryway was much the same as Derek remembered it; burgundy wallpaper, a grand staircase to their left, expensive-looking oil paintings lining the walls, and a patterned rug worth eight hundred gold that Derek had spilled apple juice on once.

"Leave your cloaks on the hanger and bags by the door. Lord Boeheart is waiting for you in the study," said the maidservant, already shuffling through the entryway and down the hall.

She led them to a closed door at the end of the hallway and knocked. A voice called out to them from the other side, and the maidservant opened the door.

The study was huge, with pale light streaming in from the high windows. The walls were covered in patterned, green wallpaper and a fire crackled in the tall fireplace. A huge painting of Aryanna Vir Fortis as a golden dragon took up much of the wall space to their left. Two couches and an armchair were set up in the middle of the room with a low table between them. Behind that, at the other end of the study, was a wide desk of dark mahogany. It almost came as something of a shock to Derek when he saw that the man sitting behind it wasn't Goldridge.

Instead, there sat a much younger man, perhaps in his thirties, with a handsome, angular face and wavy black hair. He was dressed in the red waistcoat and blue overcoat of a Mayor—the same clothing that Goldridge used to wear—and a gold ring with a red wedding gem on one of his fingers.

"Excuse me, Lord Boeheart, but the Guardians have arrived," the maidservant announced.

The Mayor looked up from where he had been writing away at the desk and something very much like boyish wonderment lit up his expression. "Guardians! Excellent." He stood from his chair and crossed the room towards them. "Thank you very much, Lilith. Could you please have the refreshments for our guests brought in now, please?"

"Of course." The maidservant—Lilith—bowed her head and retreated from the study.

"Well, as I'm sure you've already guessed, I am the Mayor of Windfell, Edmund Boeheart, and it is an honour to welcome you to our town."

"Thank you, Mayor Boeheart. My name is Cassandra Luteus, and this is Rosalie Decorus, Derek Draco and Arabelle Aloria."

"It's a pleasure to meet you all. Please, do come and sit." Boeheart gestured to the couches. "You must have had a long journey here and I'm sure you must be quite keen to give your feet a rest."

"You have no idea," Rosalie said as the four of them took a seat on one couch while the Mayor sat down opposite them.

Cassandra shot Rosalie a stern look for the remark, but the Mayor only laughed.

Lilith, accompanied by another servant, returned carrying silver trays that they set down on the table before them. There were cups of steaming green tea, a plate of powdered biscuits, honey cakes and a cheese platter with crackers and a sprig of grapes. Derek, Arabelle, and Rosalie all eyed the delectable spread hungrily. None of them had eaten since early that morning and, according to the grandfather clock against the wall beside them, it was now well into the afternoon.

"Please, help yourselves," Mayor Boeheart said eagerly. "You must be famished."

The Queen had told Derek on many occasions that it was polite to accept food from a host when offered. So, without waiting to be told twice, he helped himself. He was just digging into his small collection of honey cakes when a large, white and brown head appeared above the armrest beside Derek, startling him.

"Bear, no," said Boeheart to the dog. "Leave the boy alone."

"It's all right," Derek said, gladly indulging the dog named Bear with a pat on the head. He received a wet lick to the underside of his wrist in return.

"You won't be saying that when he steals the food off of your plate. Come on, Bear. Come over here."

Obediently, Bear moved to sit at the Mayor's feet. He was taller even than the back of the couch.

"Mayor Boeheart," Cassandra said. "If you could please tell us more about these killings that have been happening as of late? Three people have been murdered, yes?"

The Mayor's handsome face grew sombre, the smile quickly fell from his lips. "I'm afraid the number has gone up to four now. Not long after the message was sent to Ember, another body was discovered."

Before Cassandra could reply, the Mayor added, "My Captain should be arriving here shortly. He'll better be able to fill you in on the details."

Not long after he said this, Lilith entered the study once more. "The Captain has arrived, Lord Boeheart."

A tall man came striding in, dressed in the silver and blue of the Windfell Town Guard and with a blue scarf around his neck that signalled captaincy.

Derek recognised the man the instant he walked through the door.

And felt as if he had just been thrust into one of his night terrors.

He had aged visibly since Derek had seen him last. His face had more lines and his dark hair was streaked with grey—only strengthening the already striking resemblance Orville Goldridge bore to his older brother, the late Mayor Goldridge.

It wasn't that Derek hadn't expected to cross paths with his once adoptive uncle while he was in Windfell, but not like this. Not as *Captain* of the Town Guard.

Bloody hell, he thought. *How did* Orville *become Captain?*

Orville's ice-chip blue eyes found Derek straight away and he could practically feel the hatred rolling off of the older man in waves, like heat from an oven. Derek remembered the morning after Goldridge had been killed.

"You! You little cretin, tell me what happened to my brother?!" Orville had screamed at him while being held back by a Guard. *"What did you do?!"*

"Ah, Captain Goldridge, there you are," Mayor Boeheart was saying. "Come and meet the Guardians. This here is Cassandra Luteus, Rosalie Decorus, Arabelle Aloria and—"

"Derek Draco," Orville finished, his lip curling unpleasantly.

Derek felt the rest of the eyes in the room swing towards him. He plastered a pleasant smile on his face and inclined his head. "Orville. I hope you've been keeping well."

He could tell that a snide remark was on the tip of the other man's tongue, but that he must have only kept hold of it in the presence of the Mayor, who looked between the two of them with rounded eyes.

"You two have met before?"

"I grew up here in Windfell, My Lord," Derek explained, keeping his tone as conversational as possible. "After both of my parents passed away, it was the former Mayor Goldridge who took me in. When he died, I went to live with my father's people in Ember."

"I see. Yes, I do believe I heard of such a story when I first came to live here."

Derek wondered if that was all he had heard about it.

Arabelle cleared her throat. "Perhaps we could begin discussing the murders?"

"Right, yes, of course. Orville, come sit down and we'll explain everything the Guardians need to know."

Derek cast a grateful glance at Arabelle, and she returned it with a small smile.

Orville sat on the armchair beside the Mayor, his armour shifting noisily as he did so. He held a sheaf of yellowed papers in one hand. "Back in June, a Valley dweller came home one morning to work on his crops and ended up discovering a body amongst the bush."

Orville took one of the papers and laid it flat on the table. It was a drawing, done in black charcoal, of a man—middle-aged perhaps?—in nondescript clothing. His limbs were in a sprawl and his neck looked gruesomely distorted. There were black splotches covering where his left hand should have been. *Blood,* Derek thought.

"We identified him as Marc Graff, another farmer from the Valley," said Orville, and Derek felt a little shock go through him. He hadn't recognised the drawing, but he recognised the name. Marc Graff had been a friend of Derek's parents. He'd let Derek pat his dog once.

"His neck had been broken and his left hand missing," Orville continued.

"And the man who found him?" inquired Cassandra.

"We questioned him but Graff had clearly been dead for a good while before he was found and the bloke who found him was said to be at the Healing House, visiting his daughter before spending the rest of the night at the Old Stones tavern." He set down another sheet of paper on top of the first. Another charcoal drawing, this time of a young woman with a shroud of long, dark hair. Her neck also appeared to have been broken and her left hand was missing as well. Only blood.

"Cecilia La Fray. She'd been staying in Brai for a week and her body was found outside of the town gates the morning after her sisters said she was supposed to return home."

Another drawing, a fair-haired man also with a twisted neck and no left hand. Clermont Black, Orville said. His body had turned up two weeks later in an alleyway. And the fourth and last victim was an Ishlavan man by the name of Arish Sabir.

"Why are they all missing their left hands?" Arabelle wondered.

Orville shrugged. "Maybe the killer likes to take a trophy?"

"As I'm sure you can already surmise," Mayor Boeheart chimed in. "The killer remains at large."

"Have you narrowed down any suspects?" Cassandra asked, looking up from her careful examination of the drawings.

"Well." Mayor Boeheart began fiddling with the cufflinks of his coat. "The Captain does have a theory."

Orville straightened in his chair. "I believe this is the work of Lady Night."

"Lady Night?" said Arabelle, her tone perplexed. "Who is that?"

"A ghost. Or a ghost story, really," Derek answered.

"A ghost story?" Rosalie said. "I don't think I've ever heard of it."

"I don't think many outside of Windfell have," said Derek. "It's about a woman named Rhysandra, who lived here in Windfell many years ago. She was the beautiful mistress of a nobleman, who was so in love with her, he planned to leave his wife and run away with her. When the wife found out, she killed him by poisoning his wine and then claimed it was Rhysandra's doing. The nobleman was well liked among the people, so they banded together to steal Rhysandra from her home one night and hang her. She died from a broken neck and her body was tossed into the lake for the water imps and the lucaira to feed on.

However, no one knew that Rhysandra was actually a dark mage and that she'd cast a spell upon herself so her ghost would live on when she died. After that, her ghost started appearing to the townspeople at night. First to the nobleman's wife. Then to the man who put a noose around her neck. Even the little boy who laughed while she struggled. She killed them all, breaking their necks just like hers had been." He looked to Orville. "You can't honestly think some ghost from an old story is behind all of this?"

Orville shrugged. "Why not? All of these poor souls had their necks broken and Lady Night killed her victims by breaking their necks. And they've all been killed sometime during the night. Just like the victims of Lady Night."

"That could just mean that the real killer is trying to make it look that way."

"And who would do such a thing?" Orville scoffed, as if Derek were a simple-minded brat.

"I see. No wonder the Mayor had to call us in to find out instead of leaving it up to you."

Spots of colour appeared on Orville's face. His nostrils flared and Derek was reminded of the expression, 'If looks could kill.' He returned Orville's glare with a smirk while the Mayor quietly sipped his tea.

It was Cassandra who spoke. "Theories aside, I think it would be best for us to do a bit of investigating ourselves. I assume you have already spoken with the families of the victims?"

"Of course we did," Orville barked. Derek's remark had clearly soured his mood. "Although Graff had no family. Not here in Windfell anyway."

"Good. Can you provide us with names, Captain? We will speak to them come tomorrow morning."

Orville frowned. "I told you, my Guard and I already spoke with the families and all of the conversations were written down, so there's no need for you to go talk to them. We can just show you the records."

"Thank you, Captain, but as I already said, we would like to do our own investigations."

Orville's frown deepened. Derek knew that to him, what Cassandra had just said was as good as calling his competency as Captain into question. And if anyone did not appreciate such criticisms, it was Orville.

The Mayor called an end to their meeting and asked if Cassandra could stay behind to talk further with him before calling Lilith in to show Derek, Arabelle, and Rosalie to their rooms.

"Oh, please, Mayor Boeheart," Cassandra started, "we don't want to impose on you. Staying at the inn will do us just fine."

Yes, Derek thought, *please just let us stay at the inn.*

"Nonsense. We have plenty of unused bedrooms for you all to stay in and I imagine they're much nicer than the ones at the inn. Not to mention they're free!"

There were no further arguments—much to Derek's disappointment—and with that settled, Lilith escorted them all out of the study and back down the hallway.

As they left, Derek felt a heavy hand on his shoulder and a voice next to his ear whisper, "I know it was you who murdered my brother that night. And believe me, I intend to make you pay for it."

"You must feel right at home here, huh, Arabelle?" said Rosalie as they made their way up the staircase after Lilith. "Your house is probably about the same size as this, right? And just as fancy looking?"

"Mm, more or less, I suppose."

Rosalie let out a theatrical sigh. "Oh, to live as a noble. Meanwhile, I'm forced to live in a little apartment above my mother's shop."

"I've seen your home, Rosalie," Derek said. "It's hardly cramped living."

She looked over her shoulder at him, sticking out her tongue. "What about you, Derek? You used to live here. What's it like being back? Is it like you remember?"

"There's a lot less mounted animal heads and pelts around here now," Derek said, only answering the last question.

They arrived on the second storey landing, where portraits of past Mayors lined the walls in heavy frames. Goldridge's portrait hung in the same spot as six years ago. Even the painted version of him looked imposing. "Other than that, nothing's really changed."

As Lilith led them down the wide hallway, towards the guestrooms, they ran into a woman descending the third storey staircase.

"Oh! Hello," she said when she spotted them. She was tall and fair-skinned with long, sleek brown hair, green eyes and dressed in a plain, but fashionable, purple dress. A string of pearls rested against the exposed wings of her collarbones. She also wore a ring with a wedding gem that matched the one the Mayor had been wearing.

"Good afternoon, Lady Boeheart," said Lilith to the woman. Her voice had lost some of its gruffness and sounded softer, affectionate. There was even something akin to reverence on her face as she gazed up at the younger woman.

"You must be the Guardians, Edmund said would be arriving," the woman said, smiling. "I'm Anna Boeheart, the Mayor's wife."

"It's a pleasure to meet you, My Lady," Arabelle said amicably and introduced themselves.

"It's such a good thing you've come," said Lady Boeheart, a troubled frown now upon her face. "All these murders lately have got the townspeople so shaken up—myself included, actually."

"Rest assured, Lady Boeheart. We'll find the killer and put an end to all of this."

Lady Boeheart smiled, charmed. "I'm glad to hear it. I'll let Lilith get on with showing you to your rooms." With that, she glided past them.

"Hurry up, you three," Lilith snapped, now back to her cranky demeanour as she hobbled down the hallway.

"The boy will have this room," Lilith gestured to the open doorway to their right at the end of the hall. "Miss Luteus will have this one and the two girls will share this one." She nodded at the room just opposite Derek's.

"Thank you for showing us," said Rosalie.

Lilith's only response was a scowl before she left.

"Charming woman," Derek said once the maidservant was out of earshot.

"She reminds me a bit of my great aunt," Arabelle noted. "Only she's—"

"More like a walking, talking corpse?" Rosalie supplied.

"I was going to say shorter, but what you said is also true."

They retreated into their respective rooms to change into something more comfortable for dinner. Once Derek closed the door behind him, he leaned his back against it, his knees buckling and his chest tightening. His breaths sounded too loud in the empty quiet of the guest room.

"You, Derek Alexander Draco, are the strongest person I know."

Jared's words rang through his mind, like an outstretched hand pulling him out of the dark waters of his fears before he could drown.

Jared thinks you're strong. He believes in you. He believes that you can do this assignment, but to do that, you need to grab a hold of yourself and actually be strong.

It took all of Derek's willpower to get his breathing under control, to force the steadiness back into his limbs.

He would not be that defenceless little boy anymore.

He *wouldn't*.

7

Jared and Will were walking near the docks in the port town of Skree. A chilly sea breeze blew over them, stinging the skin of Jared's nose and cheeks.

"What is that smell?" he said.

"Sea water. And probably fish guts, too."

Jared scrunched his nose. "Fish guts?"

Will nodded to where Jared now noticed a big man in a dirty apron gutting fish on his front porch. When he noticed Jared and Will looking, he grinned and waggled his knife. He knew they were Guardians—not that they were hiding it, dressed in their uniforms and all—and waving the knife almost felt like a taunt.

Despite the icy conditions, the docks were still full of people, many of whom were shouting over each other or loading and unloading cargo from the vessels that were moored there. Two children sat on the edge of a gangway, poking at an ice drift in the water with the end of an oar. A dog wandered about in search of scraps.

"Are you sure this is the right place?" Will asked.

"Of course I'm sure," Jared said. "I have this, don't I?" He held up the object in his hand—a black stone with a smooth surface, no bigger than his palm. It had a symbol, a triangle with a dot in its middle, engraved upon its surface.

"Prisoners are always branded, you see," Darus had explained to them when Jared asked how they were supposed to find the escaped prisoners so efficiently. When they had all been split into groups at Black Rock, he had decided to take Jared and Will on. "With a mark that acts as a sort of beacon, so that in the event that one ever does manage to escape, they can be easily tracked down. The marks are invisible though, and the prisoners aren't aware that they even have them."

"But how do we—?"

"With this." Darus had held out the black stone that had been given to them by the guards at Black Rock. He pointed to the triangular symbol. "This is the exact same symbol the prisoners are branded with. I'm not clear on exactly how it works, but I do know that there is a sort of magical tether between the symbol on these stones and the ones on the prisoners. As long as I hold this stone in my hand, I know exactly where to find any one of the prisoners."

Now Jared held the stone in his hand and he was surprised at the instinctive way with which he knew where to find one of their escaped prisoners. As if the prisoner had told him themself that they would be in Skree. He and Will were weaving past a group of

Tybeni merchants holding a pair of goats by rope leads, when Jared spotted a familiar head of wild, red hair at the end of one of the docks.

"What are the odds?"

"Hm? Did you say something?" Will asked.

"That's the one we're looking for." Jared pointed towards where the bandit, Rall was standing in a ratty cloak, near a small cog. He appeared to be speaking to a brawny man with bare, tattooed arms that Jared could only assume was the captain of the vessel.

"You sure?" Will asked and then, when Jared shot him a glare, "I know, I know. The stone."

"C'mon, mate. Can't ya do me this one favour?" Jared could hear Rall saying once they were within earshot.

"I don't smuggle escaped convicts out of the country without an upfront payment," the brawny man grumbled, turning to spit something into the water. "Ain't worth what'll happen if I get caught."

"You—"

"I'm afraid boarding that boat or any other is out of the question for you," said Jared, loud enough to draw the two men's attention. He watched Rall's expression shift from irritation to dawning horror.

"Now, if you'd be so kind as to—"

Rall bolted. He shoved past them with enough force that Jared nearly went toppling over the edge of the gangway. Rall even knocked over a couple of nearby barrels, spilling salted herring everywhere.

"I *knew* he was going to try and run." Will's voice was full of vindication. At the same time he took out his ring, put it on and Changed into a dragon with a hide as white as the snow falling around them.

Will took to the air while Jared chased after Rall on foot.

"Excuse me! Sorry!" Jared called out as he was forced to push past people in an effort to keep up with the red-haired bandit.

The chase led them away from the docks and into the narrow streets. Rall was quick, and it was proving to be a challenge for Jared to even keep him in his sights.

Rall took a sharp turn into a much less crowded laneway. A shadow passed over Jared's head and barely a moment later, Will landed at the other end of the laneway, blocking Rall's path.

Before Rall could even skid to a halt, he ducked into an alleyway between two buildings. Jared bolted after him while Will climbed onto the rooftops. The alley was tight enough that Jared's cloak scraped against the rough brick on either side of him, pulling at the threads. He vaulted over fallen crates that Rall knocked over into his path.

The end of the alleyway brought them to the edge of the town and the woodland beyond. Rall only made it a few steps into the open before something descended upon him from above. It was not Will, as Jared would have expected. Instead, it was a yellow dragon that he knew to be Darus. He had Rall pinned flat beneath him, like a cat with a rat struggling beneath its paws.

Will dropped down beside Jared a moment later, Changing as soon as he touched the ground.

Without releasing his hold on the bandit, Darus Changed as well, giving the two of them a stern look from over his shoulder. "Too slow, boys. You need to be quicker when chasing down crooks like this. Or they'll only end up getting away from you."

Jared shrugged. "I would have been quicker, but the cold has stiffened up my joints." That earned him an exasperated eye roll from Darus.

Rall had stopped struggling, seemingly resigned to the fact that he had been well and truly caught, and was now looking from Darus to Jared. He groaned loudly. "By the Goddess's ass, why is it always *you?*"

"Well, that's rude," said Jared.

"And blasphemous," added Will. "You're lucky my grandmother isn't here, or she'd have a bar of soap in your mouth."

"You're gonna send me back to Black Rock, ain't ya?"

"Spot on," said Darus, pulling a pair of iron manacles from his belt with one hand to clap around Rall's wrists. "But first, you get to spend a night in the lovely prison cells here in Skree before being carted back to Black Rock in the morning."

The bandit looked more than a little dismayed at the thought of returning to prison. "There must be some sorta arrangement we can come to, eh?"

Darus didn't bother to respond as he hauled Rall to his feet by the manacles.

"I know!" Rall went on. "What if I gave ya the names of everyone I done business with these past months?"

"We found your ledger at Serpent's Cove. We already have all the names we need."

"Shit. Wait! What about the bloke who broke us all outta prison the other night?"

Darus paused. "What about him?"

"I saw him." Rall sounded almost proud. Jared noticed a gleam of excitement in his eyes at having found something that had caught their interest. "The cell he broke into was just across from mine. I can even tell ya what he looks like 'cause I bet ya haven't a clue 'bout where to start lookin' for him."

There was a crease between Darus's brow. He was clearly thinking over whether or not to indulge in Rall. Finally, in a hard tone, he said, "Talk and maybe I'll consider leniency."

"Well, from what I saw of him, he was pretty tall, wore a hat and a trench coat."

"That certainly narrows it down," Will muttered.

"He had dark hair, too. Down to his shoulders, I think—Oh! And he had red eyes."

That last part had an inordinate effect on Darus. His eyes went wide, and he jerked back as if Rall had taken a swing at him. His hand shot out and grabbed Rall by the front of his cloak in a tight fist.

"Red eyes?" Darus repeated. "You're sure he had red eyes?"

Rall nodded jerkily. "I swear on me ma's ashes. Never seen

nobody with eyes that colour before, so I wouldn't be about to go forgettin' anytime soon."

Darus's jaw had gone slack, his pallor almost white. He seemed frozen with shock, and Jared couldn't understand why. Until he remembered a night, some years ago, standing outside of his parents' bedroom door.

"What did he say?" his mother's voice had been soft. She'd been sitting on the edge of the bed beside his father, a hand against his back.

His father sat hunched over, his expression aggrieved. "Darus said . . . he said that Derek told him that his parents were murdered. That Alex—Alexander was the first to be cut down."

"Does he know who it was?"

Jonathan shook his head and Jared could have sworn he saw tear tracks on his father's face. "Derek had never seen the man before. He only said that he had black hair and red eyes."

Red eyes.

Jared felt as if the ground beneath him was tilting. Could it be possible that the man that Rall was talking about was the same man who murdered Derek's parents nine years ago? If Darus's reaction was any indication, then Jared would say that he, at least, was thinking the same thing. But what was the killer of Erica and Alexander Draco doing breaking criminals out of prison after all these years of going unnoticed?

"You said he broke into the cell across from yours," Darus said, having regained his composure. "Do you mean the one belonging to Nile Fera? Was he the one who killed him?"

Rall nodded.

"Why?"

"Dunno," Rall admitted with a shrug. "I was sleepin', ya see, and I heard the big commotion outside. Like some big battle was goin' on. Then it all went quiet and then that bloke in the hat showed up. He got Fera's cell open somehow, and I heard them start talkin' but I couldn't really hear what they were sayin'. I did hear them say somethin' about a mirror and shards, I think? Also, Fera mentioned somethin' about havin' a son."

"And then he killed him?" Jared asked.

"Aye. Can't tell ya why, though. Fera seemed to be blabberin' about somethin' like he normally does. Maybe red eyes got fed up with it?"

"I see." The look on Darus's face was a mixture of concern, confusion, and even anger. Then it shuttered and was quickly replaced by a mild smile. "Thank you for telling us, you've been most helpful. Now, let's get you locked up." He began leading Rall back towards town.

"H-Hey, hang on a minute! I thought we were gonna work somethin' out if I told ya what I knew?"

This time there was something about Darus's smile that reminded Jared of the edge of a blade, sharp and dangerous.

"I said I would *consider* leniency. And I did, but decided against it. Perhaps *you* should consider that next time before you start running your mouth."

* * *

After a hearty breakfast of poached eggs and toast, Arabelle made her way into town with Cassandra, Derek and Rosalie to speak to the friends and families of the four murder victims.

Captain Goldridge had been by that morning while they ate and presented them with records of their past interviews with the family and friends, but Cassandra still insisted on going to speak to them for themselves.

"Don't you trust our accounts?" the Captain had asked.

"Of course I do, Captain," said Cassandra passively. "But you can't deny the benefits of firsthand accounts. That way you can make certain that the second-hand ones haven't missed any details . . . by accident, of course."

Arabelle tried very hard not to snort in a most unladylike fashion. But she didn't miss the way the Captain's eyes narrowed, his overall expression turning quite venomous.

Their first stop that morning was to speak with those who had been closest to Marc Graff in the Valley. None of them said anything different to what was written in the Town Guard's interviews. The last person to see Marc alive was the woman who lived right next door to him. She said it had been that evening, as they were preparing to quit work for the day that she last saw him.

"We bid each other good night, and he told me he'd see me in the morning," the woman had said as she started to weep.

Afterwards, they paid a visit to the sisters of Cecilia La Fray,

90

Giselle and Linette, which had been an exasperating affair. They were hardly able to make out anything intelligible from the two young women amidst all their sobbing as they spoke of their dead sister. Arabelle knew she should probably feel more empathy towards them. They had just lost their sister after all, and maybe she would have if she hadn't got the distinct impression that most of it was for show.

Again, they said nothing different to what had already been written in the first interview, that Cecilia had been away from Windfell visiting an old friend in Brai, a town not far from here, and on the morning she was due to arrive home, her mutilated corpse had been found instead.

Next, they saw Juniper Black, the widow of the third victim, Clermont Black.

There had been the briefest of moments, when the door had opened and Arabelle had first glimpsed the woman's long, blonde hair, that she had thought, *Mother?* But no, the woman was far too young to have been Arabelle's birth mother and her eyes were brown, not violet.

The outcome of their talk with Juniper Black was much the same as the one with the La Fray sisters and the neighbours of Marc Graff. Nothing they didn't already know was divulged.

When it was over, Cassandra rose from her chair at the kitchen table they had gathered around. "Thank you for your time, Miss Black. Now we—" she paused. "Where did Derek go?"

Arabelle looked around to find that Derek was indeed nowhere to be seen. When had he managed to slip away?

The sound of children's laughter could be heard through the stairwell.

When they had first come into the small cottage, Juniper had herded her three children upstairs and instructed them to play quietly while she spoke to the Guardians.

Arabelle was the first to move, not even stopping to consider whether she was taking liberties. What she found at the top of the stairs was a small attic room, furnished with one single bed and one bunk bed and toys scattered around the room.

When Arabelle had first seen the children upon arriving, they had all looked so heartbreakingly sad. As if every ounce of happiness had been sucked out of their lives and would never be seen again.

It was hard to reconcile those solemn-faced children with the smiling, giggling bunch sitting around the carpeted floor.

And kneeling in front of them was Derek.

"Do it again, do it again!" cried the littlest boy, clapping his chubby hands.

"Look closely," said Derek, and held up a coin for them to see. He then closed his fist around it and when he uncurled his fingers, the coin had vanished.

The children looked wide-eyed at Derek's empty palm. The little girl with plaits in her hair got up and walked behind Derek, as if she would find the coin hidden in his hair or in his back pocket.

"Come over here," Derek beckoned the little boy. When he

dutifully shuffled closer, his face alight with anticipation, Derek reached behind the boy's ear and when he pulled his hand back, the coin was once again between his fingers.

The children broke into laughter and applause, both stupefied and enthralled by Derek's sleight of hand.

The little boy clapped a hand over his ear. "That wasn't there before!"

"It was magic!" The eldest girl announced as she twirled around the room. "He put it there with magic!"

Arabelle was so transfixed by the scene before her she nearly jumped when she heard a small gasp beside her. Juniper Black held a hand to her mouth, her eyes shimmering with tears as she watched her children.

"I haven't seen them that happy in weeks," she whispered.

Arabelle looked back to where Derek was trying to explain to the children that he wasn't really a mage, just a plain old magic-less magician. There was a warmth blooming in her chest, one that grew stronger the longer she watched Derek interact with these children, watched him perform magic tricks to make them smile again after losing their father.

It seemed that just when Arabelle thought she couldn't fall anymore in love with Derek, he proved her wrong.

* * *

Derek got a stern talking to by Cassandra—it seemed all he did was get stern talking to's for going off on his own lately—after they had left the home of Juniper Black. "It's unprofessional to wander off like that. And in someone else's home," she'd said. "You're just lucky Miss Black had no problems with it."

But Derek could hardly bring himself to care. When they had walked through the front door and he had seen the looks on those children's faces, looks that spoke of grief and despondency, a look that Derek recognised in himself in the days after his own parents were murdered, he felt the need to lift those children's spirits in a way no one had ever tried to do with him.

"So where did you learn that sleight-of-hand trick?" Arabelle asked him as she, Derek, and Rosalie made their way through the winding streets, towards the town square.

It was now midday and Cassandra had decided to let them have a bit of a reprieve before they went to speak to the sister of Arish Sabir, the last person to have been murdered.

"There used to be a street performer who lived here when I was eight years old," Derek explained. "I used to sneak out at night to visit him so that he could teach me some of his tricks."

"Did he teach you how to juggle too?" asked Rosalie.

"Maybe." He frowned. "Why?"

"Well, at least if it turns out the Guardian lifestyle isn't for you, you could always turn to street performing."

"Maybe you could even learn to juggle as a dragon?" Arabelle suggested brightly.

"That would be sure to draw in a crowd."

The girls laughed while Derek scowled.

They came to the square where a few market stalls were set up, It was nothing close to resembling the lively open-air markets back in Ember. A small number of people milled around, rugged up in their warmest clothes. The air echoed with the sounds of vendors trying to sell their wares and people coughing, their lungs full of the winter chill.

There was a stall selling fresh meat pies, and Derek bought one for each of them for a coin each. They found a stone bench outside of the nearby Shrine House—a place of worship for the most devout worshippers of the Goddess—to sit on while they ate. The pastry was crisp and flaky and the meat inside was warm, perfect for such cold weather.

Derek had just finished his when he heard someone say, "Derek? Is that Derek Draco?"

He looked up, puzzled to see a Guard coming towards them.

"Yes?" Derek answered uncertainly.

The Guard removed his helmet, giving a better view of the face of a young man, not much older than Derek, with short, brown hair and brown eyes and the beginnings of a beard. "It's me," he said. "Edgar. Edgar Greyhill? Don't tell me you don't remember me."

Derek stood up, realisation hitting him like a rock to the head. "*Edgar?* I—Of course I remember you. It's just—"

The other boy grinned. "Been a long time, I know."

Edgar Greyhill had been Derek's first and closest friend when he lived in Windfell. He was the son of a butcher and the town's Shrine House keeper. Edgar had always been a rather chubby boy and was relentlessly teased by the other children for it, as well as for his timidness. Now it looked as if he were made up of mostly muscle beneath his armour. When they were children, they had stood at about the same height, despite Edgar being older by two years, but now he was at least a head taller.

"Are you going to introduce us?" Arabelle asked Derek. She and Rosalie came to stand beside him now.

"Right. Edgar, these are my comrades, Arabelle and Rosalie. Arabelle and Rosalie, this is Edgar Greyhill, an old friend of mine."

"It's lovely to meet you, Edgar." Arabelle extended her hand with a smile.

Edgar returned it, briefly grasping her hand and then Rosalie's. "Likewise."

"You're a Town Guard now?" Derek remarked, eyeing the armour.

"I just joined at the beginning of the year." Edgar looked slightly abashed, rubbing at the back of his neck. "And you're finally a Guardian! I remember how much you always wanted to be one when we were little."

"Yeah."

"I knew that the Mayor had called in the Guardians," said Edgar. "But I never would have expected you to be one of them, Derek. At least not until Eugenia came running to tell me just now that she'd seen my old friend with the Guardians."

"Eugenia? She's—"

"She's around here somewhere. Eugenia? Eugenia, come out here, you little grem."

"Ma said you're not to call me that in front of company."

Derek, Arabelle and Rosalie all whirled around to see a girl of about seven or eight standing behind them, as if she had appeared out of the thin air.

The last time Derek had seen Eugenia Greyhill she had been a toddling baby. Now she was as solid as Edgar had been at her age, with wild brown hair the same colour as her brother's and a smattering of freckles across her pale cheeks.

She eyed the them curiously. "You three look a little young to be Guardians."

"Eugenia." Edgar's tone was admonishing.

Rosalie laughed."They like to get us on the job early."

"Are you going to catch the person who's been killing everyone lately?"

Edgar hushed his sister and cast nervous glances around them.

Derek looked too and noticed that Eugenia's question had garnered them a few dark looks from those standing nearby. Some angry, some worried, all scared. Not that he could blame them, really. An unknown murderer within their midst, killing supposedly at random, would be more than enough to set an entire town on edge.

"Of course we are," Arabelle said confidently. "You just leave it to us and we'll catch them in no time."

Eugenia's face split into a pleased grin. "I hope you beat them up real good."

Arabelle winked. "We'll do our best."

"Well," intoned Edgar. "I better be getting back to my post and this one needs to go home for lunch before Ma gets upset."

Eugenia poked her tongue out at her brother before she waved goodbye to them and skipped away.

"It was wonderful meeting you all and getting to see you again, Derek," Edgar said. "I imagine we'll probably be seeing more of each other while you're here what with . . . everything that's going on."

"Edgar, you're a member of the Guard. Do you have any clue about why these murders haven't been solved yet?" Derek asked, pitching his voice low enough so that no one else would hear. "Surely by now they should at least have one suspect."

Edgar appeared hesitant to answer, looking around warily before finally saying, "I really can't say. I'm still new to the Guard so I'm not exactly privy to that much information. I can say that Lady Night is a pretty popular suspect and that Captain Goldridge thinks so, too."

Derek frowned. He knew Orville wasn't the sharpest knife in the kitchen, but surely he couldn't be that dense to place all the blame on a ghost story, could he? Once again, Derek found himself wondering just how Orville managed to make Captain of the Guard.

"Listen, Derek." Edgar's voice had taken on a much more serious edge. "The Captain, he's—I think he's the one who's been encouraging the idea that Lady Night's behind the killings."

"But why?" asked Rosalie. "Does he have any evidence?"

"None that I or any of the other Guards know of at least."

"So wha—" Arabelle started but was cut off by Edgar.

"I'm sorry, but I really have to go. Just—I'm sure you don't need me to tell you this, but the Captain really isn't that much different to how his brother was." And with that said, Edgar took his leave.

"What does he mean by that?" said Rosalie.

Derek knew what it meant. Mayor Goldridge had been beloved by everyone in Windfell. No one wanted to believe that he wasn't the kindly man he pretended to be, that behind closed doors, he was a corrupt and violent man.

Derek knew that, in saying what he had, Edgar was implying that Orville was not to be trusted.

Not one bit.

8

Arish Sabir had been a dealer in magical items, despite not being a mage himself, and the owner of a shop by the name of The Silver Eye. The building was double storey, grey brick with a slanted rooftop, and used to be an apothecary's shop. Derek remembered visiting once with his mother to pick up a tonic for his father when he was ill.

A wooden sign post hung on the front of the door with the word 'closed' carved onto it. Cassandra knocked on the door. "Hello, Aryel Sabir?" she called out.

They were forced to wait a few beats before the door finally opened. Standing on the other side was a tall, slim woman with golden brown skin and the amber eyes of an Ishlavan. Her dark hair was cut short and fell straight down to the sharp line of her jaw.

"Are you Aryel Sabir?" asked Cassandra.

"Who is asking?" Her voice was low and smooth and she spoke

with a heavy Ishlavan accent.

"My name is Cassandra Luteus, one of the Guardians. And I have here with me, Arabelle Aloria, Rosalie Decorus and Derek Draco. We would like to ask you a few questions about your brother, Arish Sabir."

Aryel's amber eyes passed over each of them in turn, her face remaining impassive. "Come in then," she opened the door wider for them to enter.

The inside looked like a typical shop, if a bit overly cluttered. A variety of objects, from chipped Scrying Glasses to thick tomes with cracked spines, filled just about every available space. It reminded Derek a little of the magic shop he had visited in Florinstone some months ago. The one that had been owned by a Wood Elf.

Because the room was so cluttered, there wasn't much room to move around without knocking into something, which was how Derek inadvertently ended up bumping into an urn behind him. It overbalanced and before it could shatter against the floor or Derek could move to catch it, it simply stopped. Suspended in mid-fall.

Derek turned around to see Aryel Sabir with a hand outstretched towards the urn. Then, with a turn of her wrist, the urn righted itself.

So, she's a mage.

"Apologies for the mess," said Aryel. "My brother wasn't a very organised person."

"Miss Sabir—" Cassandra began.

"Hold on a moment. Let's have this conversation upstairs."

Aryel led them past the front counter and up a narrow flight of stairs. Upstairs opened up into a small living area, complete with a tiny kitchen, a hearth on one side of the room, and a bed on the other.

"Can I get any of you anything to eat or drink?" Aryel asked.

"No thank you," answered Cassandra. "Miss Sabir, first of all, I would like to say that we are terribly sorry for your loss."

"Really? I'm not."

This gave them all pause.

"Y-You're not upset that your brother was murdered?" Arabelle said.

"You wouldn't sound so shocked if you had known him," Aryel countered. She took a seat at the table near the hearth. "Arish was an awful man and there have been many times in my life where I was ashamed to call him my brother."

Derek folded his arms across his chest as he took up a place against the nearby wall. "So, you're pleased that he's dead?" It would be a rather bold thing to admit, considering that Arish Sabir's murderer was still unknown.

Aryel turned her gaze to him. "Not pleased, but I'd be lying if I said I was particularly saddened by it. And I can't say that I'm surprised either. Like I said before, Arish was awful and I can imagine there being many people who would have wanted to see him dead."

"Anyone you could name?" inquired Cassandra.

"No. I made it a point to keep out of Arish's business."

"I see. And is there anything you can tell us about the night he died or the morning he was found?"

Aryel shook her head. "I wasn't in town when it happened. I had not seen or had any contact with my brother for a few years. I only arrived here a few days ago after I received a message saying that he was dead."

Cassandra tapped a finger against the table, her expression pensive. "And what do you think of the theory that these murders are the work of the ghost, Lady Night? Surely you've heard about it?"

"I have heard the murmurings amongst the people in town, but I cannot say I believe it. I may be a mage, able to do what is impossible for many, but that doesn't mean I believe in the idea of a ghost roaming around. Then again, I could be wrong."

There was a pause before Cassandra spoke again. "If you don't mind my asking, why did you dislike your brother so?"

"I already told you, didn't I? He was an awful person."

"But what made him so awful? That you seem so unmoved by his death speaks to me of more than just two siblings who didn't get along. It sounds like he might have done something personally to you."

"In other words, you want to know if I had a motive to murder my own brother?" said Aryel, her face unreadable. "Do you suspect me of being the killer, Miss Luteus?"

"Regardless of what I think, it's my job to be thorough."

Another pause, in which neither Aryel nor Cassandra took their eyes off of each other. The silence was so tense that Derek almost felt as if he shouldn't dare to even breathe.

He watched Aryel take a deep breath before she spoke. "He killed my lover. That's why I hated him."

Cassandra's gaze narrowed. "And why did he kill your lover?"

"Jealousy. Arish was always jealous of me growing up because I was born a mage, and he wasn't. Then, when we both fell for the same woman and she chose me over him, he couldn't bear the thought of me having yet another thing that he wanted. He must have thought that if he couldn't have her, then neither could I."

"And how long ago did this happen?"

"Seven years ago."

"Did he ever face any sort of punishment for his crime?" Cassandra questioned.

Aryel took a moment to respond. "No. I was the one who found him standing over her slain body when I arrived at her home that night. I was . . . angry. As I'm sure you can imagine. I attacked him. I would have killed him too if others hadn't barged in to see what all of the commotion was about. Arish told them that I had done it. That I had murdered Nathalie and, of course, the sight of Arish all bloody and beaten by my hand was all it took to convince them."

"So, you took the blame for your lover's murder?" said Rosalie.

Aryel nodded and rolled up the left sleeve of her jacket, exposing her inner wrist for them all to see. On the skin there was a small, black tattoo, a triangle with a dot in the middle, bisected by a horizontal line. It was the symbol all ex-prisoners of Black Rock were marked with after their release. "I spent seven years locked up in Black Rock while Arish remained free."

"Seven years?" said Arabelle. "You mean you've only just been released?"

"Yes," Aryel answered. "Three months ago."

"You never tried telling anyone the truth?" Derek wondered.

"Just because one speaks, little Guardian, doesn't mean others are always so keen to listen."

Derek dropped his gaze to the floor. He remembered a freezing winter's night, being dragged through the streets by a Guard. *"Please! Please don't make me go back there!"* he had pleaded.

"To think he would besmirch the Mayor Goldridge's name like that."

"After all the Mayor's done for him."

"What an ungrateful child."

Cassandra leaned back in her chair, arms folded across her chest and face stony. "So your brother not only murders your lover, but then allows you to take the blame for it and spend years in prison. Then three months after you're released, he ends up dead. I have to say, that seems like a pretty big coincidence."

"I'm well aware of how it sounds," Aryel admitted. "But I did not kill Arish."

"You have to understand how suspicious it all sounds. To us Guardians especially. Do you have anything to prove that you didn't murder your brother in some act of retribution?"

"Do you have anything to prove that I *did*?" Aryel retorted.

Cassandra didn't answer.

With a sigh, Aryel pushed herself up from her chair, the legs scraping against the floor. "And even if I may have had a motive for killing my brother, what motive would I have had for killing the others?"

Again, Cassandra remained quiet.

Something passed over Aryel's face. The briefest glimpse of an expression that Derek had seen on her for the first time. An expression of triumph.

"I'll allow the four of you to show yourselves out."

* * *

Since Darus preferred not to stay at the dilapidated inn in Skree, they ended up travelling to White Lake, which was only an hour's flight away from the port town.

White Lake was a quaint but lively town, sitting beside a large lake that was now frozen over. It was nearing evening by the time they arrived, the sky tinged purple and orange. Despite this, the streets were still crowded with people and some vendors hadn't even started packing away their stalls, still readily serving customers.

Like Ember, White Lake appeared to be in the grips of Nativitas fever. Wreaths adorned doors and ribbons and tinsel decorated lampposts and fences. Jared spotted an appetising array of

Nativitas cakes in the window of a bakery they passed.

Darus brought them to an inn called The Spring Owl. Inside was a wide common room filled with people and the clang of boisterous voices. An open hearth in the middle of the room had a whole pig roasting on a spit over it. It was warm too, something Jared was grateful for after spending all day in the freezing outdoors.

"Do you have any rooms available?" Darus asked one of the serving women. "Just for one night?"

"Only got two free at the moment," she said.

"I'll take them. The boys can share."

Darus paid the coin, and the woman led them to their rooms on the upper floors. The first room they came to was Jared and Will's, while Darus's was all the way down the end of the hall.

"And just so ya know," the woman told them. "We have a bathhouse 'round the back. Figured you'd like to know since you lot look like you could do with some warmin' up."

"Thank you for letting us know," Darus said, smiling in a way that had the woman going pink in the cheeks before she left them to it.

"I think I might pay a visit to that bathhouse as soon as it takes me to walk there," said Jared, setting his pack down on one of the twin beds in his and Will's little room.

"And I think I'll join you," added Will, brushing off some of the snowflakes that still clung to his hair.

"You boys enjoy," said Darus. "I have something to take care of first. So, if you need me, I'll be in my room."

Jared couldn't help but notice that ever since their encounter with Rall in Skree, Darus had seemed distant. Distracted, more like it. He could only assume it had to do with the bandit's mention of a man with red eyes. Jared would be lying if he said that what Rall had told them hadn't been nagging at the back of his mind all day,

But, for now, there was nothing to be done about it.

And for now, all he wanted was to soak himself in a nice, warm bath.

Jared let out a relaxed sigh as he sank into the hot water. The sound was louder than it should have been against the white-tiled walls. Steam filled the square room, the walls dripping with condensation, and the fresh scent of lemon grass clung to the air.

It wasn't long before Will joined him, sinking into the water beside him until he was submerged up to his shoulders. They were the only two currently occupying the men's baths.

Will made a contented sound, leaning his head back against the outer rim of the bath. "It feels like ages since I last visited a bathhouse," he said.

"Me too," said Jared.

"Can this place even compare to your royal baths, Your Highness?"

Jared frowned. "Stop calling me that."

"But isn't that your title?"

"It is," he conceded. "But no one calls me that when I'm on

duty. When I'm on duty, I'm just another Guardian."

"What about darling Derek?" asked Will. "Does he ever call you 'Your Highness'?"

"Ha, no. None of my friends do."

"Is that why you don't want me to call you that? Because I'm your friend?"

"That depends. Do you normally go around kissing people who are your friends?"

Will let out a breath of laughter. "Is that something you'll always hold over me?"

"Maybe." Jared smiled, closing his eyes and allowing the warmth of the water and the light conversation to lull him.

"It depends."

Jared cracked an eye open to look at Will with. "What does?"

"Whether or not I go around kissing my friends. It depends."

"On what?" He asked a bit warily.

Will shifted closer, the water sloshing around them, until their shoulders were just barely touching. "Whether they want to kiss me or not."

Will was smiling at him again. But there was something about Will's smile, Jared was coming to realise, that had a strange effect on him. It was something in the quirk of his upturned lips. The way his green eyes focused solely on Jared. Not being a writer or poet, Jared couldn't quite put it all into words, but he knew that having Will smile at him like that made his face warm in a way that had little to do with the steam.

That and the exposed curve of Will's shoulder above the water. The droplet of water that travelled from a strand of his hair, and down his jaw line before dropping onto the pale wing of his collarbone—

Jared nearly jumped out of his skin when the door opened to emit two men, their booming voices carrying across the room. They said a quick hello when they noticed Jared and Will, before moving to sit at the washbasins.

"I think," Jared announced hurriedly, rising from the bath. "That I've done enough soaking."

Will watched him get out with a perplexed frown. "You know I was only teasing you, right?"

"I know." Jared picked his towel off the floor. "It's just, if I stay in any longer, I'll end up looking like a prune."

He secured his towel around his waist and padded across the damp tiles and into the change room, willing his heart to go back to its regular, calmer beat.

* * *

In a back alley, where only the prying eyes of rats and stray cats could bear witness, Draken appeared in White Lake in a burst of red flame. Adjusting the crooked lapel of his coat, he stepped out of the shadowy alley and onto the bustling streets.

As he sauntered down the cobblestones, he spotted a group of people talking and laughing raucously outside of a tavern.

"Excuse me," he said to them as he approached. "I'm looking for a Luro Fera. Can you tell me if he lives around here?"

"Who wants to know?" said the woman with a silver piercing through her nose.

"An acquaintance of his father's."

One man stepped forward until he was standing directly in front of Draken, an ugly smirk on his face. "And just why should we tell you? What are you gonna give us in return?"

Draken sighed and looked into the man's eyes and almost instantly that smirk fell from his face and a red spark glinted in his dark eyes.

"Where can I find Luro Fera?" Draken tried again.

"In a house," the man said without missing a beat. "To the west. Outside of town."

"I see. Thank you for being so cooperative," Draken added, leaving the group to their bewilderment.

* * *

Jared was thinking that perhaps he should have stayed in the baths a while longer as he and Will made their way back to the inn in the freezing night air. It was only a short walk, but already Jared could feel the warmth from the baths seeping out of him.

Stupid Will and his stupid smile, he thought crossly, rubbing his palms together.

They were almost at the front door of the inn when a man, coming round a corner from one of the nearby laneways, stepped out in front of them.

"Oh, sorry," Jared said, coming to halt before he could bump into the man.

The man seemed to eye them for a moment or two—although it was hard to be certain since his gaze was shaded by the rim of his hat—before offering a smile. "No harm done." He tipped his hat to them and continued on his way down the crowded main street.

It was only as they stood outside the front door of The Spring Owl that the realisation hit Jared like a good kick to the chest and he grabbed Will by the arm.

"What is it?" Will turned to look at him with a mixture of confusion and concern.

"That man, did you see what he was wearing?"

"A . . . coat?"

"A dark trench coat and a dark hat. That's what Rall said the man who attacked Black Rock was wearing," Jared said.

"You mean?" Will looked in the direction the man had left. "You don't honestly think it was him, do you? Jared, I'm sure there's lots of people wearing clothing that fits that description around here. And besides, what are the chances that person would happen to be wandering around White Lake?"

"I know that." But the more Jared thought about it, the more he couldn't help thinking, *what if?*

He turned away from the door and started off down the street.

"Jared, wait! Where are you going?" Will called after him.

"You go back inside the inn," was all Jared said. *I have to make sure. If that really was the man who attacked Black Rock and who killed Derek's parents . . . I can't just let him walk away.*

* * *

When Arabelle and the others returned to the Mayor's Manor that evening, they took stock of everything they had learned. Which, admittedly, was not much. No one they had spoken to could make any speculation as to who might be responsible for the killings and neither had they witnessed anything that could be of help in identifying a suspect.

Cassandra was convinced, though, that Aryel Sabir was not as innocent as she claimed to be and said that they would be keeping a close eye on her.

After dinner, they decided that their next course of action would be to launch a full scale search of the town, the Valley, and the surrounding areas, since Captain Goldridge had failed to conduct one already. Every household would be searched from top to bottom, as would every nook and cranny in the streets, every crevice around the mountain road, and behind every stone and bush in the woods. All in the hope they might uncover something that would lead them towards the killer.

"But please do not alert the townspeople of this," Cassandra had said to the Mayor and the Captain. "We don't want to give the murderer time to hide anything."

"And when will this search be taking place?" The Captain asked, sounding none too pleased about it all.

"As soon as possible."

"Tomorrow then," the Mayor said, and the Captain had dared not to argue.

Finishing up her wash before she went to bed, Arabelle stepped out of the guest bathroom, her hair still damp at the ends from her shower. With a lit candle in hand, she made her way down the corridor towards the bedroom she shared with Rosalie. The floors creaked and groaned with her every step.

The hallway was bathed in darkness, everyone else having already retired for the night, so it was easy to see the light peeking out from beneath the closed door of the library. It wasn't the white light of an illuminae crystal, either, but the orange tinged glow of candlelight.

Arabelle paused in front of the door, gently pushing at it until she could peer through the gap between the door and the wall. It was a quaint library, nothing grand like the one in Ember or at the royal palace. The floor was carpeted and every available wall space was lined with bookshelves. Plush armchairs and a couch circled the room. She spotted Derek standing in front of one of the shelves, his back to her and a burning candle on the mantelpiece above the fireplace.

She watched as he browsed through the books, taking out one book and flipping through it before putting it back on the shelf and reaching for another.

Finally, Arabelle decided to announce herself. "It's a little bit late to be up looking at books, don't you think?"

Derek looked at her over his shoulder, his blue eyes wide with surprise in a way that made him look even younger than his sixteen years. He seemed to relax when he realised it was only her.

"Maybe," he said, turning back to the books. "But I don't really feel like sleeping just yet."

Arabelle stepped further into the library, closing the door behind her as she went. She set down her candle on the mantel beside Derek's and seated herself on the armchair closest to where Derek stood, tucking her legs up underneath her.

There was already a book resting on the arm of the chair. *A History of Notable Vampires,* was the title embossed in gold lettering. She picked it up and opened it at the middle. It was the first page of the twentieth chapter titled *Emery & Alice Shade: A Bloody Couple.*

Below that were masterfully drawn portraits of the aforementioned couple. A young, handsome man with long, black hair and a woman with short, fair hair framing a heart-shaped face.

Arabelle had heard about these particular vampires before, remembered learning about them once at the Academy. They were a vampire husband and wife who terrorised the northern regions of Aloseria. Raiding towns and either slaughtering the people or turning them into vampires. Both of the Shades had also been infamous for practicing dark magic, which had made stopping them all the more tricky, but had finally been slain by Guardians in the year 358.

"That was one of my favourite books when I was a kid," said Derek as he sat down on the armrest of Arabelle's chair. There was another book in his hands.

"Really? I can't imagine this being the sort of book a child would be interested in." It was true. *A History of Notable Vampires* was more of a biography than a children's tale. And a sordid one at that.

"I went through a stage where I was very interested in vampires when I was about seven or eight—why are you smiling?"

"No reason." She did nothing to hide the smile on her face, however. It made her happy to hear Derek talk about his childhood like this with her. She could picture it: Derek, looking as he had when she'd first met him when he was nine, all skinny limbs and big, blue eyes. Curled up on one of the couches in here, with a book in his lap. "Did you spend a lot of time in here when you were younger?"

Derek nodded. "I hated this house, but I always felt comfortable in here. It reminded me of my da, actually. He used to love books, and he was always telling me stories when I was little . . . He would have loved a library like this."

Arabelle could practically feel a sombre air settle around them. She thought about Derek kneeling in front of his parents' memorial when they first arrived here.

"I haven't had the chance to ask, but how are you feeling? About being back here after all these years?" she asked.

"I . . ." Derek looked caught off guard by the question. "I'll let you know when I figure out exactly what I feel."

"Well, you know I'm right here if you need someone to speak

to."

He gave her a wry smile. "You're definitely Jared's cousin, all right."

"What's that supposed to mean?"

"Just that you're both insatiably compassionate."

"Of course." *Because I'm hopelessly in love with you.* "You're our friend."

"Mm."

Sensing that they could use a shift in the conversation, Arabelle turned her attention to the book in Derek's hands. "What's that book about?"

Wordlessly, he held it up for her so she could get a good look at the cover. It was made of unadorned, black leather with faded edges and only a single word in red lettering.

"*'Daemons'*?" Arabelle read aloud in surprise. Books about daemons were rare. Only a few had ever been written and they were only for educational purposes. Few people these days wanted to know more than they needed to about the times when horrifying creatures stalked the lands and terrorised the people. Arabelle certainly wouldn't have expected to find such a book in this library.

"The last story my da ever told me was about daemons," Derek explained. "About the daemon king, Asmydionn, and Milrath's amulet. I remember my mum got really upset at him for it. I bought this book from a Tybeni trader at the market a year after they died because it made me think of my da. I really wasn't expecting it to still be here after all these years."

"Will you read it to me?" she asked.

Again, there was that taken aback look on his face. It was only there for a brief moment before he said, "Only if you say that special six-letter word."

"Oh, Derek, won't you *please* read this book to me," she pretended to beg, in a syrupy tone she'd heard noble ladies use while flirting. She'd also seen those ladies press themselves as close as physically possible against their partners while they did so, but Arabelle wasn't feeling quite that bold.

Derek chuckled. "Since you asked so nicely."

He opened up the book to the first page, the spine crackling as he did so.

Arabelle took a moment to study the sharp angles of his profile, the straight nose and the long, down-turned lashes. The way the candlelight outlined his delicate, Elf-like features in gold.

Derek took a breath and read aloud. "This land was not always ruled by men. Hundreds of years ago, men were ruled by daemons. The most powerful and terrifying of all the daemons was called Asmydionn . . ."

9

"We've just delivered the Serpens brothers to the prison in Greengate. They'll have them carted back off to Black Rock by morning," Charles Decorus's voice was saying through the ilictio crystal—an enchanted stone that allowed Darus to communicate with his fellow Guardians while on this assignment.

Darus sat cross-legged on the narrow bed of his room at The Spring Owl. The crystal rested on the fur blankets, glowing a warm red in the encroaching darkness. No one had come to light the candles just yet, which was fine. Darus didn't exactly want someone walking in and listening to this conversation.

"It looks as though the Mendax is loitering five miles south of Ember," said Carvilla Hargrade. "My sons and I are heading there now."

"Darus?" said Charles. "You've been oddly quiet. How are you and your squad doing?"

"Hm? Oh, yes, we intercepted the bandit Rall in Skree. He'll also be taken to Black Rock by morning. He—"

Darus hesitated. Should he tell them? About what Rall had said of the man who had orchestrated the breakout? Surely that was important. Someone capable of such a thing couldn't be left unchecked.

"He had red eyes."

"Rall mentioned something about seeing who it was that killed the guards and broke the prisoners out."

"Did he tell you on the condition that you would let him go free?" Amelia Caritas asked, sounding sceptical.

"Well, yes he did," Darus admitted. "But I believe he was telling the truth."

"You believe the word of a bandit so easily?" said Carvilla.

"No, but Rall had no reason to lie. He knew that I wasn't going to let him go." Well, that wasn't exactly true, but they didn't need to know all of the details. "He said that he was in the cell across from Nile Fera's, so he saw who killed him and he said that it was the same man who broke them all out."

Charles made a considering sound. "Even if we could be sure that he was telling the truth, what can we do about it? Without a name or an adequate description, how are we supposed to go about looking for this person?"

"Rall mentioned that he had . . . that the man had red eyes." *Just like Alexander and Erica Draco's killer.* He didn't bother with mentioning that last part.

"That's still hardly anything to go off of," Alistair Hargrade's pompous voice came through the crystal. "What are we supposed to do? Check every person in Aloseria's eye colour?"

There was something about the smugly amused tone of Alistair's voice that made Darus feel a hard kernel of dislike for the young man.

"Alistair's right, Darus," Amelia was saying. "It might be worth looking into once this assignment is over with, but for now there simply doesn't seem to be much we can do."

"Indeed," Carvilla agreed. "Better to focus on the task at hand for now."

"Right," said Charles, although his voice seemed to lack the conviction of the others.

Darus sighed, running a hand through his unbound hair, mussing it slightly. "I just thought what Rall said might warrant repeating. That's all."

He'd expected this response because, well, they were right. How were they supposed to find someone when they didn't even have a name or an accurate physical description? Perhaps once this assignment was finished, they could try questioning Rall or any of the other prisoners more extensively. Have some wanted posters drawn up.

However, there was still that sense of urgency beating hard within him. *The man who murdered Derek's parents is here in Aloseria. He's here and who knows what he's really up to?*

The gem's glow faded to nothing as Darus bid farewell to the others. He picked it up and stowed it away in his pack.

He felt a strange sense of foreboding wash over him and tried his best to ignore it as he stood from the bed and stretched.

Maybe I should go pay a visit to that bathhouse after all.

* * *

Further out, amongst the hilly landscape outside of White Lake, Draken walked up the pathway covered in dirt and snow towards a ramshackle house.

It had taken a few more days after his attack on Black Rock to use his somniamancy to find the son of Nile Fera. There were so many dreams to sift through, it was like looking for a needle in a haystack most of the time. But once he found the needle, it was merely a matter of pulling on the thread of memories connected to it, and everything he needed to know was unspooled before him.

It was at the back of the house that Draken found a man dressed in a plain pair of breeches and a loose shirt that looked more appropriate for the summer months, chopping wood.

"Luro Fera?" he asked.

The man paused his wood chopping and slowly turned to look at Draken. Even in the dim light, Draken could see the perspiration gleaming against the man's sun-tanned skin.

"I am." He spoke gruffly. "Who wants to know?"

"Call me Draken. You see, I'm looking for something and I was hoping you could help me?"

Luro Fera set aside his axe and wiped his hands against his breeches as he turned to give Draken his full attention. "What is it?"

"A glass shard. Or a mirror shard, to be more precise."

He saw the way Luro's body went rigid, his skin paling. "I'm sorry, but I don't know what you're talking about."

Draken smiled. "Oh, I think you do. Your dear old father told me as much."

This also seemed to catch Luro off guard. "My father? You . . . spoke to him?"

"Indeed. We had a rather lovely chat in his cell at Black Rock. He was most helpful. Right up until I stuck my blade through his throat."

Draken observed the way the revelation hit Luro like a simultaneous blow to the face and stomach. He recovered quickly enough to take up his axe and charge at Draken.

Draken reached out a hand and Luro Fera froze in his tracks. Wisps of crimson light floated around his prone form.

"Now, now, Master Fera," Draken tutted. "Attacking someone with an axe isn't how one holds a proper conversation."

He stepped forward and gripped the other man's jaw. Felt his harsh breathing against his hand. "Now, tell me where the shard is."

Luro grunted.

"What was that?"

"I . . . don't have . . . it."

"Hm, I do believe you're lying to me." He sent Luro flying backwards, where he crashed into his pile of wood and lay there, unmoving.

Certain that the other man wouldn't be getting up any time soon, Draken made his way back to the front of the house, intent on finding the shard himself.

He heard a grunt from behind him and paused in his steps. Looking over his shoulder, he saw Luro struggling to his feet.

And when he looked up at Draken from beneath the black tangle of his hair, his eyes—which had been as dark as obsidian only moments ago—were now a bright yellow that seemed to glow in the darkness. Two long, white canines protruded from his lower jaw. His nose looked broader, flatter and before Draken's very eyes, a layer of coarse, animal-like hair began to sprout along his skin, from the open collar of his shirt, beneath his sleeves, and along his face.

Draken watched with rapt attention as Luro's clothes tore and his body changed shape, he grew taller, broader, his limbs elongating. He could hear bones cracking.

Within seconds, the waifish man, Luro Fera, was gone and in his place stood a hulking, wolf-like beast.

A lycanthrope.

"Well, this is unexpected."

With a howling roar, the lycanthrope lunged at him.

* * *

"C'mon Jared, just admit that you have no idea where he's gone and let's go back already."

He ignored Will, choosing instead to continue sniffing at the

124

ground.

"What scent do you think you're going to pick up?" Will grumbled, hugging his arms tight around himself. "The ground's covered in snow."

Jared raised his head to glare at the other boy. They had followed the man in the trench coat all the way from the inn to the gates of White Lake. It was there that they had lost him in a crowd that had gathered to watch a play by some travelling performers. Still, Jared was certain that the man had left through the gates. He'd even spotted footprints in the snow leading up a rise in the earth off of the road. Although, as Will had pointed out, they could have belonged to anyone.

"Darus is going to murder us when he realises we left," Will was saying. "And I'm far too young and beautiful to be murdered."

"Oh, will you be quiet," Jared said, Changing back. "If that man was around here, he'd probably have run off by now because of the sound of your whining."

Will pouted. "I'm not whining. I'm just trying to make sure you understand how ridiculous it is that we're out here looking for someone who might not even be anywhere near here. Really, for all we know, he could have slipped into one of those houses. Back to his family, because maybe he is just a good person who doesn't go around breaking people out of prison."

"Yes, Will, I see your point," said Jared in exasperation.

"Let's just go back. If we go now, maybe we can avoid death by Darus."

"Fine," Jared relented. "But—"

An almighty roar split the air. It sounded like the cry of some strange beast, and it sounded close, as if it had come from just over that thicket of trees beyond the hilltop.

"What in Ithulia's name was that?"

Instead of waiting around to answer Will's question, Jared Changed and took off in the direction the sound had come from. Soaring over the tree thicket, he spotted a lone house, and landed outside its front, Will following close behind.

"Warn me next time you decide to fly off into the woods alone," said Will once they landed and Changed. "I don't want to get yelled at for losing the Prince."

Jared ignored him. As he was looking around for any signs of what could have made that noise from earlier, he spotted something that looked out of place on the ground by the side of the house, a dark patch against the white snow.

As he and Will drew closer to investigate, he realised what the dark patch was. Blood. A fair bit of it, too.

Not far from the spatter of blood were gouges in the snow. As if there had been some kind of scuffle.

But it doesn't look like there is anyone else around here, Jared thought, looking around, but all he saw were bits of chopped wood scattered around the back.

"*Jared!*"

The urgency in Will's voice had Jared spinning around in time to see something leaping off of the roof.

He was only able to catch a brief glimpse of a black, shaggy coat, outstretched claws, and glowing, yellow eyes, before he was flinging himself out of the way as the thing dove towards them.

Jared rolled into a crouching position, his hand going to the hilt of his sword—only to realise it wasn't there because he had left it back at the inn. Cursing himself, he turned to see what they were now faced with.

Admittedly, Jared wasn't exactly sure what he had been expecting to see, however, he certainly hadn't been expecting to find himself looking upon the monstrous form of a lycanthrope.

Lycanthropes, along with vampires, were creatures born of a disease that was created by one of the daemon lords, Algron, hundreds of years ago. The lycan before them had the face of a wolf, but with a broader muzzle and longer ears. Although its physique looked similar to that of a man, it was covered in a thick coat of fur. And unlike a wolf, it stood on its hind legs at easily over eight feet tall.

Looks like we found out what made that noise from before.

Jared moved slowly, only a minute shift of his foot, but it seemed enough to set the lycanthrope off. Its head turned in his direction, its eyes fixed on Jared, and with a growl, it sprang towards him.

Will barrelled into the lycan before it could even reach Jared. The lycan was huge even compared to Will's dragon form, but still he managed to force the beast off of its feet and the two of them clawed and snapped their teeth at each other. In a movement so quick that Jared couldn't quite track it with his own eyes, the lycan caught Will by the throat in one massive, clawed hand.

Changing, Jared launched himself at the lycan, sinking his claws into the flesh of its back until it released its hold on Will.

The lycan rolled onto its back, crushing Jared beneath its heavy bulk, and for a brief but startling moment, he couldn't breathe, his ribcage feeling close to collapsing.

Then the lycan was back on its feet and standing over him, a crazed and pure animalistic look in its eyes as it raised a clawed hand.

Will leapt onto the lycan's back from behind with a dagger in hand and plunged it into the lycan's shoulder.

The lycanthrope howled and Will fell from the beast's back as it waved its arms about wildly, trying to dislodge the dagger embedded in its skin. Will came to kneel by Jared's side, already with another dagger in his grip.

They watched as the lycan howled and gnashed its teeth, shaking its great head from side to side before it finally tore the dagger free. The fur around its wounded shoulder was now matted with blood.

When the lycan turned to look at them, Jared thought he had never seen such unbridled rage reflected in one's eyes before.

It bellowed its fury before moving to attack them once more.

* * *

Blood poured sluggishly from the wound in Draken's side. He sat on the branch of a tree, holding his hand to the bloodied tear in his coat along the left side of his ribcage. Despite the pain, Draken couldn't stop himself from chuckling.

It had been a long, long time since he had been caught off guard like this and even longer since he had encountered a lycanthrope. He had forgotten how fast and how fuelled by their blood lust they were. Draken even had to admit that if he hadn't had his magic to help him get away, he might have ended up with worse than a bloodied scratch.

As to be expected of one of your creations, Algron, he mused.

Gritting his teeth, Draken pressed his palm flat against the wound, allowing only a small hiss of pain to escape him. Crimson light flared from beneath his hand, followed by the faintest sound of something burning.

When Draken removed his hand, the wound had closed; the blood had disappeared and the tear in his clothing had been repaired, as if it had never even been torn open in the first place.

Rising to his feet, Draken looked back to the house in the distance. He could see three figures fighting nearby. Even from this distance, Draken could hear the howls and snarls of the lycanthrope. He watched as one of the figures—a boy?—ran at the lycan and changed into what was clearly a dragon as they did so.

Guardians. Aryanna's people. Draken felt a wave of disdain flood through him. They must be the boys he had run into back in White Lake.

But this was good, he thought. With the lycan properly

distracted, Draken was free to search for the shard.

He took a step off the tree branch and plummeted towards the earth. Crimson flames consumed him before he could hit the ground and he reappeared a second later inside Luro's house.

He found himself standing in a small, sparsely furnished living room. The sounds of the lycan fighting the Guardians was muffled by the thick brick walls.

Draken looked around the room, but there weren't any obvious signs of where the shard could be, not that he'd expected it to be that easy. He clapped his hands together, the sharp sound echoing throughout the empty house, and waited.

Nothing happened. Frowning, he clapped once more and again there was nothing. Before Draken could grow frustrated that the shard apparently wasn't there, he heard it, barely audible amidst the sounds of fighting outside. It was a thumping sound, and it was coming from upstairs.

"There you are," he said to himself with a smile.

* * *

Will was thrown back against the side of the house. His body hit the brick hard enough that Jared heard the crack of the impact and felt his heart leap into his throat when Will didn't immediately get up off the ground.

With Will lying still on the ground, the lycan singled him out as the more vulnerable target and began to advance on him.

Jared ran up behind the lycanthrope until he was close enough to breathe a gout of fire just above its head, effectively stopping it in its tracks.

He didn't want to kill the lycan, he knew that somewhere beneath all of that fur and fangs and unbridled aggression was a person. A person who may be completely innocent of any sort of crime. A person who might not deserve to die because of their terrible affliction. But that did not mean he could flee while they left the lycan to roam free, either. What if it attacked someone else? What if it found its way to White Lake? How many would end up being hurt or killed or infected? Jared couldn't allow that to happen.

I have to figure out some way to subdue it.

With the lycan's attention now on Jared, it turned away from where Will was still out cold and bounded towards Jared on all fours, kicking up a cloud of snow behind it.

He leapt over the lycanthrope's head before it could reach him, but he didn't get very far. The lycan whirled around and grabbed his hind leg in a bone crunching grip. Literally. Jared cried out in pain as he felt the bones in his leg shatter.

The next thing he was aware of was the lycanthrope hurling him through the air and his body colliding painfully with the ground.

Jared didn't even remember Changing but over the ringing in his ears and the intense waves of pain that seemed to roll through his whole body, Jared was aware of his hand clutching at his leg. He could feel something hard and sharp poking through his trousers above his calf.

He felt as if he were about to faint.

Something loomed over him and he didn't even have to look up to know it was the lycan.

Is this it? The thought crossed his pain muddled mind.

Something darted towards the lycan from overhead, like a shadow detaching itself from the rest of the darkness. The lycan howled as the shadow—which wasn't really a shadow but a black raven, pecked and clawed at its face before flying off again.

Before the lycan could recover, there was a burst of violet light that slammed into its side with such force, it sent the lycan flying.

Jared looked in the direction the light had come from and saw a cloaked figure coming towards them. As the figure drew closer, Jared saw it was a woman with short, black hair. Short enough to reveal the fine, Elven point of one ear. The raven that had attacked the lycan circled back and came to rest on the woman's shoulder.

"Are you all right?" The Wood Elf asked as she came to stand where Jared was sprawled in the snow.

He didn't get the chance to reply. The lycan was back on its feet, howling its rage as it rushed towards them.

The Elf looked unfazed by the sight of a hulking lycanthrope charging at her. Instead, she lifted her left hand and dozens of heavy chains materialised at her side. She thrust her arm forward, and the chains hurtled towards the lycan. One wrapped itself around the lycan's legs, causing it to topple to the ground. The rest wrapped around its body and muzzle, holding its jaws firmly shut. The lycan growled and struggled violently against its bindings, but it was useless. The chains held, and the lycan was effectively subdued.

"Well, well," said a new voice and Jared looked to see the man in the hat and the trench coat at the front of the house, as if it were the most natural thing in the world for him to be there at this very moment.

"Aurelia Blackwood," he said, addressing the Wood Elf. "So, you're still alive? You're more tenacious than I thought."

"Well, I did not feel like dying without repaying you for your last visit," said the Elf, Aurelia, her tone laced with loathing.

"Holding a grudge really isn't a very flattering look, dear."

"And I really don't give a shit." She threw her hand up and a great spike of ice erupted from the ground and shot straight towards the man at break-neck speed.

Before it could skewer him, what looked like a bolt of red lightning travelled down the ice spike, and it shattered into glittering pieces.

"Please," the man said in a bored tone. "Not these tired old tricks again."

"Very well."

Aurelia Blackwood made another hand gesture and this time, two giant spikes of ice burst out from the ground. This time, the man only managed to destroy one of them with his strange, red magic, but had to leap out of the way to avoid being impaled by the second.

While the man in the trench coat and the Elf mage seemed

focused on trying to kill each other, Jared heard a metallic, popping sound and saw that the lycanthrope was actually managing to *break free* of the chains.

One by one, the chains snapped and fell away until the lycan was standing on two feet once again. It looked about with those baleful, yellow eyes and spotted Jared lying injured on the ground, and lunged towards him.

Everything happened so fast that Jared hardly had a chance to process it all. One minute, the lycan was almost upon him, ready to tear into him with teeth and claws, and the next Will was there, throwing himself between them in time for the lycan's claws to tear across his body.

"*Will!*" The cry tore from Jared's throat as Will collapsed to the ground.

The lycan looked as if it were about to rip even further into Will, and Jared was powerless to do anything about it, when a stream of fire cut a bright path between the lycan and Will. Darus descended with a furious cry and tackled the lycanthrope to the ground.

Ignoring the chaos of Darus fighting the lycan and the Elf woman fighting the man in the trench coat, Jared struggled to pull himself towards Will. The movement caused a fresh wave of pain to travel up his broken leg, so strong that it brought tears to his eyes. Jared ignored it, biting down hard against his lip as he dragged himself over to where Will was lying face down in the snow.

"Will?" Jared placed a hand on the other boy's shoulder. "*Will?*"

But Will was unresponsive, his face startlingly pale. And to Jared's dawning horror, he noticed that the snow beneath Will's body was slowly turning red. Red with blood. With *too much blood.*

Will's blood.

No. No, no, *no.*

This couldn't be happening. Not to Will. Not because of Jared.

No.

Behind him, part of the house's roof exploded with a resounding bang, sending shattered pieces of brick and wood raining down.

The last thing Jared remembered was an explosion of pain in the back of his head as a piece of debris struck him and the sight of Will's pale face.

10

It was one of those rare days in Windfell, where the sky was not so cloudy and the air felt as if it had thawed just a little, thanks to the presence of the sun.

Derek and the others were up at the crack of dawn, when daylight still had yet to rid the sky of all traces of night. They ate their breakfast with the Mayor, but Lady Boeheart did not join them as she had woken up feeling unwell, according to Mayor Boeheart, and would remain in bed for the rest of the day.

Shortly after, they joined the assembled Town Guard and Cassandra split them into four groups: one would search the town, knocking on doors and searching homes. The second would search the mountainside, the third would search the Valley and the fourth would comb through the surrounding woodland.

Cassandra placed each one of them in charge of a group of Guards; Arabelle would oversee the search of the town, Rosalie the Valley, Derek the woods, and Cassandra would go with the mountain group.

Derek climbed through the boughs of the trees like an overgrown cat in his dragon form, hoping it would provide him with a better vantage as he and the fifteen Town Guards assigned to him searched, for any sign that the murderer they were looking for might be hiding out here.

There were a few times as Derek moved from branch to branch that he shook down snow, sometimes onto the heads of the Guards below, causing them to shout in surprise or grumble in discontent. Derek could tell that many of these men weren't happy about this assignment, and even less so about having to take orders from a boy much younger than most of them. But the Mayor had given the search his approval as well as for the Guardians to be in charge of it, so the Guards would do as they were told—even if it was begrudgingly.

Derek leapt down from the trees and onto the ground. He looked around at the forest, at the trees with their dark trunks and bare branches, at the snow that blanketed the forest floor and seemed to sparkle in the weak sunlight. He remembered playing in these woods as a child. Running around and laughing with Edgar and the other town children. He remembered wandering these woods by himself sometimes, hoping he would spot a deer or a wolf or some other kind of animal.

Remembered running barefoot through these woods in the rain the night his home was attacked by the red-eyed man.

"Oi, I think I found something over here," called one of the

Guards from a short distance away.

"That's a fox's den, you twit," said another. "Unless the killer's the size of a babe, there's no way they'd fit in there."

The first Guard bristled. "Well, I didn't realise that what with all the snow covering it. I thought it could be—"

Derek growled at the pair, loudly enough to put a halt to the argument before it could really begin.

Moving on ahead, Derek glided down a steep incline in the ground and when he landed, he sniffed at the air. Picking up scents in the snow was difficult. In fact it was near impossible for most creatures such as dogs, but a dragon's sense of smell far surpassed that of any other beast. If the killer really was hiding out somewhere in these woods, then Derek may be able to pick up a faint scent.

On the air, beneath the overwhelming, fresh, earthy smell of snow, he caught the scents of the men behind him, the leather of their armour and even some cologne. He could smell the fading traces of a deer or two that must have wandered by not too long ago, as well as—

Derek looked to the wide trunk of a birch tree not far from where he stood in time to see something duck behind it.

Derek Changed. "All right, come on out," he said. "I know you're there." There was a moment in which nothing happened. He sighed. "Fine then, I'll just come over and drag you out—"

"We're here!" cried a boy as he jumped out from behind the tree. He had a freckled face and red curls peeking out from beneath his woollen cap. He looked at Derek with a mixture of awe and fear. "Please, don't set us on fire."

Derek frowned."What—"

"Don't be stupid, Micah," said another voice, and Eugenia, Edgar's younger sister, also emerged from behind the tree, along with another girl with white-blonde hair. "He's a Guardian. He helps people. He doesn't set them on fire."

"But what about the bad ones?" The boy—Micah—asked Derek.

"It depends on how bad they are," he said before asking, "what are you doing out here, Eugenia?"

"See? I told you he knows me," Eugenia said to her friends with a smug grin. "Micah and Emmaline didn't believe me when I told them I knew one of the Guardians that were here, so I had to prove them wrong."

"Is it true that Guardians eat raw meat?" asked Emmaline.

"What? No."

"Have you ever bitten someone's head off?" asked Micah.

"No."

"What about setting them on fire?"

"Maybe."

"Can I try your ring on?"

"No." Before they could start peppering him with anymore questions, he said. "I'm sorry, but I don't really have the time at the moment to stand around entertaining you. You should all go back home. These woods might not be the safest place to be right now."

"Because you're looking for the murderer, right?" said Eugenia. "Edgar told me there was going to be a big search today."

"But wouldn't it be hard to find a ghost?" said Micah. "Wouldn't it just turn invisible?"

"Stupid, I already told you, Lady Night's not the murderer. She's not real."

"But everyone else seems to think it's Lady Night," Emmaline pointed out. "Even Captain Goldridge has been saying so."

"I wouldn't put too much stock into everything the Captain says," Derek said, perhaps a bit harsher than he'd intended. Hearing that even the children were blindly trusting Orville's word made his temper flare. In a calmer voice, he added, "The thing is, we really don't know who the killer is, so we need to consider the possibility that it could just be a regular person."

"Maybe we can help?" Eugenia suggested eagerly.

The three of them looked up at Derek with wide, beseeching eyes that brought a reluctant smile to his lips. "I—"

The sound of snapping wood behind him, followed by the screams of a man, had Derek whirling around. All he saw was something large and winged, rising through the air with the struggling form of a Guard clutched in its claws.

The creature and the Guard disappeared through the treetops. The Guard's shouts grew distant until they were abruptly cut off.

Everything was silent.

Until something fell down from above and landed at Derek's feet.

It was the Guard's severed head.

* * *

Arabelle stepped back onto the cold streets. She turned around to face the man who had shown her and a Guard out of his house and smiled. "Thank you for your time. Have a lovely day."

"Hmph," was his response before promptly shutting the door in her face.

Arabelle sighed, her breath misting in the air. She understood that many of these people probably weren't too thrilled about having Town Guards show up on their doorsteps, unannounced, to search through their belongings and ask them questions, but at least they got to stay indoors. Even with the sun shining, Arabelle still felt as if her fingers were going to freeze off beneath her gloves.

How could anyone bear to live in a place this *cold?* If Arabelle had been brought up around here, she would have packed up and made for the warmer parts of the country as soon as possible. *Maybe I was born here, and that's why my mum left me, because she didn't want me living in such a freezing cold place. Maybe she wanted warmer temperatures for me.* The thought failed to inspire any humour in her.

She made her way down the street, pausing only when she saw Edgar Greyhill and another Guard exiting a house further up.

"Found anything of interest?" she asked as she approached them.

Edgar shook his head. "Nothing yet. And you?"

"Not a single thing."

"We've probably nearly searched all of the stores and homes in Windfell and we still haven't found anything," said the Guard accompanying Edgar.

"That doesn't mean we'll *never* find anything," said Arabelle. "If not in the town, then perhaps outside."

"Let's hope," Edgar said with a sigh. "I—"

"By the Goddess, what is that?!"

Shouting was coming from the direction of the town square. Wasting no time, Arabelle, Edgar and the Guard were racing down the street.

In the square, people were gathering to stare at something in the distance. The town square provided the perfect view of the land at the bottom of the mountain. From there, one could see the Valley stretched out beneath them, the woods, and more snow-capped mountains.

At first, Arabelle thought that what she was seeing was a huge gathering of black birds swarming around the Valley and the surrounding woods. But no, those weren't birds. Even from this distance, Arabelle could tell they were much too big to be any kind of bird.

The distant sound of screaming drew Arabelle's attention to where one of the winged creatures was lifting the flailing body of a Town Guard into the air above the trees.

Screams rang out around her as the creature tore the poor man's head from his shoulders.

* * *

Blood from the Guard's severed head seeped into the snow.

But there was no time to focus on that now. More of those creatures were bursting through the branches above their heads.

Gargoyles, Derek realised, when he caught a good look at one of them for the first time. They had long, spindly limbs and blue skin so dark it almost looked black, stretched over emaciated bodies. Their faces reminded Derek of the skull of a dog, with a pair of curled horns upon their heads. He knew them to be creatures born of magic—dark magic.

Shouts rose up from the Guards as they were set upon by the gargoyles. Some of them reached for their swords in time to try and fend off the gargoyles. Others were knocked to the ground or carried off screaming.

There was a scream from behind Derek, and he turned to see a gargoyle land in front of the children. It rose onto its hind legs, towering over them like a bear, strings of saliva dangling from its jaw full of serrated teeth. Its pupil-less blue eyes, cold and unblinking.

Drawing his sword, Derek rushed forward, placing himself between the children and the gargoyle. With a hissing growl, it swung a massive, taloned hand at him. Derek dove onto the ground to avoid the attack. While he was on his back, he swung his blade at the gargoyle's outstretched arm.

The sword sliced straight through the flesh and sinew, and half of its arm fell to the snow in a bloody heap. The gargoyle yowled as blood poured from the gaping wound in its arm in thick streams.

While it was distracted, Derek leapt to his feet and plunged his sword through the gargoyle's chest. It cried out in a high pitch that raised the hairs on the back of his neck as he pushed the gargoyle over and onto its back. When it toppled onto the ground, the gargoyle's skin went grey and shattered into chunks of stone.

Behind Derek, Eugenia and her friends were huddled together, their faces white with terror.

"*Go!* Hide!" He shouted at them just before two more gargoyles came charging towards him.

He Changed with no time to spare before the gargoyles had him on the ground.

It was like having a pair of stone statues fall on top of him. While the gargoyles certainly didn't look it, they were heavy, and it was all Derek could do to keep them from tearing into him completely as they grappled with each other in the snow. He felt claws rake across his hind leg and teeth sink into his shoulder, just above the wing joint.

With a roar that was part pain, part frustration, Derek released a breath of scorching fire. One gargoyle was unlucky enough to get caught in the it. It sprang away from Derek, turning to flee and screaming that horrible scream as flames charred its body.

The second gargoyle scrambled away to avoid meeting the same fate as the other, but was unable to avoid Derek as he tackled it to the ground and sank his fangs into its unprotected neck, like a sabre lion bringing down a deer.

The gargoyle struggled only briefly before it crumbled to stone.

A scream caught Derek's attention. A child's scream. He saw Eugenia and her friends had taken refuge in the branches of the birch tree, but had now drawn the attention of two other gargoyles. The gargoyles seemed to be egged on by the children's screams, snapping their jaws and clawing at the tree bark frantically in their desperation to reach their prey.

Derek rushed over, leaping into the air and grabbing the gargoyle closest to Micah and Emmaline, dragging it to the ground and clawing out its throat.

He was too late, however, to stop the second gargoyle from reaching Eugenia. The girl screamed as she was plucked from her branch and carried off above the trees.

Derek shot into the air after them. The gargoyle didn't make any move to kill Eugenia like Derek feared it would. Instead it continued to carry her away, high above the ground, heading. The gargoyle didn't seem to notice that Derek was following it, or if it did, it did not seem to care.

He dared not breathe any fire at the gargoyle; there was too great a chance that Eugenia would get caught in it as well. But no matter how hard Derek beat his wings, it simply wasn't enough to close the gap between himself and the gargoyle. Instead, Derek focused on propelling himself higher into the sky.

He climbed high enough until he was flying well above the

gargoyle. Then, closed his wings tight against his sides and went in for a dive.

The wind whistled in his ears as he cut through the air at an alarming speed. It was only a matter of seconds before he collided with the gargoyle in a bone-shuddering impact.

As Derek and the gargoyle grappled with each other in mid-air, biting and clawing at one another, Eugenia slipped from the gargoyle's grasp. Screaming, she plummeted toward the frozen lake below.

Derek disentangled himself from the gargoyle by breathing fire in its face. Once he was free, he dove after Eugenia, catching her by the back of her cardigan only feet from the surface of the lake.

He set her down gently on the ground by the lake's edge.

"Are you all right?" he asked, Changing and kneeling in front of the girl, checking her over for any signs of injury. "Are you hurt?"

Eugenia didn't look at him, but she shook her head. Her face was stained with tears and she was trembling harder than a newborn fawn, but Derek assumed it was more from shock than the cold.

He would have comforted her, reassured her that she was safe now, that he would protect her, had it not been for the returning gargoyle. Derek had just enough time to shove Eugenia out of the way before the gargoyle charged into him, lifting him off the ground and slamming him into the ice of the lake, which immediately cracked and gave way beneath them.

They plunged beneath the water and the coldness that hit him was like a thousand icy daggers stabbing into his skin and straight through his bones.

The gargoyle, however, seemed unperturbed by the temperatures. Its only focus seemed to be holding Derek under the water until he drowned. He noticed that the skin on the gargoyle's face and front was covered in fresh burns.

Derek Changed as he struggled to free himself of the gargoyle's hold. Fire breath wouldn't help him now—not while he was underwater—so he kicked, bit, and scratched at the gargoyle until it finally released him.

Except it wasn't that the gargoyle released him, it was more like it was *pulled* away from him. He watched as the gargoyle disappeared into the murky depths, its cries muffled by the water.

Before Derek could even think of making a break for the surface, something shot out from below him and wrapped around his tail, pulling him further down. It didn't take long for Derek to realise what had caught him. A lucaira. Through the bluish murk, he could make out the dark shape of its long, oval body and eight outstretched arms.

Derek didn't have time to stay and gawk at the beast. The ice-cold water was starting to make his body go numb, and it was becoming increasingly difficult not to try and gasp for breath.

He struggled to free himself from the lucaira's hold and when that didn't work, he Changed. With no tail to grab onto, he was free from the lucaira's hold. Derek pushed through the water, trying to make it to the surface as quickly as he could, desperate to reach that shimmering circle of light where the ice was broken above him.

He felt another one of the lucaira's arms wrap around his left ankle and another grab hold of him around the torso, squeezing tight and dragging him down into the icy depths.

This time, he didn't even struggle. He couldn't struggle. He couldn't move. He could hardly feel his body at all. He couldn't even feel the lucaira's arms around him anymore. Even the cold had left him.

Derek barely even noticed that he'd let go of the breath he'd been holding up until now, until he began to choke as water filled his lungs.

It was the last thing he remembered before everything went dark.

* * *

The gargoyle screeched as Arabelle set it alight. It plummeted down toward the earth, bursting into a shower of stone half-way down. Another came careening towards her, claws outstretched, and before Arabelle could even think to move out of the way, a purple blur sped past, right into the gargoyle. Rosalie sank her teeth into its neck, turning the creature to rubble.

Gargoyles. By the Goddess, what are gargoyles doing here?

So far, the gargoyles only seemed to be focused on attacking the Valley. They'd made no move towards the town, which was a relief in a way. However, trying to keep the Valley dwellers safe was a challenge, especially when the only ones who stood a real chance against the gargoyles were Arabelle and Rosalie. Many of the Town Guards put up a valiant effort, but the gargoyles had numbers and sheer viciousness on their side. When she'd first made it down to the Valley, she'd been too late to help as a Guard was set upon by a pack of gargoyles. She had only been able to look on helplessly as he was torn limb from limb.

Screams from below alerted Arabelle to where a trio of gargoyles were tearing into the thatched roof of a cottage.

Arabelle launched herself at the gargoyles, ramming into one and knocking it over the side of the roof and breathing fire on the others until they took off, squealing.

Peering through the hole the gargoyles had clawed open, she saw an elderly couple huddled together in the corner, their faces stricken with terror, but otherwise seemingly unhurt.

Something hard ploughed into her and she tumbled over the side of the roof, landing hard in a frozen vegetable patch.

Arabelle rolled onto her back in time to see a gargoyle diving towards her, talons extended and mouth wide open—before it broke apart.

Arabelle brought her wings up to shield herself as bits of rock rained down around her. When next she looked, it was to see that the rest of gargoyles were, one by one, exploding into chunks of stone. A man that was in the middle of being carried off by one fell to the ground as the gargoyle fell to pieces.

After the last of the gargoyles shattered apart, all that was left was a shocked stillness.

Rosalie landed next to Arabelle and Changed. "What just happened?" she asked, helping Arabelle to her feet. She knew Rosalie wasn't only talking about the sudden demise of the gargoyles.

Arabelle surveyed the destruction that was left in their wake. The ruined homes, the blood and the bodies strewn along the ground like discarded toys. She saw a Guard kneeling over what was left of one of his comrades. He bowed his head into his hands and sobbed.

"I don't—I don't know?"

* * *

Consciousness returned to Derek with a flash of red light.

No longer was he numb from the freezing water as feeling returned to his body. The water he had inhaled seemed to disappear and new air filled his lungs. He became aware of his surroundings instantly, taking in the lucaira that was still holding onto him and a red glow emanating from his chest.

But there was no time to dwell on it. The cold already beginning to seep back into his bones, and he could only hold his breath for so much longer. The lucaira had pulled him even further toward the bottom of the lake. He could now make out the reddish skin of the lucaira's body and one huge, black eye.

With his free arm, Derek reached for the dagger sheathed at his belt and stabbed the blade into the soft skin of the lucaira's arm

150

wrapped around his middle. A cloud of red blood rose up into the water and the arm quickly recoiled, as did the one around his leg when he slashed at it.

As soon as he was free, Derek Changed, using his wings and powerful tail to launch himself through the water, towards that wavering circle of white light.

He burst through the surface, through the break in the ice where he had first fallen through. Flying towards the bank, he crashed into the snow in a heap. Breathing in the cool, mountain air had never felt so incredible.

Eugenia, who had been kneeling by the lake's edge, came rushing to his side, just as he Changed back to his human form.

"A-Are you all right?" she asked between sobbing breaths.

Derek didn't answer her. Instead, he busied himself with undoing the buckles of his dripping vest with trembling hands. He pulled at the collar of his shirt to peer underneath and saw it. Glowing faintly against the pale skin of his chest was a strange red mark, made up of three swirling patterns and smaller, jagged lines cutting through them. It looked as permanent as any tattoo—or even a brand from a hot iron—but Derek had never seen it before in his life. And then, the mark faded, disappearing completely, as though it had never been there at all.

What the hell was that? Derek's mind was whirling. What was that mark and where had it come from? Did it have something to do with how he miraculously survived drowning?

There was the sound of voices in the distance and Derek looked over his shoulder to see a group of Guards appear over the cliff's edge above them. Not too far behind were two dragons, Arabelle and Rosalie.

It seemed the mystery of the mark would have to wait for now

11

When Jared opened his eyes, it was to the blurry outline of a pale face with black hair hovering above him.

Derek? he thought.

But as his vision cleared, he realised that it wasn't Derek, but a woman, one that he had never seen before—no, he *had* seen her before.

The woman's emerald green eyes flicked up to his face. "You are awake? Good."

She spoke with a distinctive Elvish lilt to her voice, and that's when Jared took notice of her ears. A Wood Elf.

"Y-You're," he croaked, "the woman from last night."

"I am," she said in a way that made Jared believe she thought that was of little importance. "You received quite a nasty blow to your head. How do you feel? Dizzy? Nauseous?"

"No." He took a quick look at their surroundings. Surprisingly enough, they appeared to be in a rather spacious room with plush, red carpeting and matching walls of hanging fabric. Jared realised they must have been inside a tent and that he was lying in the middle of an incredibly soft bed. "Where are we? Where's—Darus and—"

The memory of Will, lying still with his blood spilling onto the snow, came rushing back to him. Panic lanced through Jared and he made to sit up quickly, but the Elf woman placed a firm hand on his shoulder, easing him back down.

"Hold still," she said. "The bone in your left leg was shattered. I managed to heal most of it, but you still need to be careful."

But he didn't care about any of that right now. "Where's Will?" he demanded. "Is he here? Is he all right? He was injured, wasn't he? I have to see hi—"

"Jared?"

He lifted his head to see that, peering in through the flap of the tent, sunlight streaming in behind them, was none other than Will.

Relief swept through Jared like a strong ocean current at the sight of Will, although looking somewhat worse for wear, whole and not like he had been at death's door from trying to protect Jared.

"I thought I could hear your voice," said Will as he came to stand at the Elf woman's side. "Are you feeling okay?"

"Am *I* okay? I'm not the one who was bleeding out just before."

"And I'm not the one who had their leg crushed by a lycan and the back of their head smashed with a brick."

"Now, now boys," the woman cut in. "You were *both* in a

154

horrible condition. But thanks to me, you have both managed to pull through."

"Thank you," Jared said, because that was the least he could do after this woman went through the trouble of healing their injuries. "Miss . . ."

"Aurelia Blackwood."

Hm, Jared thought. *The name doesn't really ring a bell.*

"Darus sent me in here to get you," Will said to Aurelia. "The lycan's waking up."

Lycan? Were they talking about the same lycan who had attacked them last night? The same lycan who had nearly killed Will?

"Really? Well then, if you will excuse me." Without further preamble, Aurelia left the tent.

"Who is she?" Jared said once he and Will were alone.

Will shrugged. "Who can really say? I think Darus only allowed her to stay around because she pretty much saved our lives last night."

"That's the only reason?"

"I suppose so. Why?"

"It's just that she kind of reminds me of . . ."

"Of what?"

Jared shook his head. "No, never mind. So what happened after I was knocked out? Where are we?"

"We're in the woods near that house from last night," Will explained, taking a seat on the bed at Jared's side. "I don't know exactly what happened either, but from what Darus told me, he and that Aurelia woman managed to subdue the lycan. You and I were both in pretty bad shape, so once that was done, they started patching us up. I only came to a couple of hours ago."

"How did Darus find us?"

"He said that he started getting worried when we didn't come back to the inn, so he went looking around town. Someone told him they'd seen us leaving through the gates and then he he noticed the big magic battle happening between Aurelia and that man."

"And the man? What happened to him?"

"Apparently he just . . . vanished. That's why Darus and Aurelia want to talk to the lycan. They think he might be able to tell them something."

Jared ran a hand through his hair, messing up the already unruly curls. *Just what have we stumbled into?*

"And you?" he asked. "Are you really all right?" He kept seeing Will bleeding onto the ground. The image unsettled him more than he'd like to admit and, as silly as it might have sounded, he needed reassurance that Will wasn't in danger of dying anytime soon.

Will looked as if he hadn't expected Jared to take such an interest in his wellbeing. "I'm all right. Really," he said. He lifted the hem of his coat and shirt and Jared felt all thoughts momentarily flee his mind at the sight of Will's bare stomach.

But soon enough, his attention was drawn to the three diagonal slashes running across Will's side. They were jagged and angry-looking, but already scarred over with puckered, red skin, as if they were more than just a few hours old.

"I'm supposed to be wearing bandages, but they were getting itchy so," Will explained idly.

"You should have left the bandages on," said Jared, sounding uncharacteristically stern even to his own ears. Still, he couldn't help himself from reaching out to brush his fingers along the scar beneath Will's ribcage.

The other boy shivered, inhaling sharply at the press of Jared's fingers. The sound seemed startlingly loud within the tent. Realising what he was doing, Jared snatched his hand back, cheeks flaming. "By the Goddess, cover yourself up already. Do you want to catch a chill?" He found it incredibly difficult to look anywhere at Will's person.

What is wrong *with you, Jared?*

Will cleared his throat. "Right. Yes. You're right."

An awkward silence pervaded until Will declared he should leave and let Jared get some more rest.

Once Will was gone, Jared collapsed back against the pillow and pulled up the blanket to muffle his agonised groan.

* * *

Aurelia found Darus Flynn standing a little way away from where they had set up the tents she had conjured the night before. Behind him was the lycan, tied to the base of a tree. The air was more than a little brisk outside, and Aurelia pulled the collar of her cloak tighter in a vain effort to protect herself from the cold as she approached the two men.

Darus regarded her with cautious, grey eyes—not that she blamed him. He knew nothing of her. If not for the fact that she had saved his companions from their grievous injuries, she suspected he would have either run her off or tied her to the tree alongside the lycan. As for the lycanthrope, he was looking around dazedly, as if he had just woken up after a night of heavy drinking to find he had the mother of all headaches.

"How's Jared?" Darus asked her.

"Awake. Just like our friend here."

The lycanthrope glared up at the two of them with bloodshot eyes. Under the unkempt, dark hair and beard, Aurelia could see that he was actually quite young. Probably not even that well into his thirties.

"Who are you people?" He spoke in a deep, growling voice. Aurelia thought she could almost hear the beast in him.

"My name is Darus Flynn. I'm a Guardian."

"And I am Aurelia Blackwood. Not a Guardian."

Something in the man seemed to deflate when he heard the word, 'Guardian'. He looked almost as though he were bracing himself for a blow. "Who did I hurt?"

"No one," Darus lied smoothly.

The lycan didn't look like he believed that for one second. "I—"

"Don't worry about that now. The only people you encountered while you were transformed were the two of us, and as you can see, we're fine."

"If that's true, then why am I tied to a tree?"

"Just a precaution," said Darus calmly. "Until we figure out whether you're a friend or foe."

"Does it seem like I'm a foe?"

"That remains to be seen," Aurelia said, taking a step closer to the bound lycan so that he would turn his gaze to her. "Who are you and who was that man with the red eyes? What business did you have with each other?"

Without breaking eye contact, the lycan said, "My name is Luro Fera."

"Fera?" Darus spoke as if that name meant something to him. "Any relation to a man named Nile Fera?"

Luro nodded. "He is—*was*—my father."

"You know what happened to him then? That he's dead?"

"Yes. But only because that man from last night told me so. He told me that he was the one who did it."

"Really?" said Aurelia. "Was that the only reason he decided to pay you a visit?"

Luro hesitated a moment before answering. "No. No, he came because . . . he wanted something."

"And what was that?"

"Before I tell you, you need to take me to my house."

Later, Aurelia stood in the middle of a cramped room in Luro's house—which had only been partially destroyed during her fight with the red-eyed man. The entire ceiling was missing, however. As Luro knelt on the floor and lifted a loose floorboard after clearing away a bit of debris, Aurelia peered over his shoulder to see what was underneath—and saw that there was nothing.

Frowning, Aurelia was about to make note of this when Luro let out a humourless laugh.

"Just as I thought. He took it."

"Took what?" Darus asked.

"The mirror shard."

"A mirror shard?" Darus's tone was full of bewilderment. Of course it was. He did not understand why someone would go to the trouble to steal a broken mirror piece. But Aurelia did.

"Tell me about this shard," she demanded. "Did it have a strange energy about it? Did it make you see things when you touched it?"

"I wouldn't know," admitted Luro. "I never touched it. But my da . . . he wasn't right. Not for a long time. He was always having nightmares. Always saying he could see monsters lurking about when there was really nothing there. My mum and I knew it had something to do with that mirror shard that had been passed down through his family. One day, my mum tried to get rid of it. She thought it might make him better if she did. When he caught her doing so, he killed her for it."

"And you still kept it? Even after all of that?"

"I didn't know what would happen if I got rid of it," said Luro. "I didn't want it to accidentally wind up in some other poor soul's hands and do to them what it did to my family."

Luro's reasoning for not getting rid of the shard mirrored

160

Aurelia's own reasoning for not tossing out the one she had the first chance she got.

"All right," Darus cut in. "One of you needs to start explaining what's going on. What is this mirror shard and why would someone bother to steal it?"

"It isn't just an ordinary mirror shard," Luro explained. "It's a piece from a mirror that was created hundreds of years ago so that Aryanna Vir Fortis could use it to banish the daemons to another realm."

There was a pronounced silence as both Aurelia and Darus processed this. Could that possibly be true? Aurelia thought of the shard she had found on the doorstep of her shop in Florinstone all those months ago. If it really had been a part of some sort of portal to another realm, it would certainly explain the unsettling feeling it had given her—the strange visions when she touched the glass and the nightmares she had had for weeks afterwards. Still, to think that she had held a piece of what—supposedly—the legendary hero, Aryanna Vir Fortis, had used to vanquish the daemons was a lot to comprehend.

"A mirror?" said Darus somewhat sceptically. "I've never heard of a mirror being used to banish the daemons."

"Then what did?" Luro said in a mild voice. "Aryanna was no mage, and even if she was, there has never been a mage alive who could open doorways between realms with their magic alone. And in all of the stories and history books, has there ever been mention of exactly *how* she managed such a feat?"

Darus did not have a response because the answer was obvious; for all Aloserians loved to keep the memory of Aryanna Vir Fortis and her triumph against the daemons alive, they certainly seemed to miss a few key details.

Aurelia was no expert in history, but the few accounts that she had read about Aryanna Vir Fortis's epic, final battle with the daemon king, Asmydionn, there had never been any mention of precisely *how* she had banished the daemon hordes.

"I can't tell you why that is. All I can tell you is what my father told me and what my grandfather told him and his father before him," Luro began. "After the daemons were defeated, the mirror was broken, and the pieces were entrusted to Aryanna's closest confidants to keep safe, secret, and hidden. Since then, the shards of the mirror have been passed down to their children and then to their grandchildren and great-grandchildren and so on."

"That's—" Darus broke off with a sigh and rubbed at his temple. Snow was beginning to fall again, coming through the gaping space where the roof should have been. "I'd like to believe you, but it's—"

"I believe him," Aurelia said.

Darus turned to face her with narrowed eyes. "And why should I trust you? Where do you come into all of this, exactly?"

Without preamble, Aurelia launched into the story of how, months ago, a stranger had left a glass shard on her doorstep. How it had made her see images of a dead landscape and nightmarish creatures after she'd touched it. She told them of the man with the red eyes who appeared in her shop one night looking for the shard.

"Did you give it to him?" Luro was looking at her with growing horror.

"Of course I did not *give it* to him. I refused and then we fought, but he overpowered me and took the shard before setting my shop on fire and leaving me to die."

"Is that why you're after him?" asked Darus. "To get the shard back?"

Aurelia picked at a loose thread on her cloak. "No, I am after him because no one tries to murder me and gets away with it. I could not care less about some broken mirror piece."

"You should care," said Luro. "And you should be very concerned. Because if that man is gathering all of the mirror shards, then that could only mean one thing."

* * *

Draken fitted the shard into place. This time, when the image of a barren landscape and a crimson sky flickered to life in the mirror, it didn't fade almost straight away like all the other times. It stayed in place long enough for Draken to see the figures of a pair of hunched back daemons scuttle across the grey sand, before disappearing and leaving Draken to gaze at his own reflection in the fractured glass once again.

Draken's lips curled into a smile.

"Its power is returning," said the distorted voice in his head with a pleased rumble. *"Stronger with each shard."*

"And now there's only one more piece to find." Draken's gaze fell to the only spot in the mirror that was still missing a shard. It looked as though the next one he'd have to find would be no longer than his palm. Funny that something so important would be so small.

"And to think, it only took you nine years to get to this point."

Draken rolled his eyes at the thinly veiled jab. "Would it be so hard to show some gratitude? I've gone to great lengths for you, after all."

"Don't whine," the voice snapped. *"And do not pretend that you haven't done all of this hard work for your own benefit."*

"What would benefit me is if doing all of this could bring the dead back to life," he said as he poured himself some wine from the decanter he'd left on the small table by the window.

"Oh, and I suppose you thought tracking down and killing that Draco couple as soon as you escaped from prison would help with that?"

"We needed the boy."

"The father could have done just as well. You could have always killed the boy and the woman and left the man alive."

Draken didn't reply, only brought the goblet to his lips and tipped his head back, draining it in one go.

"I am under no illusions that you do my bidding out of loyalty to me. Nor do I really care. All I care about is that you do what I've asked of you, and soon. We have waited long enough."

Chuckling, Draken set his goblet down. "Do not worry. The

time of the daemons is almost upon us. That I will make sure of, my lord Asmydionn."

* * *

Derek was in the Valley, surrounded by the groaning of the wounded, wails from those who had lost someone, and orders being shouted at those who could still walk on their own two feet.

"A healer! We need another healer over here!"

"Mahkli! Has anyone seen Mahkli?"

"Get that one straight to the Healing House!"

Derek lay curled up on a piece of broken timber, his body wracked by shivers from his time in the frozen lake. Arabelle had insisted he remain in his dragon form, to keep himself warmer, since a dragon's body temperature was much warmer than a human's. Steam rose from his body in curling tendrils, reacting to the cold of his skin. Even so, Derek still felt as if the cold had buried itself permanently into his bones.

Rosalie knelt beside Derek, tending to the wounds on his shoulder. He growled when she pressed down too hard with the damp rag she had managed to find somewhere.

She gave him a cross look. "Well, how can you expect me to be gentle if you won't keep still?"

Well, how can you expect me to keep still when I'm still trying to thaw out my insides? He thought, hoping his words were properly conveyed in his grumpy huff.

It was also entirely possible that he felt a bit snappish because his sword—the sword that had once belonged to his father—was missing. He'd dropped it in the woods while he was fighting off the gargoyles and no one had yet to retrieve it.

He looked over to where Arabelle was tending to Eugenia and her two friends, wrapping blankets around them and murmuring words of comfort, and wished that she were the one tending to him instead.

"Eugenia!"

Derek looked up over Rosalie's shoulder to see Edgar moving through the throng of people, straight for them, followed by a short and plump woman in the white robe and headdress of a Shrine House keeper.

"Mama!" Eugenia cried at the sight of her mother and brother. She sprang to her feet and flew straight into her mother's arms, sobbing.

Edgar and his mother weren't the only ones to join them. Aryel Sabir came sauntering towards them, dressed in a long, turquoise coat with a fur ruff collar.

"What are you doing here?" Arabelle asked her.

"I came to lend a helping hand," she answered easily. "Being a mage, I'm sure I could be of much use." To demonstrate, she lifted her hands, palms up, and the broken rafters and roof tiles from a nearby house, rose into the air. Some of the tiles that had been shattered and the rafters that were snapped in two, pieced themselves back together, and as if lifted by an invisible hand, fitted themselves back into their original positions until it looked like the roof had never been damaged at all.

"That magic of yours sure could have come in handy when we were fighting those gargoyles," said Rosalie, an irritated edge to her voice.

But Aryel paid no attention to the remark. She turned to Derek. "You look like an overgrown half-drowned cat," she said in that neutral voice of hers. "Change."

Hesitantly, Derek did as he was told, Changing back into his human form, and immediately regretted it when he felt the shocking cold from his sodden clothes clinging to his skin.

Aryel placed her palm flat to Derek's forehead and slowly drew it back. As she did this, Derek noticed water being pulled from his clothes to form droplets suspended in the air in front of him. Aryel continued this until Derek was completely dry and no longer looked as if he had taken a plunge into freezing water only a short while ago.

"Thank you," he said as Aryel let the floating ball of lake water spill onto the snow at their feet.

"Oi! Guardians!"

A group of townsfolk were gathering around them and none of them looked as if they were about to sing the praises of Derek, Rosalie and Arabelle for helping to defend them from the gargoyle horde.

"What the hell happened?" demanded one bearded man Derek recognised as a farmer from the Valley. "What did you's do?"

"What did *we* do?" said Derek. "*We* just fought to save this valley and all of your lives."

"Nothing like this has ever happened in these parts," said a woman with brown, curling hair. "Never had monsters come down and attack us like this. Not until you lot showed up 'ere!"

"You think the gargoyles attacking was our fault?" said Arabelle, bewildered.

"Are you all out of your minds?" added Rosalie.

"Well, we've never had Guardians come here. Never," cried a lanky boy Derek used to play with as a child.

"You have," Derek said. "My father was a Guardian, and we lived in this valley for almost seven years and I don't remember any monsters swooping out of the sky during that time. And it was Guardians who dealt with the lycanthrope problem six years ago."

"Yeah, and then our Mayor ended up dead as well," the bearded man huffed, folding his thick arms. "Seems too big of a coincidence to me."

A quiet murmur stole through the gathered crowd, and Derek felt his throat constrict at the memories the mention of Goldridge's death brought to mind. He had to bite at the inside of his cheek to stop himself from saying anything that might aggravate these people further.

"Everyone, please," Edgar said, his tone placating. "I know we're all frightened by what happened, but it's ridiculous to lay the blame on the Guardians."

"Are you defending these outsiders rather than your own townspeople?" Another man shouted.

"I'm not taking sides! I simply—"

"Now, now, calm down, everyone."

Derek grimaced at the sound of that voice. *Oh, perfect.*

Orville and a few of his men pushed past the gathering onlookers. Derek noticed that Orville's uniform didn't have a scratch on it and nor did he appear to have a hair out of place. He was even walking with his typical swagger. It made Derek wonder where Orville had been exactly while they were all fighting off the gargoyles. Had he even joined his men in the fight? Or had he been off hiding somewhere while others died and were injured in his stead?

"It is not the Guardians' fault," Orville said. "They didn't know that they were disturbing Lady Night and that in doing so, she would visit her wrath upon us all."

Lady Night's wrath? Is he serious?

"Therefore, I think it's best that we end any and all searches."

"What? You can't do that," said Arabelle.

Orville turned to her with an arrogant grin. "I think you'll find that I can. I am Captain of the Guard after all."

"The Mayor—"

"I believe Mayor Boeheart will agree with me on this. It's for the good of the people of this town, after all."

"And wouldn't actually working to find the killer instead of just sitting around and twiddling your thumbs be for the good of these people?" Derek snarled.

He caught a flash of anger in Orville's eyes. "I wouldn't expect an outsider to know what's best for these people."

"But I'm not an outsider, *Captain*," Derek answered back with mocking emphasis on the title. He pushed forward until he stood directly before Orville, fury simmering in his veins as it always did when he spoke with Orville. "Not really. Or have you forgotten?"

Orville took a step closer, and Derek forced himself not to flinch away from the proximity.

"Oh, I haven't forgotten." Orville's voice was low. "And I'm sure you haven't either. Those most fun of days." The way he sneered made Derek want to put a dagger through his face.

"Hold on," Rosalie said. "Where is Cassandra?"

Orville straightened up and stepped away from Derek. The sneer disappearing to be replaced with a more sombre expression. "That's why I came down here. I'm afraid I have some rather terrible news. Miss Luteus is dead."

Shocked gasps and more murmurings broke out among the people around them, and Derek felt the words hit him like a dull blow. He didn't have to look to know they had a similar effect on Arabelle and Rosalie.

"You're lying," he said, the words coming out of his mouth of their own accord.

Orville merely cocked an eyebrow and turned to his men, standing behind him. It was then that Derek realised they had been hanging back for a reason. They had something with them and even with the dirty blanket covering it, Derek knew what one of the Guards carried in his arms as he strode forward and set it on the ground. Dark strands of hair fell out from beneath the covering and splayed on the white ground. The Guard pulled the blanket back and out of the corner of his eye, Derek saw Arabelle's hand fly to her mouth as Cassandra's pale, lifeless face and broken neck were uncovered.

Orville had been telling the truth after all.

* * *

"So, what you're saying is that the man we ran into last night was here to steal some piece of glass that's part of a mirror that's . . . really some kind of doorway to the daemon's realm?"

"Spot on, William," said Darus from where he was leaning against the mantel of the lit fireplace across from Jared and Will. The flame light cast deep shadows along his face, highlighting the angle of his cheekbones and the slope of his jaw.

It was nearing the day's end and they were all seated in Luro's partially destroyed living room, sharing a meal of stewed vegetables and buttered bread, which Luro himself had prepared for them. It certainly wasn't lost on Jared that only a few hours ago, Luro had been trying to kill them and now they were eating the food he had made for them.

Jared was seated on the worn couch beside Will. Luro sat cross-legged on the floor to their right, while Aurelia Blackwood sat on the window ledge to their left. Her raven, Familiar, Cora, perched on her raised knee and the empty right sleeve of her tattered brown coat dangling.

"And you think he's going to use it to try and bring the daemons back?" said Will.

"Precisely," said Luro.

"So, what do we do now?" asked Jared, trying to keep the anxious edge out of his voice. "We have to go after him, surely?"

"But how can we go after him if we don't even know where he is?" said Will.

"I know where he is."

Everyone turned their attention to Aurelia. She had her head turned and was looking out the window at the darkening sky. Again, Jared got the sense that there was something familiar about the mage, but couldn't quite place in what way.

It was Darus who asked, "How?"

Aurelia pulled something out from beneath her cloak for them all to see.

It was small, barely longer than Jared's little finger, with jagged edges and glinted silver in the firelight."A piece of metal?"

"It is all that remains of my prosthetic arm," she explained. "When that man—Draken—broke into my shop and left me for dead, he destroyed my arm before he left. If it was not for Cora, lending me enough of her strength to break free of the spell that had paralysed me, I would have died. When I escaped, I took a piece of my arm with me. You see, when he smashed my arm to pieces with his boot, he left his trace—a faint one—but enough that I have been able to use it to track him."

"If you already knew where he was, then why wait around here with us?" questioned Darus.

"Because I have faced him in battle twice now, and he has been far too strong for me to handle alone."

Darus folded his arms with a grim little smile. "I see. So, you just want to use us to get your revenge?"

Aurelia returned the smile with a bladed one of her own. "And you care nothing about this man and his schemes, Darus Flynn? I know you also want to find him."

"I want to find him and question him. You just want to kill him, don't you?"

"I can wait my turn," Aurelia said airily. "But the fact remains that through you, I will have a better chance at beating him and through me, you will have an easier time finding him. A fair exchange, no?"

For a moment, no one said anything, and the crackle of the flames in the fireplace became more pronounced. Jared kept his eyes on Darus, who was clearly deliberating on whether to place their trust in this woman, who was still very much a stranger to them.

Although he knew next to nothing about Aurelia Blackwood, Jared got the feeling that she was trustworthy, as strange as it was to admit.

"All right, fine," said Darus finally. "You can help us. Or we'll help you. Whichever way you want to look at it. You two, however," he turned to Jared and Will, "I think should head back to Ember first thing in the morning."

"What? Why?" demanded Will.

"Because from the sounds of things, this Draken is far too dangerous and unpredictable for rookies like you to be going up against."

Jared was on his feet. "Absolutely not. I am *not* leaving."

Darus let out a long sigh, rubbing the back of his neck. "Jared, this situation is unprecedented and we don't know just how dangerous it could turn out to be."

"So? We're Guardians. Danger is a part of the job."

"Yes, but you and Will are still inexperienced."

"I fought against the likes of Durbash only a few months ago and survived," Jared said, lifting his chin defiantly. "I think I can survive this."

"Jared—"

"I'm not going to run home, not when so much could be at stake," he continued, looking Darus square in the eye. "I'm not just a Guardian, I'm the Prince of Aloseria and just because I may never be King, doesn't mean that I don't still have a duty to protect my country and my people. If you really want to send me back to Ember, you'll have to put me in chains and drag me back. You might even need to lock me up in the dungeons just to be sure I won't try to sneak out and follow you, anyway."

"And if Jared will not go quietly, then neither will I," Will announced. "I'm not going to be the only one who gets sent back home while you all rush off on some exciting adventure."

"This is not an exciting adventure." Darus scowled.

"Racing off to the bad man's hideout to try and stop him from summoning daemons? Sounds pretty exciting to me."

Aurelia Blackwood started laughing. "My, my, such authority you hold over your subordinates, Master Flynn."

Darus threw his hands up. "Teenagers! Fine, if you want to join us on this incredibly dangerous mission that could end with you being seriously injured or even killed, then by all means." He turned to Luro. "What about you, Master Fera?"

The other man only shook his head. "I am no fighter. And as I'm sure you've all seen, my lycanthrope form makes me quite . . . unpredictable. I would only be a hindrance to you all."

"All right," Darus said. "We leave first thing in the morning. If anyone isn't ready by sunrise, they get left behind."

He pushed away from the fireplace and stepped out through the missing front wall to where Aurelia had magically set up the tents for them.

"Well," said Aurelia after a beat of silence. "You Guardians are much more entertaining than I thought."

* * *

When Darus entered his tent—which disconcerted him because it was far more spacious on the inside than it appeared to be on the outside—he went straight for his pack that he'd tossed on the bed and pulled out the illictio crystal.

"Darus?" It was Charle's voice that filtered through first once the crystal lit up red.

175

"Is something wrong?" Adolphus's voice.

"I'm sorry to bother you like this," Darus said. "But I need to ask you all a favour."

12

That evening, the Valley was filled with hastily prepared funeral pyres and the stench of smoke, as the bodies of all those who had died today were burned. Derek stood with Arabelle and Rosalie in front of Cassandra's pyre, watching the flames grow higher until the white cloth covering Cassandra's body was consumed. Derek still couldn't get rid of the image in his head of Cassandra's body, the broken neck, the missing left hand. The wide, glassy eyes.

"All the work of Lady Night," Orville had announced, and it had taken everything in Derek not to try and claw the man's eyes out.

Cassandra's body had been discovered on the mountain, where she had been searching, but there was no sign of who or what had killed her. No one who had been on the mountain with her had seen her die, either.

After the funeral was over, they retreated to the Mayor's Manor, where Derek and the girls took refuge in the library. The three of them sat in silence for some time, listening to the crackle of the fire in the fireplace.

"What do we do now?" asked Rosalie from her place on the couch.

"What do you mean, what do we do now?" said Arabelle. She was standing by the window closest to the fireplace with her arms folded. "We do what we came here to do. We find the murderer and put a stop to these killings."

"But is that really our duty anymore? Now that Cassandra is— well, gone?"

"That doesn't mean we should just abandon the assignment."

"We're only rookies," Derek said. He sat on the rug in front of the fire, watching the way the flames slowly ate away at the logs. "We're not supposed to be taking on assignments by ourselves."

He wondered if his voice sounded as dismal as he felt. Derek felt . . . he felt hollowed out and overwhelmed all at the same time. There were so many things playing on his mind, the gargoyle attack, Cassandra's death, the mark that had appeared on his chest.

Losing his father's sword.

Some might think it ridiculous to feel so deeply about losing a weapon, but it had been *his father's sword*. Having it felt like having some part of his father with him and when he fought with it, he could almost imagine that his father was fighting alongside him. And now it was gone.

"Since when do you care so much about rules?" Arabelle asked him.

Derek shrugged. "I don't, and in any other situation, I might even say hang the rules and let's carry on with it. But I think there's more going on here than we realise, and do we really want to get involved any further without someone more experienced to back us up?"

"I agree with Derek," intoned Rosalie.

"I can't believe this is the same boy who only months ago spear-headed a quest to find a daemonic amulet with only two of his friends," said Arabelle.

"Maybe I've matured since then." *Or maybe I'm just being selfish and I'll take any chance to get out of this damn town.*

"Are the two of you really saying we should just abandon the people of this town when they're being murdered in the streets?"

"Not *abandon* them," said Rosalie. "Just leave this situation up to someone more . . . experienced?"

"We're experienced enough. We—"

There was a knock on the door and they fell silent as it opened to reveal Lilith's hunched figure and glowering face, followed by Edgar. The other boy was dressed in casual clothes and an olive green cloak, dusted white with snow at the shoulders.

"Master Greyhill is here to see you," grumbled Lilith. She looked to Edgar. "Are you sure you don't want me to take your cloak?"

Derek noticed Edgar take an almost imperceptible step back. "Oh, n-no thank you. I'd really rather leave it on."

Lilith made a sort of grumpy croaking noise before shuffling away.

"She came with the house," Rosalie said in a mock apologetic tone once Edgar had closed the door behind him.

"Edgar, what are you doing here?" asked Derek.

"I'm sorry for dropping in so unexpectedly like this," said Edgar. "And I wanted to say that I'm so sorry about what happened to Miss Luteus."

"Thank you. But that's not all you came here to say, is it?" Arabelle wondered.

Edgar shook his head. He looked nervous, his eyes flicking from side to side as if expecting someone or something to leap out and grab him at any moment. Finally, Edgar pulled off his cloak, revealing a satchel strapped to his back.

"This is what I wanted to show you," he said, shrugging the satchel off and opening it up to pull something out.

It was a book, thick and bound in dark, featureless leather. It was large as well. The spine was easily the same length as Derek's forearm.

"What is that?" he asked, joining Arabelle and Rosalie in crowding around Edgar to get a closer look.

"According to Captain Goldridge, this book was discovered near Miss Cassandra's body."

They all looked up sharply at Edgar.

"Near her body?" repeated Arabelle. "But we didn't hear anything about this."

There was an uncomfortable look on Edgar's face. "That's

because I don't think the Captain wanted anyone to know about it."

"What?" said Rosalie. "Why not?"

"I can only tell you what I overheard, but earlier this evening, I'd just returned to the barracks when I heard the Captain speaking to another one of the Guards. They told him they'd found this book that had been lying near Miss Cassandra's body. That they thought it might've belonged to the murderer," Edgar explained. "The Captain said he'd take the book and deliver it to the Mayor. But instead, I saw him take it into his study, put it in his desk and just leave. I got the feeling that he wasn't going to show it to the Mayor or anyone at all, so I . . . I took it."

"Without permission?" Derek raised an eyebrow. That would explain why Edgar had seemed so jumpy when he first walked in.

"Such a naughty boy," Rosalie said admiringly.

Edgar's cheeks flushed pink. "I'm sure the Captain would have my head on his wall if he ever found out, but after I snuck into his study and had a look through this book well . . . I think you need to see this."

He held the book out, and it was Derek who reached out to take it. The book was heavy, so much so that it almost felt like he was holding a slab of stone. They were all kneeling in a half-circle by the fire now, Arabelle and Rosalie on either side of him, leaning in close, as he opened up the book. He opened it to a page that, at first glance, looked like a recipe of some sort, but quickly realised that it was actually instructions for a spell.

"It's a spell book," Rosalie observed.

"No." Arabelle's voice was hushed. "It's a grimoire."

Grimoires were books containing spells used for dark magic. Dark magic was a macabre imitation of natural magic. One didn't need to be born a mage to use it, but it could only be used through the death of another living thing, be it a plant, an animal or a man, woman or child. It was forbidden to practice dark magic and therefore, so were grimoires. Anyone caught in possession of a grimoire could face a lifetime of imprisonment or even execution.

Simply by reading the heading at the top of the page, Derek could tell that Arabelle was right. It was a bad luck curse, meant to bring nothing but misfortune upon the one it was cast upon. There was a crudely drawn picture of a person that appeared to be wailing in despair. Below that, it detailed the necessary ingredients to make the curse, a drop of blood from the person being cursed, the eye of a slain wolf, and the tails of four drowned rats.

Derek turned the page and found another spell for everlasting beauty, which didn't sound too bad . . . except that it required slaughtering three young women. He couldn't help but wonder if this was Orville's grimoire? Had Orville begun practicing dark magic?

"Turn to page twenty-one," Edgar said.

Derek did. On that page were instructions for a spell to resurrect the dead, along with a drawing of what appeared to be a corpse in the process of coming back to life. He skimmed through the text, reading about how the spell had to be performed on the night of a full moon on the seventh month of the year. It also needed the left hands of six murdered souls to be placed around the corpse while thrice chanting their name.

Derek looked up at Edgar, the words on the page sparking a thought in his head. "You think this spell has something to do with the murders, don't you?"

"It's only a suspicion," Edgar said. "When we met in the square the other day, I told you to be careful of the Captain and that's because I've always thought that he knew more about these murders than he let on. Like the way he blames it on Lady Night and seems content with letting the killings run their course." He gestured at the grimoire. "And now this."

"So, what you're saying is, you think Captain Goldridge is the killer?" Rosalie asked.

Edgar chewed on his bottom lip. "I think—I think he might be complicit, at the very least."

"That's very bold," said Arabelle. "Accusing the Captain of the Guard of being in on the murders."

"But it's not an unreasonable one," Derek pointed out. "Not if you know what Orville's really like."

Derek stared down at the open grimoire before him, his mind racing. Like Edgar, he'd had a nagging suspicion that there was something Orville was leaving out about these murders. Maybe he had even entertained the idea that Orville was the killer at some point, but to have what could very well be evidence proving so— well, it still came as a bit of a shock. He thought about the drawing of the rising corpse on the previous page. Who could Orville be trying to raise from the dead? His brother? The thought of the elder Goldridge alive again made Derek feel sick to his stomach.

"All right, so what do we do now?" Rosalie was saying. "Do we go to the Mayor about this?"

Edgar shook his head vehemently. "No, if you go to Mayor Boeheart, he will only go to the Captain and it will be too easy for him to deny any connection he might have to this book. You'll need more proof if you're going to bring this up to anyone else."

"But just *how* are we supposed to find more proof?" said Arabelle, sounding frustrated.

Rosalie raised an eyebrow. "Hold on, weren't we just talking about how this whole situation wouldn't be up to us anymore, now that Cassandra's gone?"

"After what Edgar just told us, you really think we should do nothing?"

"Here's what *I* think we should do," Derek interjected. "We write to Ember explaining the situation we're in, but until we hear back from them, we continue on with the assignment."

Arabelle frowned. "Do you really think it's necessary to write to them?"

Derek looked at her in surprise. "Yes. I do."

"It's just that they'll probably send other Guardians to replace us and by the time they get here, we might have already found the killer, so what's the point?"

"The point is that maybe we won't have found the killer by then and maybe it would be better to have more experienced Guardians handling things."

"I'm with Derek on this," Rosalie chimed in while Edgar looked between the three of them in silence.

Arabelle worried at her bottom lip. She looked as if she were deliberating on something. But what? It was odd that she would even speak out against one of Derek's more responsible ideas.

He wanted to know what was making her look so conflicted, but before he could ask, she said, "You're right. Writing to Ember is a smart decision." She smiled at Derek and patted him on the head. "Good thinking."

He knocked her hand away, ignoring how the gesture made his cheeks warm.

Arabelle clapped her hands together. "All right, tonight we write to Ember. And in the morning, we figure out what our next move is going to be."

* * *

Later on that night, Arabelle traversed through the streets of Windfell, heading toward the Post House with their letter to Ember clutched in her hand.

When Derek had first suggested writing to Ember, her first reaction had been to protest. This assignment was supposed to help her prove to her father that she was serious about her duties and that she was a suitable candidate for joining the Crown Guard. She knew that sending word to Ember would only result in them being pulled from the assignment and other Guardians being sent in to take over.

She rounded a corner, and the Post House came into sight. It was a slim, triple storey building made of the same featureless, grey brick as the rest of the town. She could see candlelight glowing through the front window on the first floor, and heard the muted sound of ravens cawing and clucking from inside. She was standing before the door and about to enter when she paused.

Arabelle looked down at the letter in her hand, sealed up in a crisp, white envelope, and an idea came unbidden into her head. What if she simply . . . didn't send the letter?

She could throw the letter away into the street where the wind would carry it away or the snow would soak it through until it was a soggy, illegible mess. She could turn around, walk back the way she had come and tell the others that she'd sent the letter and they'd never know any better.

It was an incredibly dishonourable thought, one that Arabelle was sure her father would scold her for if he knew. But if doing so would allow her to complete the assignment the way she wanted to and prove to her father that she was ready to take on the responsibility of a Crown Guard, then shouldn't she?

She looked to the door of the Post House and back down at the envelope.

Arabelle made her decision.

13

The days following the gargoyle attack and Cassandra's death brought nothing but a persistent and violent snow storm.

It was the kind of storm where howling winds pounded at the windows so hard, one might be forgiven for fearing they would break. The snow came down at such a dizzying speed it was near impossible to see anything past the haze of grey and white.

There had been no new murders or sightings of gargoyles, possibly because very few would dare to brave this storm for fear that they would freeze within seconds. When Derek was a child, he remembered hearing about how people lost their lives from being caught in a storm such as this one.

Derek, Arabelle, and Rosalie had, once again, shut themselves away in the library one afternoon, along with the Mayor's dog, Bear, and Edgar. Edgar had joined them earlier because apparently he was one of those fools who was willing to step foot outside in this weather. Although Derek supposed Edgar had a good cause to brave the storm. The night that Edgar had revealed the grimoire to them, as well as his suspicions about Orville being involved in the murders, they decided that their next course of action should be to search Orville's home for any evidence that might tie him to the killings.

"He lives on the Goldridge estate," Edgar was saying from his seat on the couch beside Rosalie. "It's only a short horse ride west of town."

"So, it's fairly secluded?" asked Arabelle. She was lying on her back in front of the fireplace, her yellow hair splayed out around her head. The grimoire lay open on the floor next to her, where she had been flicking through it moments ago. She'd taken an almost vested interest in reading through it lately. "Sounds like it should be easy enough, sneaking in."

"It might be if it weren't protected with enchantments to keep uninvited guests off the grounds," Derek said while reaching over for the plate of fruit mince tarts on the table by the window that one of the servants had brought by a while ago. Bear, who had his large head resting in Derek's lap, eyed the tart hungrily.

"That does complicate things," muttered Arabelle, frowning up at the ceiling.

"There is one way we could get in," Edgar said. "The Captain throws a Nativitas masquerade ball every year at the estate. It should be two nights from now."

"Perfect!" said Rosalie with cheer.

"*But*, Orville and whoever he has on guard duty that night know who everyone is because no one can get in without an invitation."

"Not perfect," Rosalie amended glumly.

"And where does one get these invitations?" Arabelle asked.

"I think the Captain sends them out himself."

Arabelle made a displeased sound.

Bear was slowly inching his head closer to the tart in Derek's hand. "Do you know anyone who does happen to have an invitation?" asked Derek, placing a restraining hand against the dog's nose. "Or is there some way we could find out who will?"

"I'm sure Mayor and Lady Boeheart are invited, as well as quite a few members of the Town Guard and their families. The La Fray sisters too."

"What are you getting at, Draco?" Rosalie asked.

"If we can't get our own invitations," Derek grunted while trying to hold back Bear, who was now attempting to climb over him to get to the tart. It was proving to be a struggle, especially since Bear was the size of a small pony. "Then maybe we should just consider stealing someone else's."

Arabelle sat up. "That's actually not a bad idea. And you said that it was a masquerade party," she added to Edgar. "That means Orville and the Guards will be none the wiser so long as we have an invitation."

"I suppose so," Edgar admitted. "Although, even with the masks on, the Guards or the Captain might still know you're not who you say you are. Remember, this is a small town and everyone knows everyone around here."

"If that's so, then why can't anyone figure out who the killer is?" said Rosalie.

"Obviously whoever it is, is very good at hiding it."

Bear finally overpowered Derek, knocking him flat on his back and stealing the tart from his hand. With a sigh of defeat, he said, "What about disguises?"

"First, we'd have to figure out who we're going to disguise ourselves as," Arabelle said.

"Well, I think Arabelle and I have a better chance at disguising ourselves as those La Fray sisters." Rosalie pressed herself against Edgar's side, smiling coyly at the blush that appeared on his cheeks. "And Edgar and Derek can be our companions."

"*You* could probably get away with it." Arabelle tugged on a few strands of her golden-blonde hair, so unlike the glossy black hair of Giselle and Linette La Fray. "But my hair colour might just give me away."

A mischievous smile appeared on Edgar's lips. "Perhaps Derek could be disguised as one of the sisters instead?"

Derek responded by giving the other boy one of his fiercest glares. Although the effect might have been dulled somewhat since he was currently trapped beneath Bear, who had not only stolen Derek's tart, but had also decided to use him as his cushion. He imagined that he didn't make a very threatening image right now.

Both Rosalie and Arabelle looked highly amused at the suggestion.

"His hair might be a bit too short, but we could just say he decided to cut it." Rosalie's smile was wicked. "I think you'd look lovely in a dress."

"If any of you come near me with a dress, I will break your knees."

"So violent. But actually, I don't think we need to worry about that. When we went to visit Aryel Sabir the other day, I saw there was a pair of desona charms in the shop."

"Really?" Derek was surprised. Desona charms were incredibly rare pendants charmed to disguise the wearer into whomever they wished. All that was needed to use them was something from the one the wearer wanted to disguise themself as, such as a strand of hair, a piece of clothing or even a tooth or a drop of blood. Very few of the charms had ever been made, hence, why they were so hard to come across.

"Are you sure they were desona charms?" Arabelle sounded a little dubious.

An annoyed look crossed Rosalie's face. "Yes, I'm sure. You're not the only one who paid attention in classes at the Academy."

Arabelle had the good grace to look sheepish.

"But what if the charms aren't there anymore?" said Edgar. "Or what happens if you can't afford them?"

"Then we steal them?" Derek suggested.

Arabelle frowned. "There's only so much stealing we can do."

"Fine, then perhaps we should try dying your hair black?"

"Or we could start measuring you for a dress?"

Derek opened his mouth to retort when there was a soft

knocking on the door that startled them.

"Yes?" Arabelle called out, snapping the grimoire closed and pushing it behind her back.

The door opened and Anna Boeheart stepped in. She looked as immaculate as ever in a red dress and a red jacket with grey fur lining on the hem, collar, and sleeve cuffs. Her long, brown hair was pinned at the back of her head in a chignon, exposing the elegant line of her neck. She looked as if she were ready to attend an evening out at some extravagant dinner, not to simply spend her day at home.

She smiled, looking as fond as a mother watching her children having fun with their friends. "I just wanted to see how you were all doing. Can I get you anything? Some hot chocolate maybe?"

"We're fine, thank you, Lady Boeheart," said Arabelle. There was a besotted look on her face as she watched Lady Boeheart, that made Derek frown. "No need for you to go to the trouble for us."

"No trouble at all, dear. I want to make sure your stay here is as comfortable as can be."

"We appreciate it."

Derek noticed Lady Boeheart do a quick survey of the room. Was she looking for something or was she making sure that they hadn't stolen or broken anything while left in here unattended?

"Well, please don't hesitate to let us know if there's anything you need," said Lady Boeheart, offering them one last lovely smile before she left, closing the door behind her.

"She's so nice," Edgar said, a moony expression on his face.

"And beautiful," added Arabelle with a similar look.

"And she has excellent taste in clothes," Rosalie remarked approvingly.

"And maybe we should get back on track," said Derek.

* * *

Arabelle awoke sometime during the night, her heart racing.

She must have been dreaming because she thought that when she first opened her eyes, she had seen a face—gaunt and skeletal—hovering over her. But as she sat up and looked around now, she saw that there was no one else in the room, apart from Rosalie, who was snoring softly in the bed next to hers.

On top of the blanket beside her was the grimoire, still open on the page she had been reading before she'd fallen asleep—about a spell that allowed you to control the minds of others. At the bottom of the page was a sketch of a person with eyes that looked as if a purple mist clouded them.

It probably wasn't right for her to be reading this, but Arabelle couldn't help but find the grimoire, full of footnotes and crude sketches intriguing—awful, but intriguing. Besides, she thought it might come in handy one day if she was at least somewhat versed in the ins and outs of dark magic spells.

Arabelle knew there would be no going back to sleep for her just yet so, gathering up the grimoire, she pushed the thick, woollen blankets to the side and got out of bed. She sought out her dressing gown and slippers, then crept silently from the bedroom.

Stepping out into the dark hallway, Arabelle noticed a light from beneath the library's doors. She already knew what—or rather, *who*—she would find behind those doors and sure enough, as she eased one ogpen, there was Derek. He was curled up on the window seat; the curtains had been thrown open and the glass panes being lashed by rain was on full display.

"Derek?" said Arabelle, stepping forward.

He lifted his head from where he'd had it resting against the glass. He turned to look at her and Arabelle couldn't help but notice straight away the dark rings beneath his eyes. He looked exhausted and . . . haunted.

"Is everything all right?" she asked, concerned.

Derek swiped a hand across his face. "I'm fine. I just couldn't sleep. That's all."

Arabelle took note of the fact that Derek was still dressed in the same clothes he had worn that day. "When was the last time you slept properly?" she asked, sitting down opposite Derek on the window seat, resting the grimoire against her lap.

He didn't respond, only continued to look out at the storm raging beyond the windows.

"Derek."

"I don't want to talk about this."

But Arabelle couldn't let it go, not when Derek was looking so clearly troubled. Not when she might be able to help him.

"I know being back here can't be easy for you—"

Derek let out a mirthless laugh. "No, you really don't know."

"Then talk to me," she pressed. "Tell me what you're going through."

"I just said that I don't want to talk about it."

"But maybe I can—"

"Maybe you can, what?" he snapped. This time he was looking at her with an expression twisted by frustrated anger. "What do you think you could possibly do for me? Do you think that you could make everything better for me with just a few pretty words and a cuddle?"

Arabelle felt herself bristling at the words and derisive tone. She sat up straighter. "I only want to help you."

"I never asked for it. So stop bothering me already."

Hurt seared through her, but her pride would not allow her to display it as anything other than anger. "Fine." She stood, glaring down at Derek, who continued to stubbornly look out the window. "Sorry my concern was such a *bother* to you," she said with as much venom as she could before stalking across the room.

It took all of her self-restraint not to slam the door on her way out.

14

The storms had completely dissipated overnight, making it safe to set foot outside once again. As such, almost everyone in town seemed to have business to attend to outside this morning, making the streets of Windfell busier than usual. This included Derek and Rosalie, who were on their way to visit Aryel's shop to see if they could purchase those desona charms for Orville's party tomorrow night.

"So, what did you do?"

Derek looked at Rosalie, who was walking alongside him. "What are you talking about?"

"Arabelle, of course. She seemed rather upset with you this morning."

"Did she? I hadn't noticed."

He had noticed.

How could he not when Arabelle had done nothing but give him the cold shoulder all morning? And he knew it had to do with their conversation the night before. Not that he could blame her, really. He knew Arabelle only had the best of intentions when she'd tried to get him to talk to her. But Derek had been so close to giving into all of those vulnerable emotions and it had been so tempting to do so in front of Arabelle—Arabelle, who was warm and kind and far too good for him. But he couldn't. He didn't want to be weak. Not in front of her.

So, he had allowed his anger to be his shield instead.

"Well, whatever it is, you should hurry up and apologise to her before someone else catches her eye," said Rosalie.

"What—?"

"Oh, look we're here!"

And so they were. Derek hadn't even noticed that they'd already walked onto the street of the *Silver Eye*.

There was already someone stepping out of the shop, a squat woman with her arms full of different items such as a lamp with an illuminae crystal that glowed pink to a clock that was in the middle of announcing the time in a rather out of tune singing voice.

Derek and Rosalie stepped inside the shop, the bell above the doorway ringing as they did so. There was no one else in the store. Even Aryel Sabir was nowhere to be seen.

"So, where did you see these charms?" Derek asked, looking around the shop.

"Right over here." Rosalie led him to one of the far corners where there was a collection of illuminae crystals of various shapes—there was even one carved into the shape of a dragon—

and memoria stones—gems that allowed one to record and store their memories—cluttered the shelves. Hanging off a nail in the wall next to the shelves was a pair of rather plain-looking lockets.

"That's them," Rosalie announced, gesturing to the lockets.

For what was supposed to be rather rare and valuable items, they didn't look like much. The lockets were made of bronzed metal with an open eye carved into the centre and hung from worn bits of string.

"Are you sure these are the real deal?"

Rosalie had now wandered over to look at a display of masks hanging on the wall. "Well, if they're not, they're a rather impressive imitation."

"So, you don't know whether these actually work or not?"

She shot him an irritated look. "How could I possibly know if I haven't even used them?" Rosalie lifted one of the masks from the wall and showed it to Derek. It was painted black with the distorted face of a bear with a snarling maw and a pair of red eyes, one bigger than the other. "What do you say we wear these to the Captain's party?"

"I wouldn't." Derek and Rosalie spun around at the same time to see Aryel standing at the base of the stairs, a steaming mug in her hands. "I think one or two of them might be cursed. Although I'm not sure which ones exactly."

Rosalie hurriedly put the mask back.

"Selling cursed items hardly seems legal," Derek observed.

"Is anything that happens in this town truly legal, little

Guardian?" said Aryel, unconcerned. She took a sip from her mug. "Besides, I'm not the one selling anything. This was my brother's shop, after all."

"No need to worry about all that," Rosalie said pleasantly. "We actually just came here to buy something."

Aryel raised an eyebrow. "Oh? And what is it you were looking for?"

Rosalie pointed at the desona charms on the wall. "How much for those?"

"Those? There's no cost. You can simply take them."

Derek was certain the look of dumbfounded surprise on Rosalie's face mirrored his own. "You're just going to give them to us?"

"They're not fakes, are they?" asked Rosalie.

"No, they're not fake," said Aryel. "I can feel the enchantment on them."

"Then why—?"

"Everything in this shop is for free. I'm sure my brother would be howling from the heavens to see all of these treasures he went to such great lengths to swindle people out of, just given away. So please, take anything and everything you'd like."

Derek thought about the woman they had seen leaving the shop earlier with arms full of items. He exchanged a look with Rosalie, who shrugged one shoulder, before reaching out grabbing both of the charms off the wall.

"All right, well, thank you very much for your time, Miss

Sabir," said Rosalie.

Aryel merely inclined her head and went back to her drink.

They were just heading out the door when Derek paused. Rosalie looked over her shoulder at him. "What's wrong?"

"Nothing. I just—you go, I'll catch up in a bit."

Shrugging, Rosalie left, leaving Derek alone with Aryel.

"What other business do you have with me, little Guardian?" She was leaning back against the front counter, staring at him with impassive amber eyes from over the rim of her mug.

Derek reached into his coat pocket, pulling out a piece of paper. "I was wondering if you've ever seen this symbol anywhere before?"

Aryel took the paper from him and considered the sketch he had done of the marking that had appeared on his chest after emerging from the lake during the gargoyle attack last week. His memory of it was a bit hazy thanks to his near drowning experience, but he wouldn't soon forget those strange, red, swirling patterns and jagged lines, glowing like hot coals.

The mark hadn't reappeared since then, no matter how long Derek stared at his reflection in the mirror and he had scoured the books in the library of the Mayor's Manor, but hadn't been able to find anything on magical symbols, let alone this one. He'd thought that, perhaps, asking the only mage in Windfell might lead to some answers.

But she merely said, "I've never seen this symbol before," and handed the paper back to him.

"I see," Derek sighed, hoping his disappointment wasn't too obvious.

"I will say, though, that it does not look like any normal symbol. The markings speak to me of a dark origin."

"You mean the symbol could be associated with dark magic?" When had he ever come into contact with dark magic before? Then again, he couldn't remember ever receiving a glowing, vanishing mark on his chest, either. Could it have had something to do with coming into contact with Milrath's amulet?

"It's possible," said Aryel. She didn't ask any further questions, such as why Derek was so curious about a symbol that could be related to dark magic, and for that at least, he was thankful.

"Well, thank you for your time. I'll be leaving now."

He was at the door when Aryel said to him, "Enjoy Captain Goldridge's party tonight, little Guardian."

Derek paused, taken aback by her words. When he turned around again, he saw only her shoes disappearing back up the staircase.

* * *

The fort sat high between two craggy, snow-capped mountains. The stonework was simple and unadorned, a building made not to welcome, only to intimidate. The heavy grey skies and blustering winds only added to its daunting air.

Jared stood with Will, Darus and Aurelia on an outcropping of rock halfway down the mountainside.

"Is this the place?" Darus asked Aurelia.

"Yes," she answered, holding the piece of metal from her ruined prosthetic arm. "He is here. I can feel it." Cora clucked and ruffled her feathers from where she was perched on Aurelia's shoulder.

The harsh winter winds whipped through their hair and flapped their cloaks. It had taken them almost four days to get here, all thanks to a violent snowstorm hindering their travel.

"All right," Jared said. "He's in the fort. How are we going to go about this?"

"I think our best chance will be to try and take him by surprise," said Darus. He turned to Aurelia. "I don't suppose you also know which part of the fort he's in?"

"No. But I am sure Cora could find out for us."

The raven took off from Aurelia's shoulder as she sat cross-legged in the snow and closed her eyes. When she opened her eyes again, her green irises and the whites of her eyes were gone, replaced with a featureless black. The look was so startling, Jared took an involuntary step backward.

"The fort looks as if it has been abandoned for many years," said Aurelia after a moment.

Jared looked up to where he could see Cora, little more than a speck against the grey sky, circling the fort. *She's seeing through her Familiar's eyes,* he realised.

"He is in the north watch tower," Aurelia announced.

"And are there any defences we aren't aware of?"

"None. Or at least none that I can be aware of at this distance."

It wasn't long before Cora returned to them and Aurelia's eyes returned to normal as she ended whatever spell she had cast between them.

"Right. As I was saying," said Darus. "Our best chance is to try and take him by surprise. Aurelia and I will distract him while Will and Jared look for these mirror shards"

"And what do we do once we find the shards?" Jared asked.

"Destroy them," said Darus. "And if you can't destroy them, take them with you and get out of there. Our priority is getting those shards away from him." He added the last part with a significant look in Aurelia's direction. "If we can manage to capture him as well, then all the better, but I don't plan on getting any of us killed just to do that. Does everyone understand?"

"Yes," said Jared and Will in unison.

"Perfectly," drawled Aurelia.

"Good. Then let's go."

* * *

Draken knew they were coming. He knew in the way that he knew everything that happened within sixty feet of this fort. It was a clever enchantment, completely undetectable and one of his own making no less.

He was seated on the windowsill in the empty room at the top of the north watchtower, with one leg drawn up in front of him and the other stretched out with his boot planted on the floor. He couldn't see them from this window, but he knew they were coming up the mountain from the west. Draken also knew without a doubt that these new arrivals were comprised of the Guardians he had seen at the lycan's house outside of White Lake and the mage, Aurelia Blackwood.

"So persistent," he murmured to himself and smiled. "But perhaps this could be fun. It's been a while since I played a game."

* * *

The true disrepair of the fort was even more visible up close. Deep cracks ran through the stonework. Broken off chunks of rock scattered the ground, shattered glass lingered in the windows.

Hiding out in an old, abandoned building in the middle of nowhere, Darus thought. *Does this man think he's a storybook villain?*

They waited a moment for Aurelia to check for any hidden traps or barriers. There were none, and somehow that made Darus feel more uneasy than relieved. They snuck in through the front gate, where one of its doors was broken off its hinges, and found themselves in the middle of an open courtyard, archways lining the surrounding walls. A group of sparrows took flight, startled by their approach.

"He keeps the mirror in a room at the top of the eastern tower," Aurelia said in a low voice. "You should find it through there." She indicated to the third archway on their left.

"You two be careful," said Darus, giving the boys a meaningful look. "In and out. Don't take any foolish risks and if something doesn't seem right, get out as quickly as you can, whether you have those shards or not."

Jared nodded before he and Will were dashing towards the archway and disappearing from sight.

Darus tried to shove down the feeling that he may have very well sent them to their deaths. *They're Guardians. They understood the risks in coming here.*

He, Aurelia, and Cora made for the largest archway straight ahead of them. He allowed Aurelia to lead him through the eerily empty corridors and up the dark, winding staircase of the north tower. They climbed all the way to the top, taking care to make sure their footsteps did not echo too loudly against the stone floors.

On the top floor, they came to a single closed door. Darus drew his sword silently from his scabbard and looked to Aurelia. She nodded, her hand already blazing with a conjured flame.

Darus placed his hand around the door handle, took a steadying breath, and pushed it open, rushing through with Aurelia quick on his heels.

But the room was empty.

Darus did a quick look around, but it was a small, circular room devoid of any furnishings. There was nowhere for anyone to hide.

He turned to Aurelia. "I thought you said he was in here?"

But the Elf looked just as perplexed as he felt. "He was. He should be. I can still sense his presence here."

That was when Darus spotted the bit of paper lying on the floor. Frowning, he bent to pick it up and unfolded it. Written in a spiky scrawl were two words:

Caught you.

And the floor fell out from beneath him.

* * *

The door opened with a muted creak as Jared peered inside. A quick scope of the room showed that there was no one inside, and he turned to say as much to Will before stepping in.

It looked like a study with two large desks and a huge arched window overlooking the snowy mountain ranges beyond. There was even a coat stand by the door. It didn't take long for them to spot something oval-shaped, covered by a velvet cloth, standing by the window. A mirror perhaps?

Will started towards it, but Jared grabbed him by the elbow. "Wait," he urged. "What if it's booby trapped?"

"What do you suggest we do, then?"

Jared looked about and spotted a pair of boots lying haphazardly on the floor by the coat stand.

"Those could have been booby trapped too, you know?" Will remarked as Jared picked up a boot.

"Shut up."

He drew his arm back and threw the boot at the cloth draped object. Not hard enough to knock it over, but just enough that the boot bounced off harmlessly and crumpled to the floor. They waited a moment, but nothing happened. The boot didn't burst into flames, no bolt of magic lightning scorched it to a crisp, and no knives came shooting out of the walls.

"Okay," Jared said. "There we have it. No booby traps."

Will let out a breath of laughter.

"What?"

"You're just so—never mind."

Jared made a mental note to question Will about it later, but for now, they had a job to do.

They crossed the room, stepping over the boot and came to stand before the object draped in cloth. Somewhat hesitantly, Jared reached out and grasped the cool and velvety cloth in his hand and drew it aside.

There was nothing beneath it.

Nothing but empty space . . . and a piece of paper pinned to the wall by a thin knife.

"What the hell?" Will said disbelievingly, as Jared stepped forward to read what was written on the paper.

So close.

Almost as soon as Jared had finished reading those two words, something unexpected happened.

The room around them began to flicker and change. The chamber with its onyx walls, bookshelves, and two desks had faded away to be replaced with the windowless brick walls and cramped space of a dungeon cell. Torchlight flickered against the walls, their only source of visibility. The floors were flooded in murky, black water that came up to their knees.

"What—" Will spun around in a circle. His expression

bewildered. "What just happened?"

"I don't . . . know?" Jared said, sounding just as disorientated as he felt. "But I think we should—"

Whatever he had been about to say was forestalled when something shot out of the water and grabbed Jared by the wrist.

15

The ground caught up to Darus in no time. It felt as if in one breath, he was falling through the air and in the next, he was hitting the floor with a jarring thud. He was distantly aware of Aurelia landing next to him, but somehow with much more grace, like a cat landing on its feet. Cora flew down shortly after to resume her perch on Aurelia's shoulder.

Darus picked himself up, ignoring the points of pain along his body from where it had collided with the hard floor. Looking around, he saw that they now stood in the middle of a great hall with stone masoned walls, and two long tables stood parallel to each other on either side of the hall, both covered in a thick layer of dust, as if they had not been touched since long before Darus was even born. There was a dais with three shallow steps at the very end of the hall. Two high-backed chairs stood side by side and seated in one of them, with their legs draped casually over one of the armrests, was the red-eyed man—Draken.

Darus was instantly on guard, pulling his sword from its sheath once more, the sound of scraping metal ringing throughout the hall.

"When I was a boy," Draken started, sounding as casual as a cordial host speaking to their guests. "My aunt taught me that it was very rude to enter someone's home without being invited first." He stood up from the chair. "She may have despised me, but she seemed determined to at least instil me with some proper manners."

"And where were those manners when you broke into my shop and burned it to the ground with me still inside of it?" Aurelia demanded.

"I said she was determined, but I never said she succeeded." Draken stood and began making his way down the dais steps, hands in his coat pockets. "Now I assume you are here to—what? Arrest me? Clap irons around my wrists and drag me off to rot in some prison cell?"

"And if it was, would you come amicably?" Darus asked, not lowering his sword.

Draken smiled, like one would at a pet they found amusing. "What do you think?"

"I like to think of myself as a fairly optimistic person, so you tell me?"

"Oh, by the Goddess," he heard Aurelia mutter to herself.

"I do have one question for you, though," Darus said.

Draken cocked his head to the side. "Hm?"

He knew that now probably wasn't the right time. That almost anyone else would tell him that he should be solely focused on capturing this man and nothing more. That what he was about to say now could wait. Only, it couldn't, not to Darus. Because how was he to know whether he would get the chance to ask again?

"Nine years ago, in the valley outside of a town called Windfell, a man and a woman were murdered, and only their son survived. Their names were Alexander and Erica Draco . . . was it you who murdered them?"

He heard the hissing of a sharp intake of breath beside him, but Darus was too fixated on Draken and what his response would be to pay it any sort of mind.

And finally, "Yes. It was me."

It was an answer that Darus had been prepared for, one he had been expecting, even. Yet hearing the words straight from Draken's mouth and knowing for sure that he stood before the man who murdered his son's parents—

"Why?" The word was out before he could even think to stop it.

"I had my reasons."

Draken had barely finished speaking before there was an explosion of fire that momentarily deafened Darus. He felt something land on his shoulder and realised it was Cora. Aurelia had conjured the sudden torrent of fire and sent it hurtling straight for Draken. It consumed him within seconds and then kept raging, lighting up the hall and searing the air.

What surprised Darus the most, however, was the look on Aurelia's face—full of unadulterated rage. He'd become accustomed to seeing Aurelia present such a calm and almost aloof demeanour, that witnessing such a change was akin to seeing a rock crack open to reveal a crystal that sparkled with a multitude of colours.

Finally, the fire ceased, leaving the stench of smoke and Aurelia's harsh breathing in its wake.

But where Draken should have been nothing more than a burnt out corpse, he stood whole and completely unharmed. Not one stitch of his clothing had been singed. He lowered his arm from where he had been using it to shield his face, as if from a mere cloud of smoke and not an inferno. Darus thought that he could see a red shimmer in the air around him. *Did he shield himself with magic?*

Draken looked at them flatly. "Rude."

An animalistic sound tore from Aurelia's throat before she was racing across the hall, more magic already crackling at her fingertips.

Darus had no choice but to charge after her.

* * *

The water splashed as Jared and Will raced through the maze-like corridors of the dungeons. They turned a corner but were brought up short when all that awaited them was a brick wall.

"By the Goddess!" Jared shouted in frustration. "How are we supposed to get out of here?"

"I don't think we are," Will said.

Almost immediately, they heard the sounds of rattling and splashing water behind them.

"Move!" He shoved Will out of the way in time to avoid being impaled by a spear-wielding attacker.

The attacker stumbled past them, their momentum carrying them forward. The torchlight illuminated their form and revealed them to be a skeleton. A skeleton with empty, black eye sockets and a ragged tunic hanging off of its brittle bones.

A skeleton that could *stand up* and *move* and *wield spears.*

And it wasn't the only one.

More animated skeletons, some carrying rusted weapons and others crawling through the water on all fours, came surging towards them.

The one that had attacked them with the spear opened its jaw and let out a rattling wail as it lunged at Jared and Will once more. Jared was the one to intercept the attack with his sword, while Will dealt with the others.

He caught the tip of the spear with his blade and felt the rough stone scrape against metal before forcing it up and away. While the skeleton's guard was open, Jared swept his sword out in an arc, severing the rotted tendons that connected its spear wielding arm to its shoulder. The skeletal arm and the spear fell into the water with a splash.

Jared moved with the speed and precision that had been hammered into him at the Academy. *"Don't give your opponent a chance to regroup,"* the words spoken by a former Professor rang through his head even now. *"Allowing them to regroup might only spell the end for you."*

He kicked out at one of the skeleton's legs, hard enough that he was sure he heard the bone crack as the skeleton was brought to its knees. Jared delivered another kick, this time to its head, sending it flying into the nearby wall, cracking in two upon impact.

The skeleton's body shuddered once before whatever was animating it seemed to leave and it fell lifeless, disappearing beneath the water.

Jared shouldn't have let his guard down. He knew that was a disastrous thing to do in the middle of a fight. Another thing he had been warned about at the Academy, yet he did it anyway, allowing one of those skeleton creatures to grab him from behind and bite down on his unprotected neck.

He cried out at the pain, but it was fleeting. He felt the skeleton being ripped away from him just as quickly as it had latched on and Jared spun around to see Will, Changed, and holding the skeleton's head between his jaws.

Its struggles ceased when Will bit down hard enough for its skull to crack and break. He let it fall carelessly from his mouth once it went still.

"Are you all right?" asked Will, Changing back and stepping closer to inspect where the skeleton had undoubtedly left a nasty bite mark on Jared's neck.

"I'm fine," he said, putting his own hand to the throbbing wound. "We should get moving, before more of those things show up. There has to be a way out around here somewhere."

A doubtful look flashed across Will's face, and Jared ignored it. He refused to pay attention to his own unhelpful thoughts that told him that whatever strange magic had gotten them down here and brought those skeletons to life might also mean they were trapped down here forever.

* * *

Darus flew out of range of the red lightning that speared his way and answered it with a breath of fire.

Draken easily blocked the fire from where he stood in the centre of the now ruined hall. One of the long tables had been thrown against a wall and the other was barely more than a mangled heap of splinters.

Aurelia conjured six daggers out of the air and sent them hurtling toward Draken's unprotected back. Before they could even so much as touch him, Draken disappeared in a burst of red fire and reappeared behind Aurelia, a huge, crimson scythe in his hands.

Darus was there, leaping over Aurelia's head and diving on top of Draken before he could use the scythe to cleave Aurelia in two. He pinned Draken to the ground as Draken, in turn, jammed the staff of his scythe between Darus's teeth. Darus bit down and jerked the scythe out of Draken's hands.

But Draken only smiled up at him. "Tell me, how is that boy doing? Derek? That was his name, wasn't it?"

Hearing his son's name spoken from this man's lips gave him pause—how did he know Derek's *name? Why did he want to know about Derek?*—and that brief distraction was enough for Darus to be caught by surprise when there was a red shimmer in the air around him and he was flung backwards, only coming to a stop when his body crashed into the wall behind the dais.

The force of it was hard enough to knock out not only his breath, but the Change from him. As he collapsed to the floor, pain echoed throughout every muscle in his body.

When he looked up, it was to see that Aurelia had once again engaged Draken. Only this time, she was attacking him with a shortsword. As she stabbed and dodged spells, she moved with the dancer-like grace and swiftness Darus had seen in other Wood Elves when they fought, and had even seen in Derek.

It looked as if Draken could only barely keep up with her movements. When he fell for one of her feints, Aurelia opened up a long gash on his face that could very well have taken his eye out had he not been quick enough to pull back at the last second.

For a moment, Darus almost believed that Aurelia would manage to overpower Draken with her speed alone. That was until a ring of crimson fire exploded to life around Draken and Aurelia was forced to leap back.

"Well, this has been entertaining," said Draken, picking his fallen hat up off the floor. "But I am getting rather bored now. I think I'll be heading off."

"Do you seriously expect us to simply let you leave?" Aurelia demanded between panting breaths.

Draken looked highly amused. "Do *you* think you can stop me? You've spent all your magic and hardly have a drop left in you."

"Don't write me off so easily," said Darus as he came to stand at Aurelia's side.

"It's too bad the rest of those Guardians didn't get here sooner," said Draken conversationally. "You might have actually had a chance at capturing me."

Darus was left momentarily gobsmacked by the statement. "What do you—?"

"They've just arrived outside the fortress gates. But I'll be long gone by the time they enter these halls." With a last, serpentine smile at Darus, he added, "Take good care of Derek for me. I'll be around to collect him soon enough."

A bolt of fear lanced through Darus as the words sunk in. Aurelia shouted a wordless cry of rage and lunged for Draken. The fire flared again, this time consuming Draken whole, and when it burnt out, he was gone.

"*Fuck!*"Aurelia cried, throwing her blade at the ground where Draken had just stood.

Draken's departing words still rang through Darus's head. He would come for Derek? But why? *Why?* What did that bastard want with Derek?

A low rumbling brought Darus out of his panicked thoughts. It was quickly followed by a shaking so fierce that it nearly knocked him off his feet.

"What is happening?" He heard Aurelia say above the noise.

Her question was answered by one of the iron chandeliers falling to the floor, along with a part of the ceiling in a shower of plaster and stone and an ear-splitting, metallic clang.

"The fort," Darus realised. "It's coming down!"

* * *

Jared slammed the skull of another skeleton against the wall—he'd lost his sword sometime ago—and cracked it to pieces easily enough.

Immediately after, another skeleton collided with him from behind, forcing Jared to lose his balance and fall through the water.

Beneath, the water was so murky that Jared couldn't see a thing except for the head of the skeleton that was pinning him down. It snapped its jaws in front of his face, as if hoping to bite a chunk out of him—and then went completely still.

Its teeth stopped gnashing and the surprising strength behind its skeletal frame vanished and Jared was able to push it away and sit up, gasping in air as his head broke the water's surface.

"Jared!" There was more splashing as Will rushed to his side and hauled him to his feet.

"Wh—What happened?" said Jared, pushing his sopping hair out of his eyes to get a look at the skeletons that now lay still in the water around their feet.

"I'm not sure," Will said. "One minute I was fighting the rest of them off and the next they just . . . collapsed."

218

"Strange. I—Is that a *door*?" Ahead of them, where only moments ago there was only an endless corridor, was clearly a wall with a door embedded in it.

"It can't be," said Will in a voice that was equal parts disbelief and hope. "That was *not* there before."

But the pair didn't waste any time in racing toward it. Jared grabbed the iron handle, and the door opened with no resistance to reveal a windowless stairwell.

Jared let out a breath of laughter.

At the same time the shaking started.

* * *

Deep cracks appeared in the walls at an alarming rate. Dust and bits of stone were raining down. Darus and Aurelia had to get out of here. Fast. Lest they wanted to find themselves crushed beneath a mountain of rubble.

He saw Aurelia stumble back to avoid the falling chunk of stone. Darus had no doubt that if her magic wasn't nearly depleted, she could have cast a spell that would've had them outside of these walls in no time.

Over the roaring of the collapsing hall, Darus heard the cawing of a raven and looked toward the other end of the hall, where he spotted Cora hopping along the sill of one of the arched windows. With an idea quickly taking root, Darus Changed and soared across the short distance that separated him and Aurelia before grabbing her and lifting her off her feet. She didn't shout or struggle, but held fast to him as he hurtled towards the window, swerving past falling debris along the way.

He ducked his head over Aurelia's just before he shot through the window, and the glass shattered around them.

* * *

Jared and Will ran out into the courtyard just as the archway collapsed behind them. From there, they Changed and flew high into the sky, safely away from the ensuing wreckage.

They watched from above as the fort collapsed at an alarming rate. One of the watchtowers fell, sending up a cloud of dust in its wake. Wasn't that where Darus and Aurelia were supposed to be? Did they get out in time, or had they been crushed beneath all of that rubble?

Before Jared's mind could race toward any more morbid conclusions, Will made a noise beside him and used his head to indicate at something below. Further down the mountain, safely out of the way of the collapsing fort, was a group of Guardians, easily distinguishable by their uniforms. Jared recognised Charles Decorus and Alistair, and Elijah Hargrade, amongst others.

With a burgeoning relief, Jared also spotted Darus and Aurelia standing with them. Both looked a little worse for wear, but they were alive. They had all made it out alive and—for now, at least— that was all that mattered.

16

The night of Orville's Nativitas masquerade party had finally arrived. Once the sun was set and Mayor and Lady Boeheart had set off themselves to attend the party, Derek, Rosalie and Arabelle snuck away from the Manor. They made their way through the winding streets, keeping to the shadows and out of sight. Not that it was too difficult, the air grew much colder at night and no one wanted to stay outdoors if they could help it.

They arrived at the home of Giselle and Linette La Fray, where Edgar was already waiting for them in the alleyway at the back of the house.

"I took a quick look inside, and it looks like they're still getting ready," Edgar explained in a hushed whisper.

"Good," said Arabelle. "Then we still have time."

They crept towards the backdoor where Derek produced a couple of lock picks from his back pocket and started picking the lock. Once it was opened, Arabelle and Rosalie slipped inside while Derek and Edgar stayed crouched by either side of the door.

Derek heard singing coming from inside the house before it was cut off abruptly. Moments later he heard a muffled thump from upstairs followed by the window above them opening and Rosalie sticking her head out.

"All clear," she whispered down to them.

Derek and Edgar found Arabelle and Rosalie upstairs and in the middle of dragging the unconscious La Fray sisters into their bedrooms. In Arabelle's arms, Giselle La Fray was even snoring as if she were fast asleep in the most comfortable bed and not being dragged across the landing like a sack of potatoes in taffeta skirts.

Derek knew it was due to the effect of the sleep tonic Arabelle had bought from the herbalist the day before. He could even smell the faintest traces of peace lily and lavender in the air.

"Instead of standing there gawking," snapped Rosalie. "Might you boys deign to help us?"

Edgar moved to help Rosalie with Linette while Derek took hold of Giselle's feet so he and Arabelle could manoeuvre her into the nearby bedroom. Once they had safely deposited her on the gaudy bed, Arabelle snapped her fingers in front of the woman's ear.

But Giselle La Fray snored on.

"She's dead to the world," Arabelle announced.

"Now let's just hope that she stays that way until this is all over," said Derek.

Arabelle didn't answer. Instead, she swept out of the room,

purposefully not looking at Derek as she walked past him.

I guess she's still upset with me, Derek thought.

He followed Arabelle back onto the landing where Rosalie was already handing two parcels in brown wrapping paper to Edgar.

"You boys go get changed downstairs. Arabelle and I will meet you once we're ready."

And so, while Rosalie and Arabelle retreated back into the bedrooms, Derek and Edgar were left to change into their party finery in the downstairs parlour.

Derek's clothes were made up of a burgundy-red waistcoat with gold brocade, a white, high-collared shirt and a pair of black trousers and a matching black tailcoat, as well as a pair of black boots. His mask was silver, only covering the top half of his face and, was made to look like the head of a wolf.

"I can't believe I'm actually doing this," Edgar was saying as he slid his arms into the sleeves of his grey tailcoat. "If we get caught, the Captain will have my head."

"We won't get caught," assured Derek, watching his reflection in the mirror on the wall as he forced his hair to lie flat using the pomade he had nicked from Mayor Boeheart's ensuite. "It's a masquerade. No one there will know who you are so long as you keep your mask on."

"I suppose you're right." Edgar chuckled, albeit nervously. "I just can't help but imagine the worst that can happen."

Derek looked through the mirror where Edgar was tying his cravat behind him. He thought of Edgar the way he had been as a child, sensitive and always seeming in need of saving, especially from the children who liked to tease him because of his weight. He remembered when they had first become friends, after he had stood up for Edgar to a group of children who had been throwing rocks at him. Even though it had left him bleeding and bruised when the children had turned their rocks on Derek instead—and made his mother angrier than he had ever seen her when he returned home— before getting bored and leaving, he had turned to the whimpering Edgar with a smile and said, "Don't worry, I'll protect you."

"I never got the chance to ask before, but why did you join the Guard?"

"Ah, that . . . it's a silly reason."

Derek turned away from the mirror. "I'd still like to know."

Edgar fiddled with the knot of his cravat. "I—You can probably imagine what the Town Guard is like under the captaincy of Goldridge. It's nothing like what I'm sure the Crown Guard is like in Ember. A lot of the men are dishonourable and the decent ones are too afraid to stand up for what's right because they know all it might achieve is a beating in the barracks by their fellow Guards." Edgar took a breath, and it was then that Derek noticed his anger. "When I was thirteen, a group of men that my da owed money to trashed the shop and beat him bloody. He knew exactly who the men were because they didn't even bother to cover their faces. The Guard did nothing about it because the men had already bribed the Captain to look the other way. And two years ago, one of my mum's friends was—she was—attacked. By a Guard. One night out in the streets."

Disgust curled unpleasantly in the pit of Derek's stomach."And nothing was done about it, was it?"

Edgar shook his head.

"So that's why you joined the Town Guard? So you can change it?"

Edgar nodded, an embarrassed tilt to his lips. "I know it's silly. How can someone like me change the ways of a corrupt Town Guard? But still I . . . want to try."

"It's not silly," said Derek, feeling pride at how much his old friend had grown. "Not at all. And if anyone can make a difference in this shitty old town, it's you."

The older boy grinned at him and for a moment, Derek saw him as he was when they had been children and he felt that same desire to protect him.

"And even if something does go wrong tonight," he said. "We'll be there to look out for you."

Edgar laughed.

"What?"

"You're still trying to protect me."

"Even though you're the older one," Derek said with a grin, mimicking what Edgar had once said to him years ago. *"You shouldn't be protecting me. I'm the older one. It should be the other way around."*

"Are you boys decent?" Came a woman's voice from the top of the stairs.

"Well, I have my faults, but I'd like to think I'm still a good person," replied Derek.

"Very funny, Draco. Really, though, you two better have everything covered up because we're coming down."

There was the sound of heels against the hardwood of the stairs as Giselle and Linette La Fray descended the staircase. Only it wasn't really the sisters, but Arabelle and Rosalie.

Both were dressed in the ball gowns the real Giselle and Linette had been wearing. Both had long sleeves and bodices that looked so tight, Derek wondered how it was possible for them to even breathe. Rosalie's—Linette's—dress was made of violet taffeta and black lace along the neckline and the hem of the skirt. She'd done up her long, dark hair into a chignon and painted her lips a plum colour.

Arabelle's dress was a striking crimson with flared sleeves. The neckline plunged so dramatically that Derek couldn't help but avert his eyes as quickly as possible. Arabelle had opted to let Giselle's hair fall loose down her back. She wore a string of white pearls around her neck and a pair of white gloves.

They both wore identical pearl-white masks that reminded Derek of the faces of porcelain dolls.

"You two look lovely," said Edgar.

"Aren't you sweet," said Rosalie. "You two don't look too bad yourselves. Don't you think, Arabelle?"

"Yes, you both look very . . . handsome." She said that last part with a glance at Derek before quickly looking away.

Derek didn't miss the way Rosalie's painted lips stretched into a knowing smirk as she looked between him and Arabelle.

Not in the mood for anything Rosalie might have to say about it, Derek quickly said, "Shall we go?"

* * *

The Goldridge estate was nestled in the woods, only a short carriage ride outside of town. It was so close by that one could walk there without growing too weary—unless they were wearing heavy skirts, however.

As their carriage approached the front gates and tall stone fence, they were halted by a pair of Guards.

"Invitations, please," one Guard asked, stepping up to Arabelle's side of the window.

Arabelle handed the Guard their invitations. "And my sister and I are accompanied by two of our friends from Brai," she said, ignoring the strangeness of hearing herself speak with someone else's voice.

The Guard looked over the invitations, deemed everything in order and waved them in through the gates.

Their carriage trundled into the front courtyard of the estate. The house itself was a grand and imposing structure, made up of dark brick and gabled rooftops dusted with snow. The front windows on the first floor were illuminated with the whitish light of illuminae crystals.

Derek, Arabelle, Rosalie and Edgar were showed inside and

ended up in an entryway with a towering, arched ceiling, illuminae crystal chandelier and white tile floors. Everything one would expect of a noble's residence.

A footman greeted them. Once their coats were taken and put away, they were led down the hall and out into the garden, full of winter-blooming flowers and stone statues of horses and men battling fearsome-looking beasts.

In the middle of it all was a tall, brick structure, with high windows and a domed roof. As they drew closer, the sounds of music and voices could be heard from inside.

The doors were pushed open to reveal a ballroom. At least seven chandeliers hung from the high ceilings and though it was nowhere near as big as the ballrooms in the royal palace, it was still spacious enough to fit quite a large gathering of people. Men and women wearing their finest attire, their faces covered by masks of all sorts, milled about the room. Servants carrying platters of finger food and flutes of champagne, weaved in and out of the crowds gracefully. They, too, wore masks.

Some guests could be seen dancing near the back of the room, where masked musicians played their lutes and their pipes. Others stood around in groups or lounged on the divans that had been placed around the room, sipping their drinks and smoking their cigars. The whole room smelled of some sort of sickly sweet tobacco.

The footman had slipped into the crowd as soon as they had arrived, only to return no time later with Orville at his side.

Orville's half mask, made of royal red material and gold lace, matched the red of his brocade and trousers and the gold velvet of his cape, which shimmered under the light.

"Giselle, Linette!" His voice boomed as he strode forward to greet them, his arms spread wide and a goblet clutched in one hand. "So glad the two of you could make it."

"Of course, we wouldn't miss it," said Rosalie in Linette's high voice.

"I only hope we haven't arrived too late," Arabelle added. She leaned over to place a hand around Derek's arm. "Our dear Ambrose and Cecil here were a bit tardy with bringing the carriage around."

Orville waved a hand. "Not to worry, the night is still young and there's still plenty of drink to be had!" He raised his goblet as if for a toast, before parading back into the crowd, calling out to someone as he did so.

"So, what is the plan again?" Edgar asked, loud enough for only the four of them to hear.

"We wait for Orville to make his speech," Derek said.

"Then Edgar and Derek use that as an opportunity to slip out unnoticed," Rosalie continued.

"And make it back to the house to search through Orville's rooms for anything incriminating," finished Arabelle.

"And until then?" said Edgar.

"We try to enjoy ourselves, I suppose."

"Wonderful idea," Rosalie said primly and latched herself onto

Edgar's arm. "Come along, my dear Cecil, let us mingle with the crowd."

"R-Right."

And they were gone, leaving Arabelle and Derek to stand around rather awkwardly with each other. Arabelle resisted the urge to pull at the uncomfortably low neckline of her gown—but did it really make sense for her to feel self-conscious if it wasn't actually her own skin that was showing?—and fiddled with the pearls around her neck instead, as she tried to look anywhere but at Derek. The way he had spoken to her in the library the other night felt stark between them—or at least it did for Arabelle.

And she hated that in actuality, it made her feel like a kicked puppy when she thought about it. Certainly, she was angry at how he had spoken to her and she wished that anger was all she felt. But really, she couldn't help but feel like maybe she had been at fault that night, too. That she might have crossed some sort of line—

"Giselle, darling!"

A man with tousled brown hair and a forest green mask and matching waistcoat approached them.

Oh, no. Arabelle grimaced inwardly. She'd been hoping that, with the help of the masks, they'd be able to avoid being noticed by people who knew Giselle La Fray.

"My dear, I was so hoping I would see you here tonight," he was saying, a broad grin on his face. "Please, won't you do me the honour of a dance—"

"I'm sorry, what was that, Cecil?" Arabelle said hurriedly, turning to Derek. "You wanted to dance? Oh, well, let's not waste anymore time then!" And with that, she dragged Derek into the throng of partygoers, leaving behind a very put out-looking green waistcoat man.

"I thought I was Ambrose?" said Derek.

"Don't worry about that now."

As they passed through the crowd, Arabelle spotted Mayor Boeheart, seated on one of the divans, surrounded by a small group of people and recognisable, even with the navy blue mask that matched his finery. Beside him sat a woman, who Arabelle was certain could be none other than Anna. Her long, brown hair was gathered into a pile atop her head and her mask was the colour of snow, as was the gown she wore, but her lips were painted scarlet in startling contrast.

Standing not too far away, by one of the windows, was a tall figure in a deep red velvet waistcoat and matching trousers. Their mask was vibrant vermillion in the shape of a bird with a curved beak, sitting over the person's nose. Even though Arabelle couldn't get a good look at the person's face with their mask on, she couldn't help but think they resembled Aryel Sabir, with their short, straight, dark hair and golden-brown skin.

She didn't get the chance to know for sure. A laughing couple walked passed and once they had stepped out of Arabelle's line of sight, the person she thought was Aryel Sabir had vanished.

She tried not to feel too unnerved by it as she and Derek came to a stop at the edge of where the dancers occupied the floor and Arabelle was suddenly very aware of her arm in Derek's, their shoulders pressed snugly against each other. Suddenly, she didn't feel like a Guardian on a covert mission or like she was still mad at Derek for snapping at her the other night. Instead, she simply felt like a young girl, flustered at the idea of dancing with the boy she loved.

Derek seemed to sense her hesitancy and said, "Would you like something to drink?"

She exhaled. "Please."

Derek gestured for one of the nearby servants to bring the drinks their way, and he took one of the flutes filled with golden, bubbly champagne and handed it to Arabelle.

"Nothing for you?" she asked as she accepted the glass.

"I really don't have a taste for alcohol."

Arabelle took a sip and was surprised to find the drink had an almost fruity taste to it, like citrus and peach. "My parents would murder me if they knew I was drinking alcohol," she said.

"You've never had any before?"

"I've never had the opportunity. What about you? Have you ever tried it?"

"No, and I never plan to."

She got the feeling that there was more of a story behind those words, if the slight edge to Derek's tone was anything to go by, but she decided against pressing the matter. *You've already done enough of that.*

"Also," he said after a few beats. "I wanted . . . to apologise for the other night. I shouldn't have snapped at you like that."

"Oh. It's all right. I shouldn't have tried pushing you so hard to talk."

"You were trying to help. I just got needlessly angry." He was fiddling with the cuffs of his coat. "It's . . . easier that way."

Easier? Arabelle was going to say, until she caught the look in Derek's down-turned eyes. Even beneath the silver wolf mask, she knew he had that faraway look on his face, like he was recalling a memory so vivid it trapped him inside his own head. The same look she'd seen on him in the library before he snapped at her. The same one she had seen so many times before. A look Arabelle had only ever wanted to be able to rid him of.

Before she could say anything else, the green waistcoat man sidled up to them, this time wrapping his arm around Arabelle's shoulders, startling her enough that she had to forcibly stop herself from applying her elbow to his throat.

"Giselle, my flower." His voice was slurred now. "I been lookin' everywhere for you. And now, here you are!"

"Yes, here I am." She tried to extricate herself from the green waistcoat man, but he clung to her like a stubborn weed.

"How 'bout that dance now? Since you appear to be finished with this chap?"

Derek stepped forward, gripping the restrictive hand the man had on her shoulder and with a pleasant enough smile. He said, "This *'chap'* is her companion for the night and would appreciate you showing some proper respect."

"Respect, huh? I'll show you some respect—"

He made to take a swing at Derek, and while the man was clearly intoxicated and she doubted he could have done Derek any real harm, Arabelle stuck her foot out and—as discreetly as possible—swept the already unsteady legs out from under the green waistcoat man. With a shout, he pitched forward, sprawling onto the floor and gathering the attention of those around them.

"Oh my," Arabelle said loudly. "I think that man's had a bit too much to drink. How embarrassing."

Two masked servants appeared and began the task of helping the man to his feet.

"Call a carriage round and send him home," Orville called out from across the room. "We don't need someone who can't hold their drink spoiling the night."

As the green waistcoat man was escorted out and the guests returned to their dancing and mingling, Arabelle and Derek were approached by Edgar and Rosalie.

"What happened?" asked Edgar.

"I think that man was in love with Arabelle," Derek explained.

Rosalie gasped, scandalised. "Really?"

"Not *me*," Arabelle pointed out. "Giselle."

"Oh."

Arabelle sighed. "Let's just get back to work."

* * *

The clanging of silverware on glass, signalled the beginning of Orville's toast.

And the beginning of their assignment.

While the gathered guests stood around to listen as Orville gave thanks to everyone for joining him in celebrating the festive season, Derek and Edgar discreetly made their way to the doors of the ballroom, with Edgar half-carrying Derek so if anyone asked where they were going, they could simply say that Derek had had a bit too much to drink and was in need of some fresh air.

Fortunately, they made it outside and back into the mansion without being confronted by a single soul.

They crept back down the hallway, past the mounted heads of stags and bears and sabre lions and oil paintings that looked as if they would earn someone a life's fortune on the selling block. They snuck past the kitchens, where some servants were too engrossed in preparing more food and mocking some of the outfit choices of the guests to notice them.

"I'm telling you, her mask was distinctly duck-shaped."

Derek had thought so when they first arrived, but this house had not changed since he had last been here many years ago. Unlike the Mayor's Manor, which had undergone some changes in decor, the Goldridge mansion was exactly how Derek remembered it. From the dark wallpaper with a pattern of gold birds in the dining area, to the grand piano that was only for show by the window in one of the front rooms and even the little dent in one of the otherwise spotless balustrades of the house's grand staircase.

There were no candles or illuminae crystals lit on the second floor. Only shafts of moonlight spilling in from the windows provided them with visibility. The end of the landing split into two separate hallways, like a fork in the road, and Derek knew that the hallway to their right would lead them to the master bedroom, which Orville would have no doubt taken over by now. He and Edgar were halfway across the landing when a voice from further up had Derek reaching around to grab Edgar and press him against the nearby wall, where the shadows were thickest.

"Did you hear that?" A man's voice.

"Hm? Did I hear what?" Another man's voice, this one with more of a lazy drawl. Derek could see their shadowy silhouettes in the doorway of one of the end rooms. Were they party guests or servants?

"I'm sure I heard something. Like someone walking down the hall."

A chuckle. "You're so paranoid. The Master's in the ballroom enjoying his party. He's not going to be roaming about the house now."

"I know that, but if we're caught—"

"We won't be." There was a break in the talking, followed by the unmistakable sounds of kissing. A gasp.

Derek suddenly wished very much to be anywhere but here. *Go back into the room. Please let them go back into the room.*

And then, as if the Goddess had decided to take pity and grant him his silent wish, "C'mon. The party won't finish until late. We have time."

"Mm. All right."

The silhouettes disappeared into the room; the door closing with a soft click behind them. Once they were sure the coast was clear, Derek and Edgar peeled away from the wall, hurrying down the hallway to their right.

The master bedroom, which had once belonged to Mayor Goldridge, was at the end of the hall. Derek placed his hand against the doorknob, ready to push it open, when he hesitated.

"What's wrong?" asked Edgar.

Derek shook himself. "Nothing," he said and opened the door.

Inside was much the same as Derek remembered it. Olive-green wallpaper, heavy golden curtains framing the windows that looked out onto the gardens. An adjoining lounge room and a canopied bed so wide it looked like three people could sleep on it comfortably and with room to spare.

"Where do we even start?" said Edgar, staring around as if he couldn't believe anyone would need such a spacious bedroom.

You should see Jared's room, Derek thought. "You search through here and I'll look through the lounge."

While Edgar started with searching Orville's bedside table, Derek stepped through the curtained doorway and into the lounge. He went to the desk first, looking through the papers on top and rifling through each of the drawers. But all he ended up finding were pens, an unopened packet of cigars, a wax seal and an old hunting knife in a leather sheath.

He even checked the hidden compartments by the fireplace, but they were both empty.

Wandering over to the bookshelves, Derek noticed that a couple of large tomes sat open on the low table in the corner by an armchair. He picked up the first book, which had the title *Vampirism and Lycanthropy: A History.*

Derek frowned. It was difficult to imagine Orville having enough of an interest in vampires and lycanthropes that he would read about them—actually, he found it difficult to imagine Orville being the reading type at all.

Setting the book aside, he turned his attention to the next one, which had its pages splayed open. Reading was made difficult, thanks to the lack of proper lighting, but Derek managed to make out a few sentences.

. . . while both magics have their limitations, there are many spells and magical feats that dark magic can achieve while natural magic cannot. Reanimating the dead, for example . . .

Derek began flipping through a few more of the pages, skimming through what words he could.

. . . dark magic was first discovered in 298 by the renowned mage . . .

. . . can alter one's appearance, while natural magic can only create the illusion . . .

Without even having to look at the front cover, it was immediately clear that this was a book with a heavy focus on the subject of dark magic.

It was certainly strange that Orville would have a book such as this in his home, but would it be enough to incriminate him? That remained to be seen. Regardless, Derek thought it would be worth taking the book with them.

He went to tell Edgar of this, when he saw what he could only describe as a shadowy figure, detaching itself from the rest of the darkness shrouding the room and moving swiftly and silently to where Edgar stood with his back to it. Something glinted, wicked and sharp in the pale moonlight at the shadow's side. A knife.

It seemed to happen all too slowly and too fast for Derek. He was aware of Edgar's name being ripped from his mouth, but as if from a distance. And that was all he could do before the shadow was upon the other boy. The knife lifting and plunging through Edgar's back.

A choked sound tore from Edgar as his body fell back.

"No." Derek was on his knees and pulling Edgar into his lap— though he couldn't quite remember how he had gotten there.

"Edgar? Hey, *Edgar?*"

The only response he got was a wheezing gasp. He could feel something wet beneath his palm where it was pressed against Edgar's chest. Blood. Far too much of it. Soaking through the front of his clothes until they were sodden with it. A dark stain spread out from the ragged hole above his heart.

No. Not Edgar. *Not Edgar.*

You said you would protect him.

Edgar convulsed, sounding as if he were trying to speak, but only blood made it past his lips.

"Edgar," it was all Derek could think to say. *"Please."*

And then he was gone.

Derek felt it. Felt Edgar's body go limp in his arms and saw his eyes dull.

Edgar who was kind and good. Edgar who dreamed of changing his hometown for the better. Who had once been his closest friend, was now dead.

Tears burned the backs of his eyes. His grief built into a hard knot in his throat that felt as if it would choke him. Derek looked up in time to see the edge of a dark cloak slip through the open window and into the night.

Rage joined the grief eddying inside of him and he didn't even realise that he had gotten to his feet and pulled his ring out from under his collar. As he launched himself out of the window, he slipped his ring on and Changed.

He ended up in the back garden, startling some of the guests who had wandered out of the ballroom. But Derek paid them no mind. Instead, all his attention was given over to the movement by the rose bushes across the yard, the cloaked figure leaping over the fence and disappearing into the forest beyond. Derek followed, ignoring the startled shouts. Nothing was on his mind except the need to catch the one who had killed Edgar.

You promised to protect him.

But you failed.

The woods at night were dense and dark enough that it would

have been difficult for a human to navigate, but not for a dragon's eyes. It took barely any time at all for Derek to spot the flash of movement that was the cloaked figure dashing through the trees. The shadows of the night faded away, and all Derek could see was red. He tore after the figure.

Grief-fuelled anger raged inside of him like a wildfire, lending him a tremendous burst of speed as he bounded across the forest ground, kicking up plumes of snow.

He was almost upon the cloaked figure. So close to pouncing on them and tearing his claws into their flesh and making them bleed, like they had made Edgar bleed, when a hand appeared from underneath the cloak, palm facing Derek, and before he knew it, he felt as if he had crashed straight into a brick wall.

The impact sent him ricocheting backwards, his back struck a nearby tree before he fell to the ground, the Change slipping off of him. Sparks of pain ran up and down his back where he had collided with the tree.

A spell?

The cold damp of the snow seeped through his trousers, as he pushed himself onto his knees. He looked around frantically, but there was no sign of the cloaked figure. He'd lost them.

"*Fucking damn it!*" The words came out in an animalistic growl as he slammed his fist against the tree bark. Pain exploded and raced up his arm, but he paid it little thought because just then, he caught sight of something lying in the snow nearby.

Even as he stood up and made his way over, Derek knew what

he was about to discover.

It was a person lying in the snow. And a familiar one.

The green waistcoat man he had last seen being escorted out of the ballroom for his drunken misconduct.

He was dead.

Blood spattered the snow where he lay, stemming from the ragged stump where his left hand should have been. His neck was twisted at an unnatural angle, and already starting to swell. His mask had been discarded too, leaving his unnaturally still features bare for Derek to see.

He had little time to ruminate on this gruesome discovery. The glow of torch light came into view, followed by the sound of pounding hooves.

Six men on horseback approached, encircling Derek and the body of the green waistcoat man.

At the head of the group, still dressed in his party finery—minus the cape and the mask—was Orville.

He looked down at Derek, a nasty smirk twisting his features. As if he had found something he was hoping for. "Well, well. What do we have here?"

17

The party at the Goldridge estate had come to an abrupt end after guests had witnessed Derek leaping out of an upstairs window, and the servants had discovered Edgar's body after hearing a commotion from Orville's bedroom.

"They endangered the lives of everyone present," Orville was ranting to the Mayor. "And one of my Guards was even killed thanks to their foolhardy actions!"

Derek flinched. The reminder of Edgar's death hitting him like a blow. From what he had gathered while they were being escorted back to town, Edgar's body had been taken away to the Crypt—along with the body of the green waistcoat man—where they would be kept until a funeral could be held.

"What of Giselle and Linette La Fray?" asked Boeheart. "Are they all right?"

"We sent someone around to their home earlier," said Rolven. "They appeared unharmed, only in a deep sleep. Most likely thanks to some sort of sleeping draught that was given to them."

"But they will wake?"

"Yes, sir."

Boeheart sighed tiredly. He sat behind his desk, still dressed in his party attire. "Why? Why would you do this?" He directed the question at Derek, Arabelle, and Rosalie, who stood before him.

Rosalie and Arabelle had removed the desona charms and were left standing in the ill-fitting dresses of the La Fray sisters. Rolven and another Town Guard stood on either side of them, as if they posed some kind of threat.

"I apologise for our unorthodox methods, Lord Boeheart," said Arabelle. "But it was the only way we could think of to conduct a necessary investigation."

"And why would you need to conduct this specific investigation?"

"We . . . we received some information that suggested we might be able to find clues about the murders at the Goldridge estate."

"And where did you receive this information?" Orville inquired with a raised eyebrow.

"We'd prefer to keep that to ourselves," said Derek hollowly. While Edgar might be gone and safe from Orville's wrath, his family was not, and Derek wasn't going to risk what he might do to them if he found out Edgar had been helping them. For now, Orville was under the impression that Edgar had merely been roped into their schemes on account of his old friendship with Derek.

"You can't say, eh?" Orville sneered. "I wonder why? Probably because you're just making the whole thing up."

"Can you at least disclose what the information was?" asked Boeheart.

"That your captain knows more than he's willing to let on about the killings," Derek bit out.

Orville's expression went stony while Mayor Boeheart's brow furrowed. "And what exactly do you mean by that?"

He saw Arabelle give him a warning look out of the corner of his eye, but he ignored it. He felt too weighed down by everything that had happened to care enough about being delicate about any of this. "Don't you think it's funny, sir, that your captain has done jack shit to put a stop to these killings? You shouldn't have had to call in Guardians to solve this problem if he cared enough to do it himself. And then he goes blaming it on a *ghost* from an old story and acts like that solves everything!"

"Get to the point, boy," Orville growled.

"My *point* is that you're involved in these murders."

"How dare you?" said one of the Guards.

"That is a very serious accusation, Master Draco," said the Mayor. "Do you have any proof?"

"Only what I saw. And that was a book in his room. A book about dark magic."

Orville barked a laugh. "That hardly counts as proof. Unless you thought to bring this supposed book with you?"

Derek said nothing, because of course he hadn't. He'd dropped it when he saw that cloaked figure attack Edgar.

And for Orville, Derek's silence was answer enough. "Of course, if it makes you feel any better," he said, turning to Mayor Boeheart, "I can send a couple of my men to search for this book—"

"No," Derek said, because he knew what Orville was up to. "Not your Guards."

"And just why not?" Boeheart's voice had taken on a hard edge.

"Because there's no way of knowing whether the Guards he sends won't just cover up anything they find."

"First, you accuse my Captain of being untrustworthy and now you say my entire Town Guard cannot be trusted?"

"Well, not the *entire* Town Guard exactly," Rosalie said.

"Mayor Boeheart," said Orville. "I believe I know what's happening here. You see, Derek and I have always had something of a complicated relationship, especially when he lived with my late brother. He was always a troubled boy who resented me for the close relationship I shared with my brother. The poor thing wanted my brother's affections all for himself."

Derek froze. A feeling akin to having been doused with cold water stole over him.

"And I fear that his feelings of resentment may have led him and his companions to do something unspeakable," continued Orville. "They wish to frame me for these murders. As some sort of twisted ploy to get back at me for something that was not even my fault."

"What?" started Rosalie, outraged. "That's not—"

"And they coerced poor Edgar into their schemes, believing that, as one of my Guards, he would hold valuable information about me they could use to serve their purposes. And I believe that tonight, Edgar, being the upstanding lad that he was, decided to stand up to them and when it was clear that he would no longer go along with their dishonourable plans, Derek removed him from the picture."

That cold feeling intensified. "Are you saying," said Derek, his voice low, "that you think *I* killed Edgar?"

"That is his blood on your clothes, is it not?"

"You *son of a b*—"

"*Enough*," the Mayor's voice was firm, cutting through Derek's words like a knife. "There is something to be said about how you make accusations of corruption against my Guard and my Captain, who has done his job well these past few years, without any sufficient evidence to back it up. Not to mention the trouble you caused tonight. As for Captain Goldridge's accusations, I will take that as mere speculation until firmer proof is brought to my attention. And until we hear back from Ember, I'm going to have to say that the three of you remain in this house at all times. You are not to get involved with these murders anymore."

"But, Mayor—" started Arabelle.

"This is *not* up for discussion, Miss Aloria. Either you agree to these terms or I write to the King to press charges and you spend the remainder of your time here in a prison cell. Is that clear?"

Derek wanted to argue further—could feel that Rosalie and Arabelle did, too. He wanted to make the Mayor understand that he couldn't trust Orville. That they couldn't just stay locked away in this house while the murderer remained at large.

That, perhaps, the murderer could be standing with them in this room right now.

It was Arabelle who said, "Yes, Mayor Boeheart. We understand."

"Good," Boeheart sighed, a breath of relief. To Orville, he said, "Captain, if you and your men could please escort the Guardians to their rooms?"

"Of course." Orville's expression was schooled into one of professionalism, but the triumphant glint in his eyes was unmistakable.

As they began to make their way out of the study, Derek felt Orville come up close behind him. Felt Orville's warm breath uncomfortably close to his ear as he whispered, "Try playing at being the big, tough Guardian all you want, but all you'll ever be is my brother's little whor—"

Derek struck Orville before he could finish.

The next few moments were a blur. It was as if he were in a kind of trance, and all Derek could comprehend was the white-hot anger searing through him with the ferocity of an inferno. His body moved of its own accord, reacting to the desperate, visceral need to tear Orville limb from limb.

Somehow, he'd knocked Orville to the floor, shattering a nearby vase along the way. Derek's fist slammed into Orville's cheekbone, once, twice.

There was shouting around them. Someone called his name. Rosalie? Arabelle? He didn't know. He could hardly distinguish any words beyond the pounding in his ears. His ragged breathing.

There was blood on Orville's nose.

Pain lanced up Derek's fist.

Strong arms wrapped around him from behind, hauling him up and off of Orville.

He fought the grip at first, until a voice, a familiar voice that was soft and commanding all at once, said, "Derek, *stop*."

Arabelle. That was Arabelle behind him. That was Arabelle holding him. That was her touch. Her arms wrapped tight around his chest. Her fingers gripping tight to the material of his waistcoat. *Arabelle*.

The haze of fury began to clear from his mind. He was breathing hard, his heart beating rapidly.

"*You little piece of shit!*" snarled Orville from where he was being held back by Rolven.

Anger and loathing were written all over his face. Gone was the smugly composed Captain of the Guard. There was blood dripping down his nose and chin, an angry red mark already blooming on his cheekbone from where Derek had hit him.

A small part of Derek felt satisfaction at seeing the blood and bruises on Orville's face.

The rest of him felt only a numb sort of anger. Where moments ago, it had burned hot and furious, it now felt like a low, simmering heat.

"*Captain Goldridge.*"

The Mayor's voice was low but carried throughout the room. He was on his feet now, chin tilted up and expression thunderous."You and your men can see yourselves out, I believe."

For a moment, Orville looked as if he were seriously considering flinging himself at the Mayor instead. Finally, he shook off the grip Rolven had on him and without a word or a look at anyone else in the study, he stalked towards the door, closing it behind him with a wall-shuddering bang. Rolven and the other Guard followed soon after.

Next, Boeheart turned his steely blue eyes on Derek, Arabelle and Rosalie.

"As for you three, you are to go straight to your rooms before I have you thrown in prison. I do believe you've caused enough trouble for one night."

* * *

Jared hissed in a breath as Will pressed a damp cloth to the wound at his neck, wiping away the blood that had dried on his skin.

"Oh, suck it up Princess," the other boy said teasingly. "I'm being as gentle as can be."

"Not very gentle then," said Jared with another flinch. Who knew being bitten by a reanimated skeleton could be so painful?

"Or maybe you're just too delicate, Princess."

250

"I think I liked it better when you called me 'Your Highness'," Jared grumbled.

They sat in front of each other on the edge of the wide bed in the middle of the extravagant tent Aurelia had conjured for them earlier, as she had done for all the Guardians that were present. "It's been a long day and I refuse to sleep on a ratty, old bedroll in the cold," she had said as she made nine, deceivingly small tents appear around their makeshift campground.

There had also been a lot of explaining to do about what the other Guardians had happened upon when they arrived at the fort only for it to collapse and Jared and the others to emerge looking as if they had just been in a fierce battle—which they had.

It had taken some time for them all to wrap their heads around being told everything Jared and the others had learned since their encounter with the lycan in White Lake, Draken, and the shards from a mirror that could very well open a doorway to the daemon realm. Carvilla Hargrade especially had been sceptical, and of course, her sons had followed suit. In the end, it was decided that there was nothing that could be done for now but to bring this matter before the King, and in the morning, Jared, Darus and Will would set out for Ember.

Once Will had finished cleaning Jared's wound, he set the wet cloth back in the basin beside them while Jared collapsed onto his back, his arm spread against the silk-soft blankets beneath him. He didn't even have to worry about covering himself back up with a shirt thanks to the crackling fire in the grate before the bed, making the inside of the tent blessedly warm. *Magic is wonderful.*

"Of all the things I could've imagined happening when we started on this assignment," said Will, leaning back on his palms beside Jared. "This wasn't one of them."

"Do you mean the part where we fought a lycan? Or where we discovered there might be some enchanted mirror that could bring daemons back and a crazy man who wants to make that happen? Or that we had to fight *skeletons,* of all things?"

"Or maybe I was talking about getting to share a bed with the Prince."

The humour drained out of Jared to be replaced with something a little more flustered. Like when Aurelia had first directed Jared and Will to the tent, she said was theirs and inside they found only one bed.

"We don't have to," Jared said, clearing his throat. "I can just sleep on the floor."

Will looked down at him, his expression serious. "Is that what you'd rather?"

He should have just said yes. But the traitorous part of him told him that no, that wasn't what he would rather. That even without the expectation of anything else happening, Jared very much wanted to sleep beside William Frain.

But what if that wasn't really what *Will* wanted?

He must have taken too long to respond, because the smile Will gave him looked tinged with sadness as he said, "Do I make you that uncomfortable?"

Jared sat up. "What?"

"Nothing." Will shook his head, but Jared didn't miss the troubled look on his face. "You know what? It might be best if I slept somewhere else tonight. You can have this tent all to yourself."

Will stood from the bed, but before he could get any further, Jared reached out to clasp the other boy's wrist. "You don't have to go."

"I think I'd prefer it."

"Why?"

"Because."

"Because why?" Jared prompted.

"Because I like you, all right! And I'm worried all I do is make you feel uncomfortable, especially after I kissed you all of a sudden that night—"

Jared didn't let Will finish. Because Will admitting he had feelings for Jared was all he needed to gather up the courage to kiss him.

Will made a soft noise of surprise against Jared's lips. He could feel the rigidity of shock in Will's body as the kiss went on. Finally, he felt Will place a hand against his chest and Jared reluctantly pulled away, but not so far that he couldn't clearly see the vein of brown that ran through the green in Will's left eye.

"Don't," breathed Will. "Don't do this just to make me feel better—"

"I'm not," Jared said, and it was true. He wanted to kiss Will because *he* wanted to. Had wanted to for some time now.

But Will still looked conflicted. "But I thought Derek—"

"I don't want to talk about Derek right now. Or anyone else." And he closed the gap between them to place his lips against Will's once more.

This time Will surrendered to it completely. His arms snaking around Jared's bare waist, eliciting a pleasant shiver up Jared's spine.

Unlike the last time they kissed, outside the ballroom on the night of Derek's birthday, Jared was able to better concentrate on the feeling of Will's lips beneath his. On how soft they were. On the feel of Will's breath when he parted his lips just slightly.

As they kissed, Jared became subsumed in the sensation of it. It chased away all other thoughts or feelings and all he could bring himself to care about was *Will*.

They found their way back to the bed, this time with Will sitting on the edge and Jared's knees bracketing his hips.

"Is this all right?" Jared asked when Will lay pressed against the bedding with Jared hovering over him. "Do you—?"

"Yes," Will's voice was husky but adamant, his eyes half-lidded and a flush across his cheeks that Jared found all too pleasing. "You?"

"Yes."

That was all that was needed for them to resume their heated kisses and surrender to each other's embraces.

* * *

Aurelia retreated to the outskirts of the campsite. It had been a long time since she had been around so many Guardians, and quite honestly, it made her feel uneasy.

While many of them simply ignored her, there were some that kept looking at her, either with curiosity or contempt. Even hiding away in her tent did little to relieve her of her unease.

As she trudged aimlessly through the snow, Cora hopping along the bare tree branches overhead, she couldn't stop thinking about Draken's admission to Darus back at the fort. Admitting to being the one who murdered Erianna all those years ago. Even now, the shock of the revelation pounded in her veins.

There was also anger. For a long time, she only ever felt sorrow at the thought of Erianna's death. But now that she had a face and a name to put to the one responsible, rage and hatred were there to take place alongside the anguish. She now knew who Erianna's killer was, knew for certain that he was still out there. And that he was coming for her son.

"Take good care of Derek for me. I'll be around to collect him soon enough."

For what? Just what exactly did he need Derek for?

Does it really matter what his motives are? Aurelia asked herself. *Whatever it is, it cannot be good.*

What mattered now was protecting the boy. Keeping him out of Draken's hands.

For Erianna.

"I was wondering where you'd run off to," said a voice from behind her and she turned to find Darus Flynn. He had his hands in his coat pockets and his long hair was unbound. "For a moment, I thought you'd decided to leave without saying anything."

"Would that have been so terrible?" Aurelia wondered.

"Well, I would have been disappointed since I never got the chance to thank you for all your help."

Aurelia leaned her back against the nearby tree. "I only helped because it served my own purposes. I wanted to get my revenge on that man for trying to kill me, remember?"

Darus shrugged, as if that was of little consequence. "Regardless, thank you."

Aurelia grunted noncommittally. She could almost hear her queen mother's voice chiding her in the back of her head. *"A princess responds with her words, always. Never with boorish grunts or sighs."*

Only I am not a princess anymore, am I? She made certain of that.

"So, what will you do now?" Darus asked her.

What *would* she do? She still had yet to exact her revenge on Draken for destroying her shop and leaving her to die. But she knew now that she had no hope of defeating him alone. She supposed she could always go back to Florinstone and see what could be done about rebuilding her shop, but . . .

You know what you need to do, said that nagging voice, so similar to Erianna's, in the back of her mind.

"I want you to bring me with you to Ember."

That answer seemed to take Darus off guard. "Why?"

"I have my reasons."

"Which you're going to have to explain to me if you expect me to bring you into my home."

Aurelia gave him a withering look. "I didn't realise one needed to complete an interrogation before being allowed inside the crown city."

"No," Darus conceded. "But I want to make sure I'm not bringing a potential threat home with me."

"Weren't you just thanking me for helping you moments ago?"

"Yes, but you also admitted yourself that you only helped us for your own benefit," Darus pointed out. "And beyond your name, I really know nothing about you. For all I know, you could really be in league with that man from before and you wanting to come to Ember could be a part of some plan to attack the city."

By the Goddess, Aurelia forgot how annoying Guardians could be. Although she supposed she could not blame him for being suspicious of her, given the circumstances.

"I need to see the boy, Derek."

It just came out. There was no thought to not say it, and when the silence that followed stretched out, Aurelia almost wished that she could take the words back.

Darus was staring at her in confused shock, as if she had just said something completely ludicrous. "Derek? As in—?"

"Derek Draco. Your adopted son," Aurelia finished for him.

The expression on Darus's face seemed to darken to something that was almost threatening. "How do you—What do you want with Derek?" he demanded. "Just who exactly are you?"

It had felt like such a long time since she had been anything other than Aurelia Blackwood, outcast Wood Elf, reclusive mage and owner of *Blackwood's Spells, Potions and Magical Objects* in Florinstone.

It had been a long time since she had not hated the idea of being who she was before she had been made an outcast. Of being Princess Aurelia, future queen of the Wood Elves. Her mother's daughter.

Aurelia took a deep breath, as if preparing to step off the edge and dive into churning waters.

"My name is Aurelia. Eldest daughter of Queen Nyalra and Prince Eldrin. I was cast out for tampering with a daemonic artefact, in order to bring back my sister, who was banished from the Great Forest for falling in love with a human—a Guardian—and bearing his child. My sister was the late Princess Erianna. Erica Draco after her marriage. Derek is my nephew."

* * *

The nightmare began in his bedroom.

Not the bedroom back in Ember or even the attic room he had slept in when his parents were still alive. Instead, Derek was standing in the middle of the room that had been his when he lived in the Mayor's Manor. It was bathed in an eerie, yellowish light from the soundless fire in the hearth, and sitting in front of it, in a wingback chair, was Goldridge.

He looked just as Derek remembered him, square-jawed and small-eyed, with a grey moustache and receding hairline. He was dressed in the red and blue of his Mayor's robes, the material straining in places over his heavy-set frame.

Just the sight of him, sitting only feet away, struck Derek with a bone-chillingly deep fear. He wanted to run, wanted to get as far away from Goldridge as possible, but his feet were rooted to the spot.

Goldridge was staring into the flickering fire and sipping from a glass of red wine. Slowly, almost dazedly, he turned his head and fixed his dark eyes on Derek.

"Derek," he said in that deep voice that seemed to echo throughout the room. "Come here, my child."

"No," said Derek. He took a step back.

Goldridge held a hand out. "Come here."

"No." Another step back.

"I said, *come here*."

"*No*."

A thunderous look crossed Goldridge's face. He set his glass down and rose from his chair. Derek's heart pounded hard with fear as Goldridge approached.

"Stay away from me," ordered Derek.

But Goldridge kept walking towards him. "Why must you always disobey me, Derek?" he asked. "Why must you always make things so difficult?"

"I said stay away!"

There was a sick gleam in Goldridge's eyes. "You bring this on yourself."

This time, Derek turned and ran to the door. It was closed and when he tried the handle, it wouldn't move. He tried shoving at the door, but it wouldn't budge.

Trapped. Trapped, a desperate voice chanted in his ears. *You're trapped with him again.*

Derek cried out for someone to help him.

Behind him, Goldridge chuckled. "Look at you. All those years spent training. All those years trying to make yourself strong and nothing's changed, has it?" Goldridge's voice morphed from a deep rumble to a higher, raspier tone. Orville's voice.

Derek pounded his fists against the door. He called out for his mother. For his father.

Goldridge drew closer. "You trained for so hard and for so long. You became a Guardian, but you're still just as you were nine years ago."

Derek's knees gave out, and he slid to the floor. He shouted for Jared and for Arabelle. He shouted for Darus. For somebody—*anyone*—to save him.

"You're still nothing but a *weak* and *pitiful* little boy. You still can't protect anyone. Just like you couldn't protect your father or your mother or Edgar. Just like you can't protect yourself."

Weak and alone.

"And you still can't escape from me."

Derek came awake with a gasp and bolted upright.

He was in his room—the guest room he had been sleeping in since they had arrived in Windfell. There was no fire going in the hearth, leaving the room cold and shadowed. Goldridge was nowhere to be seen.

The air had a frosty bite to it, but despite that, Derek felt as if every inch of him was covered in sweat. His breaths left him in quick gasps, struggling past the tightness in his chest. He could still hear Goldridge's voice taunting him. Could still feel his hands—

Derek tore the blankets off of him and leapt up from the bed. He had to get out of here. He couldn't stay in this room. Flinging the door open, he stepped into the hallway.

He made for the bathroom at the end of the hall and, without even stopping to check if it was occupied, pulled the door open and went for the sink, turning on the cold water with a twist of a handle. Dipping his still trembling hands underneath the fall of water, he splashed it onto his face, uncaring of the way droplets dampened his hair and the front of his shirt.

He kept his hands pressed to his face for a few moments and focused on taking deep, steadying breaths. When he brought his hands away from his face, he stared down at them, feeling half-dazed as he watched them wracked by tiny trembles.

"You're still nothing but a weak and pitiful little boy,"

Goldridge's—or had it been Orville's?—voice had said to him.

He's right, Derek thought to himself. He thought things had changed. He thought he was finished feeling like this.

But nothing had changed. He was still the same weak little boy he had been all those years ago under Goldridge's care.

"Derek?"

Derek startled badly. It appeared that in his haste to get to the bathroom, he had forgotten to close the door behind him and now whirled around to find Arabelle standing in the doorway behind him.

She was dressed in a plain nightdress beneath an untied dressing gown, her hair loose and slightly mussed. Even in the dimness, Derek could see the concern on her face as she looked at him. He could only imagine what he must have looked like to her at that moment.

In a voice that was barely above a whisper, she asked him, "Are you all right?"

And all Derek could do was crumble.

They went back to his room. They sat on the edge of his bed. Derek was distantly aware of the sound of the beginnings of rain tapping on the glass. Candlelight illuminated the room, flickering thanks to the draft coming in from beneath the closed door. Arabelle was close, but not touching him, and that was a comfort.

Derek kept his eyes on the carpeted floor as he told Arabelle the things he had kept hidden for so long.

He told her about life with Goldridge after his parents died. How, in the beginning, everything was fine. Goldridge acted as a kind and caring father figure, but after a while, everything changed. He told Arabelle about Goldridge's violent moods, especially when he drank, about the nights when Derek was forced to hide under his bed while Goldridge yelled and pounded on his door.

And he told her about how Goldridge betrayed him. How he had felt ashamed for so long, because he was a boy and that wasn't supposed to happen to boys. How no one believed him when he told them because Goldridge was the kindly and beloved Mayor of Windfell. What was Derek's word, the word of an orphan boy, against that of the esteemed Mayor Goldridge?

By now, tears were sliding down Derek's cheeks, but he made no move to hide them or wipe them away.

"And then I killed him," Derek said. "I still remember it—stabbing him over and over again. I thought that would be the end of it. After I killed him. I thought the nightmares would stop after Darus took me away. But they didn't. I thought once I became a Guardian, the nightmares would stop scaring me so much. I thought I had stopped being that weak little boy. But I haven't." He dropped his head into his hands, his shoulders began to shake. "I'm still so . . . pathetic."

"Derek," Arabelle said. He felt her slide off the bed so that she could kneel in front of him. Gently, she reached up to pry his hands away from his face. He let her.

"You are *not* pathetic," she told him in a firm, but gentle, voice.

Derek made a disbelieving sound in the back of his throat.

"I mean it. You're not pathetic or weak just because you're still affected by the things that you've been through. This," she said, indicating his current state, "doesn't mean you're weak. It just means that you're . . . human."

Derek looked down at his lap, where Arabelle's hands were clasped warmly around his own. "But I let him—for years . . . I didn't stop—"

"You didn't let him do anything to you." Arabelle's voice was fierce and unyielding, as was the look in her eyes. "You were a *child*. Nothing that he did to you was your fault."

"You weren't there. You don't know—"

"You've already told me everything I need to know," interjected Arabelle. "I know that you were young and alone and you had just lost your parents, and he took advantage of that. I know that in the end, he deserved what he got and much worse."

An unnamed emotion was beginning to well up inside of him. He found it hard to look at Arabelle because of it.

But when Derek turned his face away, he felt Arabelle's fingers, light as a butterfly's wing, touch his cheek. Surprisingly, the touch didn't make him startle. Didn't make him flinch or pull away. Quite the opposite actually, and just that light touch of fingers against his cheek sent a rush of warmth throughout him.

Arabelle was kneeling now, so that she was eye-to-eye with Derek. Shadows and candlelight danced across the planes of her face. Her expression as she looked at Derek was hard to describe, but it made his throat feel tight.

"Derek," Arabelle's voice was soft and steady and filled with another emotion that Derek couldn't quite place. "You are one of the strongest people I have ever met. Being strong doesn't mean being unaffected. It doesn't mean that you have to be made of stone. It means surviving and learning how to keep going after all the bad things have happened. You've done that, Derek. You've been surviving all this time, and you still are. That's a true testament to your strength. And it's all right that sometimes it gets too overwhelming for you. Just know that I . . ." She paused here, as if steeling herself. "Just know that I'll always be here for you. Whenever you need me, I'll stay by your side. Always."

It was—he was—Derek couldn't form a proper thought. He felt too overwhelmed. All he could do was stare at Arabelle. The fall of her golden hair over one shoulder, the shimmer in her violet eyes that never once left his. As he looked at her, he felt a new pressure in his chest, one that he didn't feel mentally or emotionally stable enough to discern.

Fresh tears welled and spilled and, unthinkingly, Derek leaned forward until his forehead was pressed against Arabelle's shoulder. He closed his eyes, and he felt her slowly—hesitantly—place her arms around him.

"Arabelle . . ." He began, his voice sounded choked. "Arabelle, I—"

"Shh," she hushed him gently.

"Don't leave me," said Derek. "Stay with me." A distant part of himself knew he was speaking nonsensically. Knew that he probably sounded like a needy child. But he couldn't help himself. Couldn't stop himself from voicing the thing he wanted—*needed*—the most right now.

Derek thought he heard Arabelle make a sound akin to laughter.

"Didn't you hear what I just said?" She spoke softly and with absolute tenderness. Her cheek pressed against the top of his head. "Always."

18

It took Arabelle only a handful of seconds after waking to realise the bed she was lying in was not her own.

Or that she was the only one in it.

Lying opposite her, under the same coarse blanket, with his face only scant inches away from hers, was Derek.

Her cheeks flamed and Arabelle nearly scrambled up and away, until she realised that Derek was still sleeping, and rather peacefully, by the looks of it.

Seeing the unguarded expression on his face kept her fixed in place. Even when she realised their hands were pressed against each other's in the small space between them. She didn't want to do anything that could disturb that look on his face.

He looked so young, Arabelle thought. With his mouth parted and his hair falling into his face even more than it usually did. His long, dark eyelashes brushed the tops of his cheekbones and Arabelle was struck by how beautiful he was. Surely it was strange to think of a boy as beautiful? But she couldn't think of another word to describe his appearance. 'Handsome' just didn't seem to do Derek justice.

In sleep, he also looked . . . vulnerable.

Memories from last night came flooding back and Arabelle felt a surge of anger and sadness and protectiveness well up within her.

She wouldn't lie, it had been hard hearing Derek recount those events from his past. To know just what he had gone through. To know that a man could do that to a child. Sickness roiled in the pit of her stomach at the thought.

She remembered the sobs that had wracked Derek's body. How he clearly thought so little of himself because of what happened to him—what was *done* to him. It not only broke her heart to witness, but made her wish she could bring the former Mayor of Windfell back to life, only so she could be the one to drive a knife through that dark heart of his.

But that would never happen, so instead, all she could do was hold Derek and try to make him understand that he was so much more than what some monster did to him. That he wasn't weak. He wasn't broken. He wasn't tainted. That it was all right for him to let his walls down and be vulnerable from time to time. It didn't make him any less, and certainly not to her.

Then there had been that moment where he had leaned into her. *"Don't leave. Stay with me."*

And so she had.

She had held him as his body shuddered with heaving breaths.

Even as she felt the exhaustion finally drag him down into sleep, Arabelle didn't leave his side. How could she? Especially after he had asked her not to.

Even now, she felt guilty at the thought of getting up to leave, so she could return to her own room before he woke up. But would Derek even be bothered if he woke to find he had been left alone?

Arabelle didn't have to wonder for long. She held herself still as Derek started to come awake, unsure of how he would react when he saw her, especially when he realised they were lying *so close* together, their hands barely touching.

His eyes fluttered open and she couldn't help but smile at the way he blinked blearily, a slight frown on his face. Then, as he seemed to become more aware of his surroundings, his eyes landed on her and any traces of a frown disappeared.

"Good morning," said Arabelle steadily, although she felt anything but. By the Goddess, she was lying in a bed with Derek. *Imagine what my father would say if he saw this,* she thought wryly.

Derek was looking at her as if he couldn't quite figure out whether she was real or a figment of his imagination. "You stayed?"

She smiled at him. "Of course. You asked me to stay, didn't you?"

"I—You didn't have to." He looked somewhat abashed and was that a blush she could see?

"How are you feeling?" She asked.

"I feel—not great, but . . . better. Lighter, I think." He looked up at her then. Sincerity shining in those blue eyes. "Thank you. For—For being there, last night."

"Of course," Arabelle said firmly. "You're one of my best friends and I—you can talk to me about anything. I'll always be here to listen."

"Mm." He looked so calm and carefree. Hair tousled from sleep, eyes glittering with amusement. One corner of his mouth turned up in a small, boyish smile.

It made her heart flutter.

It could have happened then. In that moment, Arabelle wanted it enough that she would have tossed out all thoughts of caution or self-preservation and closed the short distance between them so that she could touch her lips to his.

Instead, the bedroom door was pushed open and Rosalie walked in, dressed and hair brushed into glossy black waves.

When she saw the two of them clearly lying next to each other on the bed beneath the same blanket, she raised a dark eyebrow.

"Well, don't you two look cosy," she remarked.

Oh, by the Goddess.

"Good morning to you too, Rosalie," said Derek. "And how are you on this bright winter's day?"

Rosalie smirked. "Oh, I'm fine, but probably not as fine as you both are."

Arabelle felt her face burn at Rosalie's implication. "*Rosalie!*"

"What?" That smirk didn't leave Rosalie's face as she stepped further into the room. "I wake up to find your bed is empty and when I come to see if Derek knows where you are, I find the two of you curled up on the bed together? Forgive me if that puts certain assumptions in my head."

Arabelle pulled the blanket away to reveal that they were both still fully clothed. Derek made a disgruntled sound.

"Nothing happened."

Rosalie looked at them, consideringly. "But you cou—"

"*Nothing happened.*"

"All right, I'll take your word for it," Rosalie sighed. "Now, will you both get up so that we can get some breakfast already? I'm starving."

"Why don't you just go down by yourself?" asked Derek as he sat up, scratching at the back of his head.

"No one else seems to be up yet. I'd feel awkward going down to the dining room by myself."

"Really? What time is it?" said Arabelle, rising from the bed.

"Almost ten o'clock, I think?"

Odd, Arabelle thought. In the time they'd spent here at the Mayor's Manor, she'd found that the day always started early for those that lived and worked here.

Indeed, as she made her way back to her and Rosalie's room, she noticed a distinct lack of activity around the house. Curtains had still yet to be drawn open. The sound of house staff going about their day went unheard. Arabelle wondered if perhaps the servants had a day off?

As Arabelle changed her clothes and combed her hair, Rosalie continued to pepper her with questions about what she was doing in Derek's room, but she refused to give the other girl an inch. She didn't want to encourage the ideas that were no doubt running amuck in Rosalie's head, but she also wouldn't tell her what had really happened. That was something only Derek could do if he chose to.

"If you didn't want me to know, you should have been more discreet," said Rosalie from where she sat on her bed, examining her nails. "I saw you leaving this morning."

"What?" Arabelle turned away from her reflection in the vanity table mirror so she could look at Rosalie. "What do you mean you saw me leaving this morning?"

"Exactly what I said. I woke up because I heard you going through your things and then you left. Even though I tried calling out to you. A bit rude not to even acknowledge me, by the way."

Arabelle was baffled. She had been in Derek's room since around midnight. "But you couldn't have—" Her eyes went wide. She shot up from her seat and went to her knees at the side of her bed, pulling her pack out from underneath.

"What's wrong?" Rosalie asked her while she searched through her things.

It didn't take long for her to realise that, with a sinking feeling, her suspicion was correct.

"The grimoire," she said. "It's gone."

The heavy sound of the doorknocker downstairs echoed

throughout the house.

Arabelle and Rosalie exchanged a look before they were both heading for their bedroom door. They found Derek had already emerged from his room as well, and together, they made their way down to the foyer, where they were just in time to see Lilith open the door to two Town Guards in their silver armour and blue capes.

After a quick exchange with Lilith that was too quiet for them to hear, the Guards stepped inside.

When the first Guard caught sight of Arabelle, Rosalie and Derek still standing on the stairs, he turned to them and said in a clear voice, "Guardians, you are under arrest for the murder of Captain Orville Goldridge."

* * *

The first thing Jared was aware of when he woke up was the distinct lack of another person's warmth beside him.

The blankets slid down as he propped himself up on his elbows and he shivered as bare skin met the chilly morning air seeping into the tent. The fire had gone out sometime in the night. Jared looked around blearily but quickly deduced that he was alone and that only his clothes lay in a haphazard pile on the floor by the bed. Will must have slipped away while Jared was still sleeping. The realisation caused Jared a twinge of disappointment; he would have enjoyed waking up beside Will—or better yet, with Will in his arms.

Jared got up and set about putting on his discarded clothes, but with his mind on other things as he did so. Primarily on Will, and what had happened between them the night before. Last night hadn't been the first time Jared had ever slept with someone, but it had been the first time it had felt like *that*. As if something had fallen into place. Some missing piece that, now that it had been found, left him feeling lighter and happier. When he remembered the feel and taste of Will's kisses, the press of Will's body against his own, the sound of his name on Will's lips, it filled him with a warmth and desire so strong it nearly robbed him of breath.

Jared pulled out his travelling cloak from where he had stuffed it, none too neatly, into his pack and pulled it around his shoulders. Once he was sufficiently rugged up, he made his way out of the tent.

It was still early in the morning, the sky a mottle of pinks and soft blues. The outside of the camp was deserted apart from Adolphus standing at the far end, keeping watch. He didn't see Will anywhere. Adolphus clearly hadn't noticed Jared emerge, so he took the opportunity to slip away quietly. He wandered aimlessly through the woods, being careful not to stray too far from the camp and almost stumbling at times when the snow deepened unexpectedly.

Jared paused beneath the overhanging branch of a tree and gazed up at the icicles hanging along its length, glittering in the rising sunlight.

Was he falling for Will? He didn't know for certain whether this was simply a new infatuation or the beginning of something more, but what he did know was that, more than anything right now, he wanted to see Will. Wanted to be with him and to run his fingers through that tawny hair and kiss him.

He was about to head back to the camp to see if he could find Will when he heard the murmur of voices close by.

Moving to investigate, Jared soon caught sight of the familiar blond head of Elijah Hargrade. He was standing underneath one of the beech trees, with a hand leaning against the trunk. That's when Jared noticed the other person Elijah was with. Will.

Will had his back against the tree, looking at his feet as Elijah towered over him. Was Elijah bullying him? It looked that way at first glance, but Will's posture and expression seemed far too relaxed for someone who was being hassled. Even Elijah didn't look as antagonistic as he normally did. Still, Jared couldn't say he cared much for the way he was looking down at Will.

"You sure moved on quickly," Elijah was saying. "And with the Prince too."

"Shut up, Elijah."

"What? I'm only teasing." He grinned. "But really, though, I'm a bit hurt. Have you forgotten me so quickly?"

Will, who had been keeping his eyes lowered, looked up at Elijah's face. "How could I do that?"

Something unpleasant curled in Jared's stomach now and it only grew stronger the longer he looked at the way Elijah and Will stood so close to each other, the way they looked at each other, and listened to the way they talked.

"I miss you." Elijah's voice was so low, Jared barely caught the words. "And I know you miss me, too. C'mon, Will, let's be together again."

Jared barely dared to breathe as he waited for Will's answer to come. He hoped, more than anything, that Will would say no. That he would turn Elijah down and walk away. In that moment, he wanted that more than anything.

But it didn't happen. Will didn't say anything. The look on his face was one of hesitation, but it was also mixed with one that looked almost like yearning. Like Will wanted it. Wanted to say yes. Wanted *to be with Elijah.*

Finally, Will opened his mouth to speak. "I—"

That was all he managed to say before Elijah kissed him.

Jared was unprepared for the awful feeling that crashed over him at the sight. He had half a mind to storm over there and pull Elijah away and throw him to the ground and he might have done it had he not noticed that Will was kissing Elijah back.

Jared felt something inside of him crumble. Will was kissing Elijah. Will, who had kissed Jared only last night.

He couldn't look anymore. He couldn't be here anymore. Couldn't be—He couldn't—

Jared stumbled blindly through the snow, back towards the camp. His breath was coming out heavier than it had been before, in small plumes of mist. He couldn't get the image out of his mind. Of Elijah and Will together. His throat felt tight and—

"Jared!"

He came to a halt. His body responded instantly, as if on instinct, to the sound of the voice more so than the call of his name.

Jared turned around and sure enough, there was Will standing before him. His cheeks were flushed pink, and he was breathing heavily, as if he had just been running. Or—no, Jared didn't want to think about any other potential reason for his exertion.

Clearing his throat, he said, "So, you and Elijah?"

Will paled. "No. Well—not really."

"What the hell does that mean, Will?" Jared snapped, his patience frayed. "Are you together or not?"

"We're not. We used to be, but not anymore. We—*I* broke it off weeks ago."

"Well, it doesn't sound like it's over. I heard him say he wants you back."

Will stayed quiet.

"Is that what you want? To be with Elijah again?" Jared asked.

"I—I never said that's what I—"

"You let him *kiss* you."

Will was becoming fidgety, running his hand through his hair and looking anywhere but at Jared.

"*Will.*"

"I don't know, okay?" He ground out. His green eyes were wide. "I don't know what I really want, I—I've been in love with him for five years. It's not so easy to put aside those feelings."

In love with him. The words pierced through Jared like an

277

arrow. Will was in love with Elijah.

"So all this time, I've just been some . . . some distraction?" demanded Jared, trying not to sound as gutted as he felt. "Just some passing fling to help you forget about someone else?"

"*No.*" Will's voice came out adamant and without hesitation and Jared wondered if that should've made him feel better. It didn't. "Jared, no. That's not how it was."

"Then what was it like exactly? What do you really think is between us? Last night, did you . . . did it mean something to you? Because I—" *I thought it did.* He couldn't bring himself to say those words.

"Yes," Will breathed out, sounding desperate. "It did, Jared. It was all real. I promise."

"But Elijah . . . You still have feelings for him, don't you?"

This gave Will pause and Jared choked out a humourless laugh.

Will's eyes narrowed. "Oh, don't act like it's such a crime for me not to have all of my feelings sorted out. Besides, you're one to talk. Aren't you in love with your good friend, Derek?"

"That's different," said Jared.

"Really? How so?"

"Because I never kept my feelings for Derek a secret from you. I never kissed him, only hours after *we slept together!*"

His words rang out, and he didn't care if the entire camp heard it and came running. A startled bird took flight from a branch, scattering flecks of snow to the ground. Will was looking at him, open-mouthed, as though he hadn't been expecting such an outburst.

Before he could voice any of the other angry words that clawed up the back of his throat, Jared turned his back on Will and walked away.

"Jared, wait. Please, just—Jared!"

This time, he didn't look back.

* * *

"Hello? Is anyone there?" Arabelle called out, leaning against the iron bars of their dark and cramped prison cell. "Anyone who wants to explain what the *hell* is happening?"

Rosalie sighed from where she sat on the rickety bench by the back wall. "You might as well just give up, Arabelle. No one's coming."

Arabelle turned away from the bars with a growl—only to turn back around so she could kick them for good measure. "This is ridiculous. How can the Guards just show up like that, accuse us of murder and toss us in prison without even explaining anything?"

"To be fair, they didn't toss us in here exactly. We did agree to come quietly."

"Only because we didn't want to cause trouble! They still could've given us a proper explanation while they were locking us up here. Right, Derek?"

But he was hardly paying them any attention. Huddled in his own corner of the cell, ignoring the jagged edges of the rock wall stabbing into his back, Derek's mind was a tangled web of questions. Orville was dead? How? And how exactly did the Guards come to the conclusion that *they* had murdered him? Was Orville even really dead? What if this was all some ruse? But if it was, then to what end?

And if Orville really was dead, then that would mean that Derek had been wrong all this time, that Orville wasn't the killer in Windfell.

Derek was startled out of his thoughts by the sound of approaching footsteps. All three of them were on their feet, just as two Guards appeared at their barred door.

"Are you here to finally explain to us why we're being accused of murder?" demanded Arabelle.

"Shut up," one spoke gruffly while the other pulled a ring of keys from his belt and began unlocking the cell door. "You three are coming with us, and don't even think of trying any funny business."

"What funny business could we possibly do when we're in irons?" Derek asked innocently, rattling the heavy chains of his handcuffs. Indeed, all three of them had been clapped in irons when they were taken into custody. Not only that, but their rings had been taken from them as well.

"I said shut up." The door clanged open and the Guards stepped aside, hands on their swords. "Let's go."

They were led in single file, down the dimly lit corridor, past more cells—all of which were empty. They stopped at a door at the end of the corridor. The Guard up front opened it and brought them down a narrow staircase. The way down was made visible only thanks to the torches along the wall. Were the Guards leading them into some underground torture chamber?

They were indeed brought to a chamber, windowless and lit by torches imbedded in the jagged stone walls. However, it didn't look to be a torture chamber. In fact, it was completely empty, except for a single table that stood in the middle of the room. On the table was something covered by a brown hessian blanket. Something that was distinctly human-shaped.

Mayor Boeheart and two other Guards, one of which was the Grey Elf, Rolven, were waiting inside.

"You're here, good," said Boeheart, but he sounded much less than pleased. "Now we can address the matter at hand."

"Yes, we would like that very much," said Arabelle, and beneath the outwardly calm facade, Derek could tell she was seething. "What's all this about accusing us of a murder and locking us up in your prison?"

"Be quiet," growled Rolven. The look on his face was thunderous. "You don't get to demand any explanations, murderers."

"But we're not," Rosalie protested.

"I said be quiet!"

"Enough!" snapped Boeheart, and the room fell silent.

After a moment, Derek spoke up. "Is that him?" he nodded at the table.

Rolven exchanged a look with the Mayor and when he nodded,

Rolven stepped forward and uncovered what lay beneath the hessian blanket.

Derek had known, even without seeing what was underneath. He'd known, deep in his gut, and yet it was still a shock to see Orville's face, cheeks already hollowing and skin tinged with the grey of death. Rolven pulled the sheet down to Orville's waist, revealing a bare torso littered with ragged, bloody marks. Stab wounds. There was hardly any skin visible beneath all the dried blood.

For a moment, Derek was taken back to another time, another place, an opulent bedroom, smelling of bourbon and sandalwood and blood. Staring at another body, lying on a bed instead of a table, but also covered in bleeding stab wounds. Ones of his own making.

"What—What happened to him?" Rosalie's voice was barely above a whisper.

"Hmph, don't act as if you don't already know," said one of the Guards standing behind them.

"Captain Goldridge was found deceased in his home early this morning," explained Mayor Boeheart.

"And you think we're responsible for this?" said Arabelle.

"Seems like an awful big coincidence that the Captain is murdered the morning after your boy here attacked him." Rolven glared hatefully at Derek.

"That still doesn't prove anything," he argued.

"No, but this does." Rolven reached for something behind the

282

table. He held it up for them to see and Derek's breath caught as the torch light gleamed off of the blue metal.

"That's my—"

It was his father's sword.

He felt both Arabelle's and Rosalie's eyes on him, but he couldn't tear his gaze away from the sword he'd thought was lost.

But how . . . ?

"This sword was found by the Captain's body, covered in his blood." Rolven looked to Derek. "This sword belongs to you, doesn't it? I remember you carrying it that day those gargoyles attacked."

"I—It is. But I haven't seen it since that day. I lost it during the battle."

"What a convenient story."

Derek bristled. "It's the truth."

Rolven gave him a contemptuous smile and set Derek's sword down on the table by Orville's body. "You'll forgive us for not being eager to take your word for it."

Derek took half a step forward and heard the sounds of the other Guards reaching for their swords, as if Derek were a genuine threat, with his hands shackled and no weapon. "You said *I* was the one who attacked Orville last night, and you have *my* sword as the murder weapon. So what about Arabelle and Rosalie? Why have they been arrested as well when there's nothing to suggest they were complicit in this?"

"Because there is nothing to suggest that they *aren't*. And, of course, there's the matter of no message really being sent to the Guardians."

"What?" Rosalie spoke up. "Of course there was."

Rolven gave her a curious look. "Are you sure about that?"

"Yes," said Arabelle firmly. "I sent it myself just days ago."

"Then how do you explain this?" Rolven produced a crumpled sheet of paper from the pouch at his belt and held it out for them to see.

The paper was all but ruined, wrinkled, and torn in places. It looked as if it had been dipped in water and then left to dry. The writing was a smudged mess of ink, but some words were still legible. Enough that Derek could recognise the handwriting as his own.

"Where did you get that?" Arabelle asked.

"We found it discarded in a gutter," said Rolven. "Why would you throw away a letter to your people? Could it be because you didn't want more Guardians to come to Windfell? To make it easier for you to get away with the grisly murder of our Captain?"

"Do you really think it's necessary to write to them?" Arabelle had asked in the library the night after the funeral for Cassandra and the others who had died in the gargoyle attack.

An awful thought dawned on Derek. Had Arabelle not delivered the letter? Had she lied to them? But why?

Arabelle was shaking her head, her brow furrowing. "No. No, I delivered that letter to the Post House." She looked at Derek as if sensing his gaze. Her eyes were beseeching. "On my life, I swear I did."

And Derek couldn't find it in himself not to trust her.

"Then why was it lying in a gutter?" questioned Rolven.

"Ask the Post Master, I gave it to him myself."

"The Master claims to never have seen you set foot in the Post House."

"No . . . That's—"

Rolven turned his attention toward the Mayor, who had remained silent until now. "Lord Boeheart, with the evidence that has been presented, can there really be any doubt that these three were involved in the murder of Captain Goldridge?"

Boeheart looked dismayed. He looked as if he didn't want to believe it, but could not think of a way to refute all that he had heard. "I'm afraid my hands are tied in this," he said with a deep sigh. "Word will be sent to the Guardians in Ember about this and until we hear back from them, the three of you will remain imprisoned here."

This time, Derek, Arabelle and Rosalie had no qualms about making a fuss as they were shepherded from the chamber.

They were confined to their cell once more.

"We were framed." Rosalie said into the silence.

"Of course we were framed," said Derek. He'd resumed his spot in the corner of their cell, elbows resting on his knees.

"But who could have done it?"

"My money's on whoever's behind the murders."

"I think we can safely rule out Orville Goldridge as the murderer now."

"Quite."

Rosalie sighed. "So, where does that leave us now?"

"Stuck in a prison cell."

Rosalie sighed again.

Sitting huddled against the cell door, Arabelle hadn't said a word since they had been escorted out of the underground chamber.

Derek stood up and went to sit beside her. "You don't happen to have a hairpin, do you?"

She gave him a quizzical look. "No, why?"

"I was just thinking that if you did, I might be able to use it to pick the locks. Like when we were kidnapped by the Serpens brothers."

"Oh. I hadn't thought of that."

"Should I feel hurt about that? Was our time together in that dark, smelly hole of a room so forgettable?"

That at least got a tiny smile out of her. "I don't think I could forget about it even if I tried."

"Being forced to eat nothing but bread and cucumbers for days certainly leaves an impression."

"That's not—Never mind."

Derek allowed the conversation to lapse into silence before speaking again. "We'll find a way out of this."

Arabelle was quiet before replying, "But I don't have a hairpin on me."

"Yes, that's very remiss of you, honestly."

Arabelle laughed. It was quiet and short-lived, but it made Derek feel lighter inside, despite their circumstance.

19

For the next two days, they were left to languish inside their prison cell. During which, they were given meals of gruel in the mornings and at night by Guards with eyes full of malice.

From the waning light that filtered in through the miniscule window of their cell, Arabelle could tell that their second day of imprisonment was already ending.

Rosalie was curled up on the bench and had managed to fall asleep. Derek looked as if he was about to join her from where he sat in the back corner. Arabelle, however, was far too agitated to even contemplate falling asleep.

She kept thinking of Rolven holding up the crumpled letter. *"The Master claims to never have seen you set foot in the Post House."*

But how could that be? Yes, she had hesitated. Had thought about throwing the letter away herself, but in the end, she'd decided against it. When she entered the Post House, she'd given the letter to a short man who'd identified himself as the Post Master. He'd taken the letter himself and assured her it would be sent with haste.

If it wasn't really the Post Master I spoke to that night, then who could it have been? But no matter how hard Arabelle pushed herself to think of a way to unravel this mystery, an answer would not come.

Arabelle felt the burn of frustrated tears at the backs of her eyes and pressed the heels of her palms into her sockets, willing the tears away. She had been so determined to do well on this assignment and then, when Cassandra had been killed, she had only seen it as an opportunity to further prove herself—as terrible as that may have sounded—by taking matters into their own hands. They would be the rookie Guardians who ended the murders plaguing Windfell all on their own. Surely that would have shown her father that she was fit to join the Crown Guard and make him listen when she said she did not want to marry some pompous noble boy.

Instead, here they were, sitting in a prison cell, being accused of murder. By the Goddess, what would her father think once he got word of all this? Surely he wouldn't believe that Arabelle was really complicit in a murder, would he? But with no concrete evidence to prove otherwise, what did it matter?

This is what you get for aspiring to be more than the future wife of someone you hate, she thought glumly.

Arabelle must have dozed off because the next thing she

remembered was whispering in her ears.

Join me.

Arabelle startled, looking up and around, but there was no one there and Derek and Rosalie were still huddled by the back wall.

Then the whisper came again.

Join me.

We'll take the world for our own.

Join me.

You'll never have to prove yourself again.

You can have everything you want.

Just join me.

And the more the voice whispered, the more Arabelle *wanted* to listen. She wanted to do as it said and join them. She didn't know who she was joining or what she was joining them in, but all she cared about was doing as the whispers told her. Nothing else mattered.

It was a stroke of luck—at least, Arabelle would certainly think so when she looked back on this. At some point, she must have tried to stand up and placed her palm flat against the wall behind her to help push herself up. A sharp bit of stone stabbed into the meaty part of her hand just below her thumb and sent a spike of pain through her hand.

The whispering died down in an instant and Arabelle felt as if she were waking from a nap. She hadn't even noticed that the world had taken on a blurred, dream-like edge until it bled away and her mind felt like it had been cleared of a fog.

"What in Ithulia's name just happened?" She muttered to herself, frowning down at her bleeding hand.

When she looked up, she saw that Derek and Rosalie were on their feet, but completely motionless. Their expressions blank as slate.

When she stepped closer to them, the first thing she noticed were their eyes. Wide and unblinking, both of their eyes looked as if they were clouded by a swirling violet mist.

"Derek? Rosalie?" She tried waving a hand in front of their faces, her chains rattling as she did. But there was no reaction from either of them, not even a blink. Could they even see her with their mist-shrouded eyes?

"Snap out of it," Arabelle said, a little louder this time, shoving Derek in the shoulder. "Hey!"

Again, no reaction.

Arabelle took a step back, wracking her mind to think of some way to wake her friends up, when again she looked at the still bleeding cut along her palm. She must have been in the same sort of strange trance that Derek and Rosalie were now in, but she'd come out of it when she'd cut her hand. The pain had startled her out of it.

An idea forming, Arabelle stepped directly in front of Derek and gazed upon his relaxed features . . . before slapping him across the face.

"Fucking hell!" Lifting a hand to his no doubt stinging cheek, Derek looked at her with *blue* eyes. No weird purple mist in sight.

"Arabelle? What the—"

"Sorry," she breathed with a relieved smile and fought back the urge to try and hug him even with the handcuffs."But hold that thought."

While Derek nursed his cheek, Arabelle stepped in front of Rosalie and slapped her too.

The other girl cried out just like Derek had, and when she looked at Arabelle this time, her eyes were back to their usual brown.

"I'm sorry," Arabelle said to them both. "But it was the only way I could get you to snap out of it."

Rosalie glared petulantly. "If you say so."

"Just what was that?" said Derek. "What happened?"

"I don't know? I think I was asleep and then it sounded like someone was whispering in my ear and it woke me up," Rosalie explained.

"Was the voice saying, *join me, join me*?" Arabelle asked.

They both nodded.

"I think it was a spell," she continued. "I remember reading about something like it in the grimoire. A mind-control spell. It compels you to do whatever the caster wants by offering to give you your heart's desires. And the both of you even had the clouded purple eyes like in the grimoire."

"I guess that just leaves the question of who cast the spell and why?" said Rosalie.

"And if we were the only ones affected by it," Derek added.

Arabelle turned and walked up to the bars of their cell. "Hello?" She called out, her voice ringing out through the corridor. "Anybody there?"

There was no answer.

Rosalie came to stand beside her. "We would like to confess to murdering your bastard of a Captain! We murdered him because he was a bastard. A big one!"

"Rosalie!"

"That should have brought the Guard on watch running by now," said Derek. "And they would've heard us from the barracks too."

Derek was probably right, but all they were met with was eerie silence.

"Wonderful," sighed Rosalie. "So, if everyone else is under some mind-control spell, where does that leave us?"

"Still stuck inside a prison cell," Derek said.

They could do nothing but sit around for what felt like an age. By now, the sun had completely set and their cell was lit only by the dim flickering torchlight in the corridor. In the silence that swallowed them whole, other noises seemed much louder, the whistle of the wind through the miniscule window. The scurrying of rats in the hallway.

The creaking of a door being opened from up the stairwell outside their cell.

Arabelle was on her feet and at the cell door in two quick

strides. Was it Guards? Or could it be whoever cast the spell earlier, come to see if they had missed anyone?

It was neither. Instead, it was three children with familiar faces.

"Eugenia?" Derek's voice was coated in surprise at the sight of Edgar's younger sister and her two friends. "What are you doing here?"

Under the glow of the torch's flame, Arabelle could see that the kids were white with terror and their eyes red with tears.

"We're here to free you," said Eugenia. Her voice sounded much stronger than she looked. She held out a ring of keys, similar to the one Arabelle had seen on the Guard that had been on watch, and began fumbling with the keys to unlock the door to their cell.

"S-Something's happened to everyone in town," said the boy, Micah. "But we don't know—we don't know what . . . Even my mama and papa are . . ."

Eugenia finally found the right key to unlock their cell. Opening the door, they stepped out into the corridor. Arabelle and Rosalie turned their attention to Micah and Emmeline while Derek helped Eugenia find the right key to unlock their handcuffs.

"What do you mean something's happened to the townspeople?" asked Arabelle.

"We were out playing in the woods," said Emmeline, the torch in her hand wavered. "We snuck out because no one wanted us going out there alone after what happened with the monsters. Then when we came back to town, everything was so quiet and people were just—just standing there."

"No one would look at us when we tried talking to 'em," said Micah. "And their eyes were all funny and purple too."

By now, Eugenia had freed Derek of his handcuffs and came over to unlock Arabelle's and Rosalie's. It was a relief when the iron manacles finally fell from around her sore wrists.

"While we were coming here, we also saw that mage, the Ishlavan lady, walking around."

"Aryel?" said Rosalie. "She wasn't affected by the spell?"

Emmeline shook her head. "Don't think so. We saw her go into the Mayor's house."

What would Aryel be doing at the Mayor's Manor? Arabelle exchanged looks with Derek and Rosalie. "You don't think?"

A deepening crease formed between Derek's brow. "When Rosalie and I went to the Silver Eye to get the desona charms, she knew we would be at Orville's party. She told me, 'enjoy Captain Goldridge's party tonight, little Guardian.'"

"At the party, I . . . I *thought* I saw her. But I wasn't sure. I thought maybe I might have just been mistaken."

"And whoever it was who—" Derek cut a quick glance at Eugenia. "Who attacked Edgar and I in Orville's rooms, it couldn't have been a random attack. They must have known who we were and targeted us. And when I was chasing them down in the woods, they used magic to repel me and escape."

"And Aryel Sabir is the only known mage in this town," Rosalie said. "She was also nowhere to be seen when those gargoyles attacked. Would make sense if she was really the one behind the attack."

"But if she's a mage," said Arabelle. "Then why would she need a grimoire full of dark magic spells?"

"Because one can't bring the dead back to life with normal magic," Derek said. "It was in the book on dark magic I found in Orville's room. Only dark magic makes necromancy possible."

"And we know that Aryel did lose someone." The memories of their first meeting with Aryel Sabir in the living quarters above her brother's shop came flooding back to Arabelle. "Remember, she said that her lover died a few years back?"

"And that it was her brother who killed her," Rosalie said.

"Her brother, who ended up as one of the murder victims not long after she was released from prison," Derek added grimly.

Was it possible? That Aryel Sabir was the killer? Had been all along? All the evidence they had seemed to point to none other than the mage.

"That's why we came to get you." Eugenia said. "We don't know what's happening or how to fix it, but you're Guardians and—and my brother, he would've—" she broke off with a hiccoughing sob.

Without a thought to spare, Arabelle went to her knees and pulled the younger girl into her arms, holding her as she shook with sobs she tried so hard to repress. After a moment, Arabelle pulled back, but kept her hands on Eugenia's shoulders and offered her a comforting smile. "Of course we'll help you. We'll find out what's going on and get this whole mess sorted out, all right?"

Eugenia nodded and quickly wiped her nose on her sleeve.

"First things first, though," Rosalie said. "We need to get our rings back."

"We already got them for you, from the Captain's office." Eugenia stuck a hand into one of her coat pockets and fished out three rings, one black, one green and one purple. "And Micah's got Derek's sword, too."

"Oh, you wonderful little thieves," Arabelle said with a grin and, despite everything, the kids beamed.

Outside, the moon hung full and bright in the starry sky, lining the silent town of Windfell in silver. None of the streetlamps had been lit and not even a single window was lit up with candlelight. Arabelle would have almost thought the town deserted if not for the few figures that stood along the pathways, still as statues.

"It's best if you three stay here," she said, turning to the children. "Wait inside the barracks. You should be safe in there."

"But can't we help you?" asked Micah.

"You'll help us just by keeping safe."

"Whoever's behind this is the one who killed my brother, isn't it?" Eugenia said.

"We . . . don't know that," Rosalie admitted hesitantly. "But . . . maybe."

"Then I hope you kill them."

"Eugenia!" Emmeline gasped, as if horrified to hear her friend say such a thing.

"I mean it. I hope you stab them through the heart ten times over." Tears were spilling down her face, but she seemed not to notice. Instead, she kept her head held high, a stubborn jut to her chin.

It was Derek who stepped forward, kneeling in front of Eugenia, and Arabelle was hit with the memory of Derek with the children of Juniper Black, showing them his sleight of hand and making them laugh for the first time since their father died.

"I'll make them pay, Eugenia," he said, his tone a comforting antithesis to his words. "I promise."

Afterwards, they flew straight for the Mayor's Manor. When they arrived, they landed in the front garden where Rolven and two other Guards stood along the pathway. Had they been paying the Mayor a visit when the spell was cast? A servant stood by the rose hedges, a pair of hedge clippers lay forgotten at his feet.

Rosalie walked up to Rolven, considered him for a moment, before reaching up to slap him across the face.

The sound echoed in the quiet, but that was all it did. Rolven didn't wake with an indignant shout or glare at them with clear, stony eyes. Instead, his eyes remained clouded with the violet mist.

Rosalie turned to Arabelle. "I thought you said slapping them works?"

"It worked on you two." She shrugged.

"Maybe they've been left like this for too long?" Derek suggested.

Arabelle looked around at the Guards, and the servant in the gardens, and the few people that lingered on the streets outside. What did Aryel have in mind by putting the entire town of Windfell under her control?

We'll find out soon enough, she thought determinedly. *Tonight, this whole damn mystery comes to an end.*

A raspy cackle filled the air.

Arabelle turned, hand reaching for the sword at her hip as she did so. She didn't have to look to know that Derek and Rosalie had reacted similarly.

Standing before the front doors of the Mayor's Manor, was the elderly maidservant, Lilith.

Each time Arabelle had seen Lilith since arriving in Windfell, the old woman had looked nothing but disdainful. Barely uttering more than a few short words and fixing anyone in her line of sight with her baleful squint.

Now she stood before them with a new animation about her. Her skin was as deathly pale as ever, especially in the moon's light, but her expression was lit with a manic euphoria. Her dark eyes were wide and her lipless mouth spread into a smile that made her look like a grinning skeleton. It sent a chill down Arabelle's spine.

"Little Guardians managed to escape, I see." Her voice was a high rasp. "Come to cause my mistress trouble, I see."

"Your mistress?" said Derek. "Lady Boeheart?"

Lilith cackled again. It was a terrible sound, like the rattling cough of someone about to die. "Not Lady Boeheart, no."

"Then who?"

"My mistress has worked too long and too hard for the little Guardians to ruin her plans with their meddling," she said, and with a gnarled hand she pointed. "Kill them!"

And as if a match had been lit, everyone who stood in a magical trance close by came to life.

The scraping of metal blades rang out as the Guards drew their swords from their scabbards. Arabelle turned to see Rolven reaching for her, face still wiped clean of emotion and eyes still clouded. She was quick enough to duck out of the way, but not quick enough to avoid the servant charging into her.

She fell flat on her back and when the servant tried to climb on top of her with his hedge clippers in hand. Arabelle slammed the heel of her boot into his gut, kicking him away from her.

She scrambled to her feet just in time to stop Rolven from running her through with his blade. Their swords bounced off of each other and Rolven's sword arm was momentarily flung backward. Arabelle took that opportunity to shift her gaze towards the house's front doors, but Lilith had already vanished. She didn't have long to wonder where the old woman could have gone before Rolven and the servant were on the attack once again.

Trying to fight as one against two was tough, but it was especially so as Arabelle did not want to kill either of her opponents while they had no such qualms. Rolven and the servant came at her with their full strength, while Arabelle could do no more than block and dodge their attacks.

Fortunately, the servant had none of Rolven's strength or skill with a weapon, and attacked her with pure adrenaline. It wasn't long before she was able to find an opening and use it to incapacitate the servant with a swift blow to the neck.

But that still left her with Rolven to contend with. Arabelle hadn't realised just how close they had drawn to the Manor's walls until she felt the backs of her shoulders collide with the brick. Rolven swung his sword in a long arc and Arabelle ducked before the blade could shear through her neck.

She got behind him and just when he turned to face her, Arabelle reached out with the speed and surety of a snake striking its victim, and grabbed Rolven by his forehead. Using all the strength she could muster, she pushed Rolven back into the brick wall, so hard, the back of his head bounced off with an audible *smack*.

Without making a sound, he slumped to the ground. He didn't get back up and Arabelle dearly hoped he was only unconscious.

"Arabelle, over here!"

She looked up to see Derek and Rosalie making for the front doors. The bodies of their attackers lay strewn across the lawn. But she did not have time to check to see if they were all still breathing. Instead, she sprinted to join Rosalie and Derek and together, they burst through the front doors and into the dark foyer inside.

"We need to find Lilith," said Arabelle. The old maidservant clearly knew more about what was happening than they ever could have realised. If they could just find her and make her talk.

A bark and the sound of something crashing resounded through the house.

"The study," Derek said, before they were all rushing across the foyer.

Halfway through the hallway that led towards the study, they found Mayor Boeheart standing still with violet clouded eyes.

When they reached the Mayor's study, it was to find the once immaculate room in complete disarray. Books had fallen from broken shelves and the desk and couches had either been overturned or flung across the room. Dark stains were spattered across the floor. Blood stains.

Lying amongst the wreckage was Bear. Arabelle almost thought the poor thing was dead, until she heard the low, plaintive whines. Derek was at the dog's side in seconds.

"Is he all right?" Rosalie asked Derek.

"His back leg is wounded. But it doesn't look too bad."

Indeed, Arabelle could see an open wound on the dog's hind leg, the white fur darkened with blood. She looked around at the sizeable splatters of blood staining the carpet. The wound on Bear's leg didn't look deep enough to have caused this much of a mess. So what—or who—had?

Arabelle tore off a piece of fabric from one of the shredded cushions and handed it to Derek. "Wrap his leg up with this for now."

While Derek and Rosalie saw to Bear, Arabelle wandered over to the bookcase that still stood against the wall behind where the desk used to be. It might have simply been a trick of the shadows, but Arabelle was sure she had seen a flicker of movement behind the bookcase.

She drew closer.

"Arabelle? What are you—"

The bookcase was flung to the side, revealing a gaping black doorway in the wall, and out of that doorway leapt Lilith, a knife in one skeletal hand.

Lilith moved with surprising speed and Arabelle reacted on instinct, lifting her sword just in time for it to run through the maidservant.

Time seemed to stop, and the knife fell from Lilith's hand with a clatter. She made a horrible rasping sound before coughing up a glob of blood.

Arabelle withdrew her sword, and Lilith crumpled to the floor.

Rosalie came to Arabelle's side and kicked the old woman's body over onto her back. Blood coated her chin, stark against her paper-white skin and a blossoming stain was soaking through the front of her maid's uniform, where Arabelle's sword had gone in. But it was her eyes, wide and lifeless, that really convinced Arabelle that she was dead.

"So much for questioning her," Rosalie noted.

"We might not need to anymore," said Derek, coming over to observe the newly revealed passageway in the wall. Bear was up and moving gingerly by his side.

"Did you know about this?" Arabelle asked him.

Derek shook his head. "I could probably count on one hand the number of times I ever came into this study while I lived here."

There was no light whatsoever through the passageway, and it looked like a void into complete darkness.

"Aryel has to be through there. I'm sure of it," Arabelle said. "It's time to put a stop to whatever game she's been playing."

* * *

They wound up walking through what Derek could only assume was an underground tunnel, judging by the cavernous walls and lack of any natural light. Thankfully, there had been a lantern hanging on a hook in the rocky wall at the entrance, and they were able to use it to light their way through the tunnel.

Rosalie, who was walking in the front with the lantern held aloft, came to a stop.

"What is it?" said Arabelle in a hushed voice, her hand already going for the sword at her belt.

"Do you feel that?" Rosalie asked.

"Feel what?" asked Derek.

"Wind. Like there's a draft in here."

"Maybe we're approaching the end of the tunnel?" Arabelle suggested.

"No, I don't see any light up ahead. Also, it feels more like—" Rosalie took a step forward so that she could face the wall to their right. She held the lantern higher so that she could inspect something.

"Rosalie?"

"The draft," she said. "It's coming from this crack in the wall."

Derek and Arabelle stepped closer and sure enough, Derek could feel a weak, cold wind slipping through a sizeable crack in the stone. But that wasn't all. Derek noticed that the crack not only ran all the way down to the floor, but it also cut a jagged path upwards, close to the ceiling, before creating a wide arc and continuing back down to the ground. It looked almost like—

"I think this is a door," he said, reaching for a dent in the stone that looked almost like a handhold, and pushed.

With a scraping groan, the wall—the door, really—came open and a rush of ice-cold winter air blew into their faces. They weren't quite outside though, instead the hidden door opened up into a shallow cave and beyond the mouth of the cave was a view of the night sky and the Valley and the surrounding woods blanketed in snow.

"We must be in one of the mountain caves just outside of Windfell," Derek surmised.

"Cassandra was here in these mountains when she died," said Arabelle, tendrils of hair drifting into her face thanks to the wind. "This must have been how the killer got to her unnoticed."

"Come on. Aryel's obviously not here. Let's keep going."

Closing the door, they continued the rest of their trek through the tunnel in silence, none of them wishing to make too much noise and alert Aryel of their presence. They weren't sure what they would find at the end of the tunnel, Aryel most likely, but if so, would she be alone?

Finally, the tunnel came to an end, opening up into a huge, circular antechamber. The walls were hewn from jagged rock, and the ceiling formed a towering dome above them. Silver shafts of moonlight streamed in from the skylight above.

The antechamber was also filled with gargoyles.

The sight of the beasts brought the three of them up short, but it became quickly apparent that none of the gargoyles seemed to be awake. Instead, they stood as motionless as any statue, each one of them crouched on individual podiums and lined up in rows. There had to be thirty of them at the very least.

Derek was the first to take a slow, cautious step forward, his eyes darting between the rows of gargoyles for any sign of movement. There was none.

As Derek, Rosalie and Arabelle moved further into the chamber, there was a sudden burst of light as iron braziers circling the walls were lit. The lingering shadows withdrew, and the rest of the antechamber came into view.

On the other side of the antechamber was a tall, granite staircase leading up to some kind of altar.

There was also someone standing at the bottom of the steps.

At first, Derek thought the figure was Aryel. But no, it was not her. The ivory dress did not belong to Aryel. Nor did the fair skin, revealed by the shoulder-less garment. Or the long, brown hair—

"Lady Boeheart?" The confusion in Derek's voice was clear as it echoed across the chamber.

Anna Boeheart, wife of Mayor Edmund Boeheart, turned to face them, looking as immaculately beautiful as ever, as if she had just come from an evening dinner party with friends.

She surveyed them with green eyes before a smile alighted on her face."Good evening, children."

"What are you doing down here?" said Rosalie uncertainly.

"Oh dear, I thought that would have been obvious." Her smile broadened.

That's when Derek saw it. Something wrong with Lady Boeheart's smile. Where her canine teeth should have been, were instead a pair of pearl-white, elongated fangs, as sharp as needle points.

The realisation struck him like a dull blow. "You're a vampire."

Anna's expression took on a distinctly predatory quality. "Clever boy."

"It's you," said Arabelle. "You're the murderer, aren't you?"

"Well, I suppose there's no point in denying it now, is there?" Anna said with a dainty shrug of her shoulders. "I suppose I might also reveal to you that my name isn't really Anna Boeheart. It's Alice. Alice Shade."

The name struck a chord in his memory. Derek thought back to his old vampire book, *A History of Notable Vampires,* and to the chapter about the vampire lord and his wife, Emery and Alice Shade, who were notorious for tormenting the small and isolated towns in Aloseria's northern regions until their demise at the hands of the Guardians, seventy years ago.

"But that's impossible," said Rosalie. "Alice and Emery Shade were killed years ago."

Derek also remembered the sketched portraits of the vampire husband and wife. Emery Shade had had aristocratic features and long, black hair. Alice with a long face, pointed chin and fair, wavy hair. Her resemblance to the woman that stood before them could not have been any less.

Anna—Alice?—chuckled, as if Rosalie had told her a joke. "No, dear child," she said. "My husband died on that night seventy years ago. I was fortunate enough to be ferried away to safety by my loyal servant, Lilith. However, I was injured." She pulled down the collar of her dress, just enough to reveal a hint of blackened, puckered flesh below her collarbone. Burn scars. "Enough so that I could not leave the safety of my hideout for quite some time. But it was lucky, I suppose. Being gone for so long led everyone to assume that I had perished, along with my husband."

"If you really are Alice Shade," Derek said, in a wry tone that he probably shouldn't have been using at that moment. "Then you've certainly changed a lot in the last seventy years."

Alice's green eyes flashed. "Well, after everyone thought I was dead, I couldn't risk being recognised and have a pack of Guardians hunting me down again, could I? I had my appearance altered to prevent that." She traced her fingers along her own cheekbone. "Normal magic would not allow for such a permanent change of oneself. But with dark magic, the possibilities are limitless."

"That still leaves a lot to be questioned," he pointed out.

"Would you like me to tell you the whole story, then?" asked Alice. "Oh, very well, since you've all come this far, I guess you deserve a reward. After my husband was killed, grief consumed me, the way water consumes a drowning man or fire a brittle old tree. I didn't want to go on without my beloved Emery. But I didn't want to die either. Then, one night, the answer came to me in the form of a grimoire I found after feeding off some traveller. In it was a necromancy spell, and I knew right away that this was the chance to return my husband back to my side. So I recovered his remains from the ruins of our castle and brought him here to Windfell."

That was when Derek's eyes drifted up to the altar behind Alice and, for the first time, he took a proper look at the stone slab on top of it. From this angle, he was just able to make out the dark shape of what looked to be a blackened corpse. The remains of Emery Shade.

"Why here though?" Arabelle demanded. "Why Windfell?"

"Because it's such a wonderfully secluded town," answered Alice, as if that were obvious. "Because the sun is a rarity in these parts. Because this town is just teeming with all kinds of unsavoury sorts no one would really miss."

"And the Mayor?" questioned Rosalie. "Why marry him and become Lady Boeheart?"

"Just another guise, dear. When the murders started, who would even think to suspect the Mayor's demure lady wife?"

"It was you who killed Cassandra, wasn't it?" said Arabelle. "And you were the one who killed Edgar at Orville's party? When you walked in on us in the library the other day, you had been listening in? That's how you knew we'd be at the party."

Alice smirked, flashing another glimpse of her pearlescent fangs. "Yes, I killed Master Greyhill and Miss Luteus. She didn't give me much of a choice, see. Not after she stumbled upon my little hideout in one of those mountain caves and broke my control over the gargoyles. After that incident, I couldn't risk being discovered again and relocated to this charming place, which I believe was built as the town's hideaway from daemons back in the day. Sadly, though, in my haste to leave, I left behind my most precious grimoire." She held up the large, leather-bound tome she had been holding all this time. "Which is how, I believe, you managed to come into possession of it. Until I had Lilith take it back, of course."

"So, that was actually Lilith I saw leaving our room the other morning? Not Arabelle?" said Rosalie.

"Afraid not, dear."

"And was it also Lilith I spoke to at the Post House?" demanded Arabelle. "Who I gave our letter to, trusting that it would be delivered to Ember?"

Alice laughed. "No, that was me. I had to make sure that message didn't go through and bring even more Guardians racing here, after all."

"And Orville?" asked Derek. "You were the one who killed

him, too?"

"Indeed. Nothing else I had done up until then seemed to scare you off. Not setting my gargoyles on you, not killing your dear friends, Edgar and Cassandra. I knew I had to perform the spell soon, and I didn't want you three getting in my way, so I thought, what better way to eliminate you without too much fuss than framing you for the murder of Captain Goldridge? Especially when the animosity between Master Draco and Orville was no secret, and I'd already planned on disposing of Orville once his usefulness ran out, so really, I must thank you for providing me with that opportunity."

"Orville was working with you?" It was somewhat vindicating to know that Derek had been right in suspecting Orville all along.

"Yes, he managed to catch me in the act on the night I killed Master Graff," Alice explained. "Before I could kill him too, he told me that he could help me. That, as Captain of the Guard, he could cover my tracks for me. He was the one who came up with the absurd idea to blame killings on Lady Night."

"But why would he want to help you?" Arabelle said.

Alice sounded almost bored as she answered, "He'd hoped that in bringing back my husband, I might also do him the favour of bringing back his dead brother. Which I had no intention of doing, of course." Something in Alice's expression hardened. "Enough. The time for talk is over. I have everything I need and soon I will have my darling Emery back and together we will finish what we started. I already have an army outside just waiting to do our bidding. We'll avenge ourselves upon those who thought they could defeat us. We will raze your precious city of Ember to the ground. We will slaughter every man, woman, and child. We will feed on their corpses before mounting their heads on our wall."

It was Arabelle who spoke next. "Those are some pretty confident words."

"But I think you're forgetting something," said Rosalie.

Derek unsheathed his shortsword; the blade came free with a metallic hiss. The blue metal gleamed in the firelight. He pointed it directly at Alice and said, "That we're going to stop you."

"Oh dear, I don't think I'm the only one speaking with overconfidence." Alice's face broke out into a wide smile. It wasn't the charming, dainty smile that had belonged to Anna Boeheart, nor was it an amused or even a sardonic smile. Instead, it was twisted, transforming her face in such a way that she appeared far more monstrous than she ever had with only her fangs on display.

The sound of shattering rock echoed throughout the antechamber. Followed by another. And another.

All around them, the gargoyles were coming to life. Bursting out of their stone casings, which cracked and crumbled to the floor as the creatures leapt from their podiums and moved to surround the young Guardians. Two of the gargoyles were already blocking their path to Alice and the altar.

It appeared that if they wanted to stop Alice, they were going to have to go through these monsters first.

As Derek readied his sword, both Rosalie and Arabelle

Changed.

And when the first gargoyle moved to attack, Derek was ready to meet it.

20

The antechamber was chaos. The sounds of fighting echoed through the cavernous space as Derek, Arabelle and Rosalie fought off Alice's gargoyles. Derek ran his sword straight through the heart of one gargoyle. The creature turned to rubble and straight away more were closing in on him.

Beyond the roiling tide of the battle was Alice. Unbothered by the battle going on around her as she ascended to the steps towards the altar, towards the remains of her husband.

Using one of the larger pieces of scattered gargoyle stone, Derek propelled himself into the air and landed on the back of one offending gargoyle. He plunged his sword between its shoulder blades and leapt off of it before it burst into stone. While in midair, he Changed in time for two gargoyles to collide into him, knocking him to the ground.

They didn't have him pinned for long. There was a flare of heat, and the gargoyles were caught in a torrent of Rosalie's fire. They squealed, trying to scramble away from the fire. Derek grabbed one by the neck before it could get away and tore out its throat. Then Arabelle seemed to drop out of the sky, her blade flashing and her hair like a streak of golden fire, and dispatched the other gargoyle by severing its head from its body.

But it didn't stop there. More gargoyles descended upon them, snapping their teeth and flashing their razor-sharp talons. The number of gargoyles was quickly proving to be overwhelming for only the three of them to handle. It felt as if for every one they managed to kill, another two took its place.

Derek spared a glance at the altar where Alice now stood, grimoire open and levitating in the air beside her as she arranged the hands of her victims around Emery Shade's corpse.

He made an attempt to fly for the altar, only to have his path barred by a group of gargoyles.

They swarmed him like ravens to a newborn lamb. Slamming him back down to the ground and more quickly began piling onto him, clawing and biting in a vicious frenzy.

There was a flash of blinding white light, and a thunderous crackling sound filled the air. Derek could only catch a glimpse of bolts of lightning spearing through the gargoyles surrounding him before they exploded into showers of stone.

A lull fell over the antechamber, and even the remaining gargoyles had gone still. All eyes were on the new arrival.

Aryel Sabir stood at the entrance, one hand raised outwards and still crackling with magical lightning. Her other hand was pressed against her side, where the fabric of her clothing was torn and most of it stained with blood. Derek remembered the bloody spatters they had found around the Mayor's study.

Alice's scream tore through the chamber. *"Kill her!"*

The gargoyles snapped back to attention, many of them moving to attack Aryel.

None of them even made it within five feet of her.

Aryel thrust both of her hands forward, and a wave of roaring blue fire erupted from her palms. The gargoyles closest to her were consumed within seconds.

With nowhere to flee, Derek lifted his wing in an effort to shield himself as the wall of fire came racing towards him. But there was no feeling of being consumed by burning flames. Instead, there was only the sensation of warm air blowing past him and when he lowered his wing, he saw the flames had avoided him completely, curving around him as if he were a rock in the middle of a stream.

When the fire dissipated, there was only silence. Derek saw Arabelle and Rosalie, standing a short distance away from him, both looking unscathed from the fire.

The gargoyles were gone, and such was the ferocity of the flames that not even shattered stone was left of them, only ashes.

Alice stood at the altar, her face a mask of shocked fury as she stared at the ashes of her gargoyle army. With a hiss, she pulled something from the pockets of her dress—a little brown pouch— and threw it. It landed at the bottom of the steps, exploding in a small cloud of pink dust as soon as it hit the floor. The cloud expanded, stretching to either side of the walls before growing upwards, climbing all the way to the ceiling, creating a barrier between them and Alice.

"Get to the altar!" Aryel shouted. *"Quickly!"*

Derek, Arabelle, and Rosalie were already sprinting across the chamber before Aryel had even uttered a word.

The barrier was growing taller and taller with rapid speed. Derek threw himself into the air, higher and higher, until he shot through the gap between the dust-like barrier and the ceiling with only seconds to spare before it closed up.

Alice, having wasted no time to continue with her ritual, whirled around to face him, her eyes wide and wild. She bared her fangs at him and screamed her rage.

But Derek did not hesitate. He opened his jaws and let loose a stream of blazing fire. Alice leapt out of the way at the last minute as Derek's fire engulfed the altar, the hands, the grimoire, and the remains of Emery Shade.

Distantly, he could hear Alice's screams, but all Derek could think of as he burned it all was that this was for Cassandra. For Eugenia and Edgar. For everyone who had had their lives torn apart for this insidious spell and its caster.

The heat of the flames intensified enough that they started to turn blue, and when they finally stopped, Derek dropped to the altar steps, Changing, hands braced against his knees as he fought to catch his breath. The altar itself was barely more than a charred ruin and Emery Shade's corpse was no more than a scattering of smoking ashes.

Behind him, the barrier had dissolved, and he saw Arabelle and Rosalie move to where Alice was crouched at the bottom of the altar steps, weeping quietly. The bloodied dagger lay on the ground in front of her.

"Get up," Arabelle snarled, her sword pointed at Alice's neck.

But Alice continued to weep. "Emery . . . My Emery . . ."

"I said *get up*."

"You killed him . . ." She lifted her head and her red-rimmed, tearful eyes found Derek. "You killed *my Emery!*"

In her rage, the guise of the beautiful Anna Boeheart was ripped apart and the monster that lay underneath emerged.

Derek had seen drawings and read stories about the true forms of vampires. The terrifying spectacle of witnessing one transform from human and into something like a daemon itself. Her shimmering brown hair fell away as her skin turned a sickly grey. Grotesque black claws grew from her fingertips. Two leathery wings sprouted from her back with the sickening sound of cracking bones, ripping her dress apart to reveal only a semblance of a human form beneath.

Her face looked like some sort of monstrous mimicry of a bat's. Her aristocratic nose had vanished, replaced by two diagonal slits. Her green eyes were now a luminous yellow, set into deep, black sockets.

Alice leapt from her position on the ground and hurtled towards

Derek with an inhuman shriek, her mouthful of needle-sharp teeth on display and her jaw opened far wider than was possible for any human.

Derek didn't even have time to react before her claws dug into the front of his shirt and carried him off his feet.

Air rushed through his ears as Alice lifted him higher and higher, up through the skylight and into the frigid night air.

Once they were high enough above the mountaintop, Derek whipped out his sword and slashed at one of the hands gripped in the material of his shirt. Alice cried out and released her hold on him.

He sheathed his sword as he plummeted, before he Changed and his open wings caught him. When he turned back to face Alice, it was to see her coming for him once again, claws outstretched and her howls of rage ringing through the night.

A torrent of fire surged past Derek and towards Alice, who rolled out of its path.

Arabelle and Rosalie had joined him and together they launched themselves at Alice.

One would think that three dragons should have been more than a match for one vampire. But that was not the case. Alice dodged their attacks with astounding speed and countered them with brutal strength. Even their fire breath wasn't quick enough to touch her.

She delivered a swift kick to Derek's mouth, and fiery pain exploded beneath his skin. She punched Arabelle so hard in the chest, she went flying back several feet in the air. When Rosalie attempted to sneak up on her from behind, she somersaulted over Rosalie's head, landing on her back and tearing her claws through Rosalie's skin.

Rosalie let out an agonised cry before she plummeted down toward the mountaintop, the Change leaving her as she did.

Derek dove after her. Thoughts of fighting Alice fled. Only the determination to catch Rosalie before she could hit the ground remained.

He grabbed her just before they broke through a tree canopy. By which point, he had only seconds to pull her against him and shield her body with his as they crashed through the branches, their descent only coming to a halt once Derek hit the ground.

He lay there for a moment or so, his body singing with the pain of the impact, before he Changed, still cradling Rosalie in his arms.

"Rosalie?" he called to her, gently shaking her shoulder.

That earned him a moan of pain, but no other kind of response. That's when he felt something warm and wet against his arm, where he had it wrapped around her back. Blood. Lots of it, pumping through the eight vertical gashes along her back.

"*Fuck.*"

"Little Guardian."

He whipped around, adrenaline coursing hard through his body, but he quickly realised it was only Aryel coming towards them. How she managed to make it here, he did not know and nor did he care when she went to her knees beside Rosalie, her hands going to the wounds on her back at the same time he felt some of the tension leave Rosalie's body. Aryel was healing her.

He had little time to revel in his relief. There was a cry from above and through the broken canopy, Derek caught sight of the moonlit figures of Alice and Arabelle falling through the sky.

* * *

Fury roared through Arabelle's veins as she saw Rosalie fall and Derek race to catch her. She did not wait to see whether Derek would save Rosalie, instead she hurled herself at Alice.

The vampire evaded her once again, but this time, Arabelle clamped her jaws around Alice's leg and drag her down through the air.

Alice raked her claws against the back of Arabelle's neck. The flare of pain caused Arabelle's jaws to slacken, and Alice managed to pull free.

But Arabelle would not be deterred. Before Alice could move out of reach, Arabelle latched onto one of her outstretched wings, shredding through the skin with her teeth.

Screeching, Alice seized Arabelle by the throat. She allowed Arabelle to struggle in her vice-like grip for a moment before using her tremendous vampiric strength to *throw* Arabelle.

They had moved close enough to the ground now that Arabelle didn't even get the chance to right herself before she hit the first tree branch, snapping it under the force of her fall and crashing to the ground.

The last thing she saw before the edges of her vision darkened and blurred was Alice touching down in front of her.

* * *

Derek arrived in time to witness the scene of Arabelle lying motionless in the snow while Alice advanced on her.

Derek leapt off of the rocky ledge, sword drawn, before Alice could take one more step towards Arabelle.

Alice showed no sign of having noticed him, other than to step nimbly out of the way of his attack. She'd moved behind him and Derek was just quick enough to block her claws from slicing through his throat with the flat of his blade.

So Alice settled for slamming her fist into Derek's stomach. The punch was strong enough to send him flying backward, his body colliding with a tree. She was on him in seconds, pinning him by the throat.

"I've never had a taste of Guardian blood before," she said. This close, Derek heard the crack and pop of her jaw unhinging as her mouth opened gruesomely wide. Her breath smelt of decaying flesh and her rows of spine-like teeth prepared to sink into his neck.

"I wonder if it tastes any different—"

She broke off as Derek plunged his sword into her side, between the bones of her ribcage.

"I'm sorry," he said. "Were you saying something?"

He was back-handed and sent flying once more. Derek landed face first in the snow, only a hairsbreadth away from the edge of the cliff. He spat blood from his mouth.

Alice seemed to materialise at his side and slammed her foot down on his right shoulder so hard he heard an internal snap. A snap that reverberated through his whole body right before the blinding pain that forced a low cry past his lips.

"That isn't even the worst to come, little boy," Alice spat. "You took my Emery away from me. I'll make sure you all suffer for it."

"He was already gone," Derek gasped out as Alice pressed down on what he was sure was a dislocated shoulder. "All I did was clean up that mess you still called a husband."

Hissing, she reached down and lifted his head by his hair. "*You stole my chance. My only chance to bring him back.*"

"Sorry . . . but I'm not sorry."

Alice made a sound of irritation and slammed his head back down against the ground. "Impudent little beast. The chatty ones always annoy me the most."

"I'm not chatty. I'm . . . just trying to distract you."

Arabelle appeared behind Alice, after having crept up behind her as silent as a ghost, until she was ready to pounce. She didn't give Alice any time to react before she had her teeth in Alice's neck and tore out a chunk of it.

Blood sprayed, staining the white snow dark red.

Alice was screaming, but she did not go down. With a hand pressed against the open wound at her neck, streams of blood trailing down her body in rapid torrents, she turned to face her new adversary and made a clumsy swipe with a clawed hand. Arabelle easily evaded, and when Alice attempted to fly away, Arabelle grabbed her by the tip of one of her wings, dragging her down until she was flat on her back with Arabelle on top of her.

Arabelle wasted no time in releasing a scorching breath of fire directly into Alice's face.

Alice's screams took on a hysterical pitch as the fire spread across her entire body. Catching alight the way an oil-soaked cloth would. Arabelle leapt away and together, she and Derek watched as fire consumed the vampire

And between one breath and the next, Alice Shade was nothing but ashes.

* * *

It was past midnight by the time Darus, Jared, Will, and Aurelia returned to Ember.

They were walking the path towards the palace, with Darus at the head of their small procession, Aurelia with her hood drawn up and a tense set to her shoulders, and Jared and Will walking with as much space between them as possible. Darus had noticed a distance between the two boys ever since the morning after Draken's fort. He wasn't exactly sure what had caused it and nor was it his business to find out, but he had enough experience with them to recognise a lover's spat when he saw one.

They were halfway towards the palace gates when Darus noticed another group—Guardians—coming their way. As they drew closer, Darus noticed a familiar head of auburn hair.

"Lila!" he called out.

"Darus!" Lila broke away from her companions and came rushing towards him. "What are you doing back so early? No, never mind that now. You're here and I think you best come with us."

"Come with you?" The rest of the Guardians were now filing past Darus and the others. "Where are you going? What's happening?"

"We received a message. Not too long ago. It came from Windfell."

* * *

The world seemed to fall into stillness as the ashes of Alice Shade settled.

Arabelle was by Derek's side in a heartbeat. Changing, she threw her arms around him and, although unexpected, Derek thought he wouldn't have minded having Arabelle so close to him, if it weren't for the pain it sent through his shoulder.

"Arabelle," he hissed, and she immediately drew away from him.

"Sorry! I'm sorry!" Her eyes were wide as she looked him up and down. There was a suspicious shine in her eyes. "Are you all right? Are you hurt? I was so—I was—"

"I'm fine. My shoulder might be dislocated though," he added when Arabelle gave him a disbelieving look. "And you? Are you okay?" He gave her a quick once over and he spotted blood oozing from what must have been a wound at the back of her neck. Apart from that and a few other scrapes and bruises, there didn't appear to be anything seriously wrong with her.

Arabelle breathed out a sigh of relief. "I'm okay," she said. Her hand came up to grip the material of his shirt, just above his heart. "We're okay." She sounded unbearably grateful for that.

Derek felt the overwhelming urge to put his arms around Arabelle and hold her close. To press his cheek against the soft, yellow hair on the crown of her head. He might have even done so if it weren't for his damn shoulder.

So instead, he settled for tipping his forehead against hers. "We're okay," he said, his voice barely above a whisper. A whisper caught only between the two of them.

From where they sat by the cliff's edge, they had a perfect view of the entire town below, including the town gates, where Derek caught sight of a bright, white light forming in the air. He didn't realise it was actually a portal until he saw people step out of it.

And thanks to the portal's illumination, he was able to make out what clothes—uniforms—these people were wearing.

"Guardians," Arabelle breathed out with more than a little relief.

Arabelle Changed and flew down to greet the new arrivals and when she returned Derek was more than a little surprised to find Darus, Jared and Lila were part of the group. Aryel arrived to join them at that same moment with a pale-faced, but alive, Rosalie leaning against her.

Darus was by Derek's side in no time, looking at him with

worried, grey eyes and fussing over his injuries. For once, Derek didn't mind the fussing.

Lila and another Guardian rushed to see to Rosalie while Jared stood with Arabelle, his hands cupping his cousin's face while he spoke to her in worried tones. A few of the other Guardians were inspecting the sizeable patch of Alice Shade's blood and ashes in the snow.

Having Darus and Jared, and Lila here filled Derek with a strong sense of relief. And he knew it must have been the same for Arabelle and Rosalie, too.

So they allowed themselves to be worried over and have their injuries tended to, knowing that this whole ordeal was finally over.

They remained in Windfell for three more days, following the battle with Alice. Partly so Derek, Arabelle and Rosalie could recover—especially Rosalie whose wounds had been quite severe—and partly so that Darus and the other Guardians could see to the townspeople, who were all frightened and confused about what had transpired the night Alice Shade tried to resurrect her husband.

Many of the other Guardians had already returned to Ember— there was no need for such a large group to remain in Windfell— only Jared, Darus, and Lila had stayed behind.

Finally, on the fourth day, it was time for them to head back to Ember. They'd arranged for Aryel to conjure up a portal, since Rosalie still wasn't in any condition to make the journey back by flying. It was an unusually sunny morning, but no less cold, as Derek stood at the edge of the double bed in his room, making sure he had all of his belongings packed.

With his good hand, he lifted his father's sword, tucked away in its black sheath with a pattern of silver stars. It was a comfort to be able to hold it and feel the weight of it in his hand once again. He slipped it into his pack; the hilt sticking out of the opening, before lifting it off the bed.

Derek took the time to pause and look around the room, taking in the cream walls and gilded skirting boards. It felt almost strange to be leaving again. While he was certainly relieved, he still felt strangely sad in a way that he couldn't put into words.

There was a knock behind him, and Derek turned to see Darus standing in the doorway. Unlike Derek, Darus was dressed in uniform, along with his cloak. He gave Derek a fond smile. "Are you ready to go?" he asked. "Everyone's waiting downstairs."

By the set of Darus's features, Derek could tell that there was more he wanted to say. Questions like, "how are you feeling?" were probably on the tip of his tongue. He didn't say it though, and Derek was glad. Those weren't questions he felt like answering just yet.

"I'm ready," was all he said, dragging his pack over to Darus by the door. He couldn't carry it properly thanks to his dislocated shoulder and his arm cradled in a sling against his chest.

"Here, let me carry it before you ruin these expensive carpets and we have to pay to replace them," said Darus, tugging the pack out of Derek's grip and hoisting it over his own shoulder.

They made their way down to the foyer where Arabelle, Jared, Lila and Rosalie were already waiting, along with Mayor Boeheart and even a few of the house staff. With Alice's death, the possession spell she had cast on the townspeople had come undone.

Bear was there too. He came limping over to Derek, tongue lolling and tail wagging lazily. With a smile, Derek indulged him with a good rub behind one ear. If there was one thing he was going to miss about Windfell, it was this giant, mince tart-stealing dog.

"I would just like to start by saying," Mayor Boeheart began, "that I and all the people of Windfell owe you three a great debt." He was looking pointedly at Derek, Arabelle and Rosalie "I'm not sure where we'd all be right now if not for your efforts."

"Part of a mind controlled army led by vampires, probably," muttered Jared.

Arabelle elbowed him in the back.

However, the Mayor didn't seem to hear. He looked exhausted, but more than that, he looked like a man in grief. Derek had seen little of the Mayor these last few days, but he had come to see them the day after they had thwarted Alice. By then, Boeheart had learned everything that he needed to know—including how his beloved wife was really the infamous vampire, Alice Shade, and how she had been behind the murders to bring her first husband back from the dead. Despite everything, it was clear that he was still grieving Lady Boeheart, not just her death, but also perhaps the person he thought she had been.

"So on behalf of the people of Windfell, I say thank you." And then Mayor Boeheart bowed to them and the house staff standing behind him followed suit. They bowed as if they were bowing to their King and not just three inexperienced teenagers trying to do their job.

Derek could see that Arabelle and Rosalie were both as taken aback by the gesture as he was. Darus and Lila looked almost like proud parents, and Jared gave him a congratulatory nudge on his good shoulder.

Finally, it was time to go, and Derek stepped out of the Mayor's Manor for the last time.

They met Aryel in the Valley, under the cherry blossom tree that had been planted in honour of Derek's parents.

Eugenia, Micah and Emmeline were waiting there as well, the children rushing to greet Derek, Arabelle and Rosalie with hugs as soon as they approached, while Aryel hung back.

It wasn't the first time Derek had seen the mage since the fight with Alice. Not only had she been in and out of the Mayor's Manor for the last few days to heal Rosalie, she had also helped answer some of the questions they still had surrounding the events of the past week. Such as how she'd come to suspect Alice in the first place.

"Lady Boeheart always gave me a strange feeling," she had

explained. "But it wasn't until the gargoyle attack that I realised that feeling came from her use of dark magic. At Orville Goldridge's party, I noticed her slip out not long before there was a commotion and the bodies of Master Greyhill and another guest were discovered. And when she used that mind-control spell on the rest of the town, I went straight for the Mayor's Manor, where, sure enough, I found Alice and her horrible servant were behind it. Before she injured me, she mentioned how it was a shame no Guardians would be on their way to help. Once I managed to escape her, I sent an urgent message to Ember before returning to the Manor and well . . . you know the rest."

"But how did you know we would be at Orville's party?" Derek had asked.

She'd nodded her head at Rosalie. "I heard that one mention wearing one of those hideous masks in the shop to the party."

"And why didn't you show up until after the gargoyles had attacked?"

"Believe it or not, I'd actually slept through the whole thing."

Now, Lila said to Aryel as they approached, "Thank you for doing this for us."

"It's no trouble," she replied. "I wouldn't want all my hard work tending to Miss Decorus to be for naught, after all."

Rosalie offered her a smile, albeit a tired one. "I'll send you a thank you gift when I return home. A new dress maybe? Or shoes?"

Aryel looked decidedly unenthusiastic. "That won't be

necessary. Besides, I don't plan on staying in Windfell for much longer."

"Where will you go?" Derek asked.

"I think I may travel back to Ishlav. It's been a long time since I last visited my homeland and my family." With that said, she pulled out a tiny glass vial filled with a iridescent purple liquid and turned her back on the small party of Guardians. Aryel stepped closer to the cherry blossom tree, unstoppering the vial and tipping it until two black drops spilled onto the snow.

A shimmering white doorway opened up against the trunk of the cherry blossom tree. Through it, Derek could see the city gates of Ember.

Home.

"Oh, I wish we could come with you," said Eugenia, looking wistfully through the portal.

Derek reached out to ruffle her hair with a smile. "Maybe one day you can come visit."

"And maybe I'll even send a royal invitation myself," Jared added with a wink and a dimpled grin.

There was a lightness in Derek at the sight of Ember. At knowing that home was just a few steps away. He looked up at the tree branches stretching out above their heads, dotted with soft, pink blossoms that refused to wilt and die even in this cold. Derek could almost imagine that the spirits of his parents and his sibling resided in this tree. This was where their cottage had once stood. Where he and his parents had lived happily together. It was also where Alexander and Erica had died. The only kind of memorial there was for them.

It added a bitter sweetness to leaving Windfell. This town that he loathed, but that still held happy memories amongst all the bad ones.

Lila went through the portal first, helping Rosalie. Darus went next, and before Arabelle and Jared could follow, they both turned back to look at Derek.

"Hey." Jared's voice was soft and wary, as if Derek were a deer that would startle and bolt if he so much as moved an inch. "Are you coming?"

The wind picked up then and for a moment, it was strong enough to make Derek stumble forward a step. It died back down almost immediately.

He took one more look at the cherry blossom branches, wavering gently in the breeze, and smiled.

"Yeah," said Derek. "I'm coming."

They all went their separate ways not long after returning to Ember. Darus and Lila had been rather insistent that Derek, Rosalie and Arabelle all return home for some well-deserved rest. That they would take care of writing and submitting the assignment report in place of Cassandra. They didn't have to worry about a thing. They had already done more than enough.

"There are . . . a few things we need to talk about, Derek," Darus said as the two of them walked along the cobblestone streets towards their house.

"What things?" Derek asked tentatively. Darus sounded uncharacteristically serious. Nervous, even.

"We'll talk about it once we're home."

Not that it took long. They walked up the snow-blanketed lawn and stepped onto the front veranda. Darus opened the door, allowing Derek to step inside first. As soon as he walked in, Daisy came bounding down the stairs to greet them, her tail wagging furiously.

"*No.* No jumping," Darus told her sternly, holding out an arm to stop her from jumping up on Derek and jostling his shoulder. Derek reached over Darus's outstretched arm to give her a pat, anyway.

The sound of a bird's caw startled Derek, and he looked up to see a raven perched on the banister of the stairs, ruffling its feathers.

He blinked at it, confused. Where had the bird come from? And how did it even get in? Derek was sure he would have noticed a raven flying in when Darus opened the door.

That was also when someone stepped out from the kitchen. A tall, willowy young woman, with short black hair and the pointed ears of a Wood Elf. She was instantly familiar to Derek, and it only took a moment for him to remember why.

"Aurelia Blackwood?" The mage from the magic shop in Florinstone.

Aurelia inclined her head. "It is good to see you again." She was dressed in a simple pair of trousers and a grey shirt. The right sleeve hung loose and empty at her side.

"You know her, Derek?" said Darus, sounding honestly surprised.

"I met her in Florinstone in February."

Darus turned to Aurelia. "You didn't tell me you'd already met him."

Aurelia shrugged her shoulder, that wasn't leaning against the doorway. "I did not think it mattered."

Wait, what?

"So he doesn't—?"

"No."

"Does anyone actually want to explain anything to me?" Derek demanded. "Because I'm a bit confused right now."

Darus sighed and placed a hand on Derek's good shoulder. "Let's take this into the lounge. There's . . . a lot we need to tell you."

* * *

Jared sat beneath the boughs of the orange blossom tree in the gardens, watching as his mother's dogs snuffled around the grevilleas.

It wasn't quite the weather to be sitting outdoors. There was a bone-penetrating chill in the air that made Jared shiver every now and again, despite his thick coat. Still, he couldn't bring himself to go inside. These gardens were where he felt most at peace, surrounded by vegetation, breathing in the scent of grass and dirt and, in the winter, the clean smell of the snow.

He thought that sitting in the gardens might help lift this depressive stupor he'd found himself in since he'd returned home— since that morning he'd last spoken to Will—but it did nothing to lift his mood. He still felt just as glum as ever. With a sigh, Jared shifted, so that he was lying down along the stone bench, staring up at the bare tree branches intertwining above him. The weakest glimmers of sunlight shone through the grey sky. Jared wondered if this black cloud that had fallen over him would ever leave.

Who would have thought that I would be struck down with heartbreak over a boy? I'm Prince Jared Tobias Alaric Regalias, for Ithulia's sake. I should be the one breaking hearts.

Spot came scampering over to Jared, tail wagging, and licked at his dangling fingers. Jared scratched her under the chin in return.

He heard the crunching of snow and it wasn't long before his sister's face was looming above his. "Do you mind scooching over a bit?" she asked.

"No."

"Move over, or I'll sit on your head instead. Like when we were kids, remember?"

Jared grumbled but obliged, sitting up and moving over so that Julianna could take a seat beside him.

Neither of them spoke for a bit, Julianna choosing instead to give her attention to Beth, Spot, and Lucie, who had all come over to greet her.

"Mother and Father are worried about you, you know?" she said.

"Why ever for?" said Jared, although he had a good idea why that might be.

"I think something happened on your last assignment," Julianna said, lifting Lucie up onto her lap. "And I don't just mean that business with the escaped criminals and all that. I think that something, or rather some*one*, hurt you, didn't they?"

"And what makes you say that?"

"I know the look of a broken heart when I see it. I've even worn it myself once before."

Jared looked at her in surprise. "You've had your heart broken?" He asked, feeling a twinge of guilt for having never noticed. Julianna was infuriating most of the time, but that didn't mean Jared wouldn't wring the neck of anyone who hurt her.

"It was a few years ago," she explained, her breath a puff of mist in the air. "Looking back, it was only a childish infatuation, but at the time, I honestly thought it was true love, so I was quite crushed when it didn't end with us riding off into the sunset, toward our happily ever after."

She smiled and Jared tried to return it, but knew it came out weak.

"My point is, I know what's been making you mope about lately."

Jared looked away from his sister, placing his gaze instead on a blade of grass peeking out from beneath the snow. "I don't really want to talk about it."

"That's fine," said Julianna. "You don't have to talk about it. But you can't keep spending your time dwelling on it. I mean really, Jared, it's not becoming of a prince to mope."

"Then what do you suggest I do instead?"

"I think helping me plan the upcoming Tournament would be a good way to take your mind off of it."

That had Jared looking back at his sister in a heartbeat. "I— What?"

Julianna looked back at him with one eyebrow raised. The look on her face seemed to say, *You heard me. I'm not repeating myself.*

"But . . . why would you want my help?" he asked. "Surely you'd have no problem planning it on your own. And you've got the royal event planners helping you out. Father too."

"That is true." Julianna lifted Lucie up and off of her lap. "But I thought it would be nice for you and I to work on it together. Unless, of course, you don't want to?"

It wasn't that he didn't want to. It was only that Jared had never really been involved in something like this before. He was the spare heir; he wasn't required to take much of an interest in the preparations of important events such as the Tournament. All he had to do was be present when it was underway, smile and make polite conversation (and try not to get caught when he and some noble's son decided to sneak off together).

And Julianna was a monster of a perfectionist. He couldn't imagine them planning something like this without butting heads at least once or twice.

But then he thought of Will, thought of kissing Will in that tent. Of Will kissing Elijah the very next morning, and the hurt burned hotter.

Julianna was right. He needed a distraction, something that would take his mind off of Will and his wounded heart. And what better distraction than helping to prepare for one of the most highly anticipated events in all of Aloseria?

In his head, he tucked away all thoughts of Will, like one might tuck away an unwanted letter into the bottom drawer of a desk, out of sight and soon to be forgotten.

"All right," he said at last. "Let's plan a Tournament."

21

Nativitas Day arrived in what felt like the blink of an eye for Arabelle. She had been up since early that morning, helping Amara to prepare for lunch.

While Arabelle would have liked nothing better than to stay in bed for half the day, wrapped up in her bedsheets, she instead found herself dressed in one of her best dresses—white with a blue lace trim and a matching jacket—that Amara had asked her to wear because it matched the white coats her brothers were wearing.

She was now seated at the dining room table between Jared and Amias. Sitting opposite her was Julianna, and beside Julianna was Callum. Further down, Amara and Aunt Charlotte sat across from each other while her father and Uncle Jonathan sat at opposite ends of the table.

The feast was laid out before them and consisted of all the traditional Nativitas foods; a whole roast duck on a silver platter, glistening with butter sauce and sprinkled with herbs. Creamy mashed potatoes, green beans, corn cobs and carrots and crackling pork.

"The food is delicious, Amara," Charlotte announced.

"Thank you, Charlotte," said Arabelle's step-mother serenely while she tried to coax her youngest son into eating his beans. Amara was dressed in a vermillion gown that complimented her dark skin exquisitely. Her black hair was pulled up into a braided knot above her head and she wore a thick gold necklace around her neck, her wedding gem resting against the hollow between her collarbones.

"So how have you been, Arabelle?" Uncle Jonathan asked her as he set his wine goblet down. "I hope you've recovered well after the ordeal in Windfell?"

"I've been well, thank you," she replied. It had been almost a week since returning from Windfell, but she felt as if she would need another month to fully recover from everything that had transpired there. Not that she would admit that aloud.

"Well, that's good to hear. I'm sorry I couldn't come and pay you a visit sooner, but my duties as King have gotten even busier as of late. What with the Tournament coming up soon."

Arabelle was halfway into lifting a spoonful of potatoes to her mouth when she paused. "The Tournament? That's happening this year?" She had completely forgotten about it.

"Of course it's happening this year, Arabelle," Callum said to her in that know-it-all tone that grated on her nerves. "The

Tournament comes around every six years and this year is six years since the last."

"Exactly, Arabelle," Jared teased. "How could you forget?"

"Try not to stress yourself out too much, Father," said Julianna. Her dangling emerald earrings swayed with the turn of her head. "After all, you'll have Jared and I to help you with the preparations this year."

"Father wants to give us a shot at being more hands on with our royal duties," Jared explained when Arabelle gave him a questioning look. "Organising everything for the Tournament in September is a good opportunity, apparently."

"When you're Queen," Jonathan was saying to Julianna with a wry smile. "You'll see that even having others around to help you will do little to keep you from stressing."

Arabelle was just about to ask more questions about the Tournament, when her father rose from his seat, clearing his throat to garner their attention.

"There are a couple of things I would like to announce," Victor Aloria began. "But first, I'd like to start by saying happy Nativitas, everyone." He raised his glass in a toast and they all echoed the gesture—except for Amias, who was being grouchy about not being able to bring his kitten to the table.

"I'd also like to let you all know that Arabelle has decided to join the Crown Guard and she will begin her training next year."

There was a small chorus of, "Well done," and, "Congratulations, Arabelle," and "How exciting," that went around the table. Jared even bumped his shoulder against hers with a grin and pride bubbled in Arabelle's chest.

She hadn't expected her father to make an announcement like this in front of everyone. However, she couldn't deny that she was more than pleased that he had. Clearly, he was proud of her.

Her father was *proud of her*.

Arabelle couldn't help but sneak a quick glance at Amara and found that she was busy wiping gravy from Amias's mouth with a napkin and didn't appear to be showing Arabelle any sort of recognition at all.

Arabelle tried to quell the pang of disappointment.

"I'm sure Arabelle will make a fine addition to the Crown Guard," said Jonathan with a wink in her direction.

"Thank you, Jonathan. I expect nothing but great things from her," said Victor. "And last but not least, I am pleased to announce that there will be a marriage. Between Arabelle and Alistair Hargrade."

Arabelle's good mood vanished, like a candle being blown out.

She barely heard the delighted gasp leave Julianna's mouth. Nor the congratulations from her aunt and uncle. She barely paid attention to the uncertain look Jared was giving her or the indecipherable one from Amara.

No. *No.* Her father hadn't even spoken anything more about it with her. The last time they had talked about it, she'd told him she *didn't* want to marry Alistair. She'd thought that, since he hadn't brought the subject up again, he had actually *listened* to her and decided not to go ahead with the marriage arrangement.

But here he was, announcing it to their entire family.

Without even having asked her about it first.

She felt sick.

"What?"

She mustn't have sounded like an excited, soon-to-be-bride— no, she *knew* that she didn't sound excited. Not in the slightest— because everyone, even Callum and Amias, turned surprised looks at her.

Well, everyone except Amara. She was watching her step-daughter with something like curiosity. Or was that wariness?

A slight furrow appeared between her father's brows as he took his seat again. "You heard what I said, Arabelle," he said calmly. By the look on his face, she could tell her father knew she wasn't pleased by this development, but he expected her not to kick up a fuss about it.

"But—What about my Crown Guard training?" She asked. "Shouldn't I be more focused on that rather than a wedding?"

"There's no reason why you can't be married and pursue a career as a Crown Guard." The furrow between Victor's eyebrows was deepening, and Arabelle knew that wasn't a good sign.

"But I—" *I thought you'd actually listened to me the last time we talked about this. I thought you finally understood that I don't want an arranged marriage. I don't want to get married yet and certainly not to someone I can't stand. I won't go through with this! I won't!* But all she ended up saying was, "I can't marry Alistair."

Her father's face hardened even further. "And why not? I thought we'd been over this already?"

So did I. There were so many things she wanted to say in that moment, but she knew that they were all more likely to make this situation worse, not better.

Thinking fast, she said the first thing that came to mind. The only thing that she could think of that might help her out of this predicament. "Because I'm already walking out with someone."

A stunned silence surrounded the table. Julianna had a wide-eyed expression on her face, as if she were witnessing a dramatic play. Even Callum and Amias were beginning to look interested in what was going on around them.

For a moment, Victor looked surprised. The furrow disappearing as his brow lifted a fraction or two—before immediately lowering again. "Who are you walking out with?" He demanded.

Who indeed? Once again forced to think on her feet, Arabelle blurted out the first name that came to her. "Derek."

Beside her, Jared made a half cough, half choking sound. Charlotte's mouth formed a surprised 'o' shape. Amara looked as indifferent as ever, but her father looked thunderous. For half a second, she thought he was about to storm out of the house to hunt Derek down.

Excellent work, said a dry voice in her head. *Tell your father you can't marry the man he picked out for you because you're courting one he isn't particularly fond of.*

"You're walking out with Derek Draco?" her father said, his tone perhaps a notch higher than it was before. "When did this happen?"

"In Windfell," explained Arabelle, thankful beyond measure that her voice remained steady. "It's a fairly recent development. Which is why we didn't say anything sooner. With everything that happened while we were there, we wanted to take some time to ourselves before we announced anything."

She was a bit surprised with herself at how smoothly the lie fell from her lips. It was as if she had rehearsed it and not simply made it up on the spot.

Victor's scowl deepened. "He should have come to me straight away if he had intentions of courting you."

"I know, I'm sorry, Da. I was the one who told him not to say anything for now." For good measure, she added, "But he wanted to tell you straight away."

Still, her father didn't look at all pleased and she worried that he might tell her she was to marry Alistair Hargrade regardless of who she was (supposedly) courting.

Before her father could say anything else, Amara spoke up. "Well, I think that is wonderful news and I'm very happy for you, Arabelle."

Arabelle stared at her step-mother, speechless. She hadn't expected Amara to make any comment about this, and certainly not to say that she was *happy for her.*

"I agree," said Jonathan. "Derek's a fine young man."

"He's a sweet boy," added Charlotte. "Why he and Jared have been thick as thieves for so long, he practically feels like a second son!" She smiled brightly at Arabelle. "I'm delighted to hear about this match."

Arabelle managed a smile that she could only hope came off as more shy than tremulous.

"He's young," Amara began saying. "So, of course, they'd have to wait at least two more years before they could marry. But I believe you told me that your parents began courting when they were not much younger. Isn't that right, Victor?"

Almost a little reluctantly, Arabelle's father nodded. "That's right."

"And they always said that the wait to marry only made them that much more eager to spend the rest of their lives with each other," Charlotte said with a wistful smile.

"How romantic," Amias sighed with a dreamy smile.

Arabelle stared. *What is happening?*

"I think it sounds like a wonderful match. Don't you think so, dear?" Amara asked Victor.

They were all waiting with bated breath for Victor's response, but none more so than Arabelle.

Under the table, she gripped the material of her skirt so tightly it was in danger of being torn by her fingernails. Her father had to agree to this, didn't he? It wouldn't be considered acceptable to go through with this arranged marriage if Arabelle was already seeing someone. Surely he wouldn't force her to go along with it now and certainly not in front of Uncle Jonathan and Aunt Charlotte, the King and Queen. Still, there was a whisper of doubt in the back of her mind.

That doubt turned to fear as Victor turned his hard, brown-eyed gaze on her. "I want you to bring Derek over tonight and he's going to ask Amara and I properly for the right to court you."

A wave of relief washed over Arabelle, so strong she nearly sagged under the weight of it. She broke out into a broad smile. "Yes, of course. Thank you, Da."

Victor made a rumbling noise of satisfaction before he returned to his meal. And just like that, their Nativitas feast resumed.

As Arabelle returned to cutting into her roast chicken, she was torn between feeling relief—she wouldn't be pushed into marrying Alistair now!—and dread. What had she just gotten herself into? She'd just announced to her entire family that she was walking out with Derek when they most certainly weren't. She was supposed to bring him over tonight to stand in front of her parents and state his intentions to be with her romantically.

She was going to have to tell him. She was going to have to go to Derek and convince him to go along with this mad charade of hers and, oh, how mortifying it would be. But she had to do it. If she didn't, she would end up having to marry Alistair Hargrade instead. She couldn't—*wouldn't*—marry him.

"So," said Jared. His voice was low, but he startled her enough that she nearly clattered her cutlery against her plate. "You and Derek? That's . . . unexpected."

I'll say, she nearly answered. She hated to lie to Jared like this, especially since it did involve his best friend, but she certainly couldn't tell him the truth, right here and right now.

"Sorry," she said. "Like I said, it just happened while we were in Windfell. You're not upset, are you?"

"Of course not," Jared said with a smile on his face that looked more than a little forced. "I'm happy for you. For both of you. I was just . . . surprised, is all."

Arabelle got the feeling that Jared wasn't being entirely truthful, either. As he returned to the food on his plate, Arabelle stole side-long glances at her cousin. There was an unusually cheerless set to his features. His gaze was listless as he pushed the remains of pork and potato around his plate with his fork. There were the faintest traces of dark rings beneath his eyes.

How long has he been like this? Arabelle wondered. Since returning from Windfell, she hadn't had much of a chance to catch up with Jared, but she'd heard that he had also been sent on an assignment. Something to do with the escaped prisoners at Black Rock. She hadn't heard any of the details yet, though.

Did something happen on the assignment to make him look so dreary?

Looking away from Jared, she chanced a glance at her father to find that he was already looking back at her.

And there was something in the hard lines of Victor Aloria's face. Something that looked an awful lot like suspicion.

Derek sat on the roof outside of his bedroom window, with one of his old and tattered—but still warm—coats draped over his shoulders and a bottle of ginger beer in the hand that wasn't in a sling.

It was one of those rare winter days where the cold had lost some of its bite, which meant being outside was tolerable. Still, tiny flakes of snow drifted down lazily from the grey clouds.

All over the city were the sounds of people celebrating Nativitas with their families. Derek could hear distant voices and laughter on the air. In one of the houses in front of him, he could see a group of children playing in the backyard, crying out with delight as they ran around, throwing clumps of snow at each other.

Derek almost envied their carefree happiness.

He'd retreated up here after what had been a rather strained Nativitas lunch.

Admittedly, things had been strained in their household since Aurelia Blackwood had started living under their roof.

Aurelia Blackwood. His mother's sister. His *aunt*.

He had an aunt.

After all these years of believing he had no family left, to now know that he had an aunt, well, it was still taking some time for Derek to wrap his head around.

He wasn't sure if he'd ever entertained the idea of meeting some long-lost relative before, but if he had, he would have imagined that it'd be a joyful occasion. That he would have been thrilled to meet someone who shared his blood. To know that he wasn't alone.

Instead, all he felt was . . . angry.

The day he had arrived home from Windfell, Darus had left him and Aurelia alone to talk.

She'd started by telling him who she was, that she had been the Princess Aurelia, eldest daughter of the Fair Lady and her consort and sister to Princess Erianna. Derek's mother.

"The last time I ever saw Erianna in person was the day she was made an outcast," Aurelia had explained, sitting in the chair across from him. "It had just been discovered that she was carrying the child of a human. That she was carrying you. I begged her not to go through with the pregnancy, but she would not hear it. She was adamant that she would have you and so she chose to live the life of an outcast. Over the years, I checked in on Erianna from time to time with my Scrying Glass. I knew she married her human lover, and that they had built a life in Windfell. Then one day the Glass stopped showing her to me and that is when I learned Erianna had . . . that she was gone."

"So . . . you knew about me all this time?" Derek said once Aurelia had finished her story—which ended with her trying to use Milrath's amulet to bring back his mother. "When we met in Florinstone, you knew who I was, didn't you?"

"I did."

"Why didn't you say anything?" He demanded. "Or more importantly, why didn't you ever try to come find me before? You knew about me since before I was even born and you knew about what happened to my parents. So why—how come you never came for me? Did you even know what happened to me after my parents died?"

"No," Aurelia admitted.

"Why not? Didn't you care about m—about what happened to your sister's son?"

Aurelia looked him straight in the eye and answered, "I did not."

Derek certainly hadn't expected the answer to hurt as much as it did. For it to feel like a punch to the gut. "So if you didn't give a shit about me back then, what's changed now? Why are you here?"

"I've realised that my sister would have wanted me here protecting you."

Derek laughed, which seemed to catch Aurelia by surprise. "Oh, you've *just* realised that, have you?" he said, pushing himself up from the couch. "Well, I'm sorry to tell you, but you're a little too late for that."

He'd turned on his heel and left the lounge as fast as he could, ignoring Aurelia calling out to him.

Derek hadn't had a proper conversation with Aurelia since then, and quite frankly, he didn't want to. She'd made it quite clear that she didn't care about him beyond some sense of responsibility she felt because of his mother.

Some sense of responsibility, Derek thought bitterly, glaring down at the ginger beer bottle in his hand. She wanted to look out for him *now*? Why hadn't she thought to do that nine years ago?

When he was a child whose parents had just died. When he was left all alone with no one to turn to except for Goldridge. When Goldridge had—

Before he could continue that line of thought, Derek took another drink from the bottle. The ginger beer went down his throat strong and sweet.

Not only did he have Aurelia Blackwood to deal with but also the knowledge that his parents' killer had made himself known when Darus and Jared had encountered him on their own assignment. Now Derek knew for certain he was still out there.

Something landed on the roof not far from him and Derek looked over to see that it was was Cora, Aurelia's raven Familiar.

The raven cocked her head from side to side, regarding him with her keen eyes. Derek scowled at her. "Leave me alone," he said. Likely, Cora was up here because Aurelia had sent her to keep an eye on him.

Cora didn't budge.

"I'll throw snow at you."

Still, she didn't move.

So Derek picked up a handful of the snow that coated the roof tiles and tossed it at the bird.

Cora hopped back, shaking the snow off her feathers with an indignant squawk.

"I warned you."

Apparently in no mood to tolerate having snow thrown at her, Cora stretched her wings and flew off.

Barely a moment later, Derek's bedroom window was pushed open and a familiar blonde head poked itself out.

"Arabelle?"

"Hello, Derek." She looked as if she had just come from a party—which, he supposed, she would have. It was Nativitas after all—With her hair pinned back in a simple bun and her lips painted a dusky pink. Tiny flakes of snow were already getting caught in her hair.

Just looking at her made him feel like a fist had reached inside of his chest to squeeze at his heart.

"What are you doing here?" He asked.

A worried look crossed Arabelle's face. "Could you come inside, please? I . . . I have something I need to tell you."

"You . . . told your family that we're *walking out*?"

They were in Derek's room now. He was seated on his desk chair while Arabelle paced back and forth in front of him, which she had been doing for a while now.

"Yes."

"And your father wants me to come to your house tonight and state my intentions for *walking out* with you?"

"That's right."

"But we're not walking out!"

"I know!" she said, a guilty edge to her voice. "I'm sorry, I panicked!" She halted her pacing and cast a hesitant look in his direction. "You're not—are you upset?"

Derek considered this for a moment. "I'm not upset. I'm just . . . surprised."

Arabelle nodded and started fiddling with the sleeve of her white jacket. "That's understandable." She sounded almost relieved.

They were both quiet for some time.

"So what happens now?" Derek asked. "Do you—we're not actually going to start walking out now, are we?"

He'd meant it half jokingly, which was why Derek was more than a little bit surprised when Arabelle replied, "We are."

"What?"

Arabelle turned to face him, her expression beseeching. "I know this is going to sound a bit . . . crazy, but I was thinking if you and I could just *pretend* to be . . . together. Just for a little while."

"A fake courtship?" Derek cocked an eyebrow.

"Well, I can't exactly go back and tell my parents that I made it all up. My da will just make me marry Alistair anyway, and I just—I don't want to be married. I'm not ready. Not yet."

She sounded so miserable that for a moment, Derek actually contemplated getting up and crossing the space between them to hold her.

Then he thought about leaving to find Victor Aloria and give him an earful for being the one to put that miserable look on Arabelle's face.

Obviously, he did neither.

Instead, he said, "Can't you try talking to your father? Make him understand that marriage isn't something that you want right now?"

"I've already tried telling him that and he just went ahead and arranged the marriage, anyway." She sat herself down heavily on the edge of his bed. Finn—who was curled up on the blankets—raised his head from his paws and squinted at Arabelle with sleepy eyes. "My da, he's—he's so stubborn. When he gets it into his mind that something is right, there's no dissuading him. He can be absolutely impossible to talk to sometimes. Please, Derek," she said. "I know this is a lot to ask, but could you please pretend to walk out with me? At least until I've figured out a way to make sure my da won't try to marry me off again?"

Derek opened and closed his mouth, unsure of what to say. The idea of pretending to court Arabelle filled him with apprehension. He wondered if it had something to do with how he was fairly certain he was beginning to fall for her?

When he didn't say anything, Arabelle got up from the bed and came to kneel in front of him. She looked up at him with pleading eyes. "It'll just be for a little while, I promise," said Arabelle. "And it'll all be pretend. We won't actually end up getting engaged and I—I know you don't feel that way about me. That we don't feel that way about each other, so it's fine, right?"

We don't feel that way about each other. Those words made something inside of him sink. Was that why Arabelle had chosen him for this scheme? Because she thought that since they didn't care about each other romantically, that made him the perfect pretend partner?

He knew it was nothing to feel hurt by, but he couldn't help feeling a twinge of it.

He nearly told her no, but when Derek looked at her kneeling in front of him, her white dress belled out around her and the way she looked up at him with imploring eyes, he felt his refusal melt away.

In the end, Arabelle was still his friend, regardless of how she did or did not feel about him, and he wanted to help her. He didn't want to see her forced into a marriage she wasn't happy with. And if he was being honest with himself, Derek did have a more selfish reason in mind. And that was that the thought of seeing Arabelle married off to someone else—especially someone like Alistair Hargrade—made him feel much more than a little jealous.

By the Goddess. I really am falling for her, aren't I?

"All right." With his mind made up, Derek took Arabelle's hand in his, holding it between them like any gentleman would do to his sweetheart. Not taking his eyes off of hers, he said, "Arabelle Aloria, will you walk out with me?"

EPILOGUE

The wind was unforgiving so high up on the mountains, where once an old fort had stood, but now there was only rubble.

"I don't know what they're hoping we'll find here," said one of the two Guardians that patrolled the wreckage.

"Something suspicious probably," said his companion.

The other Guardian snorted derisively. "We've been over this whole place at least twice now and the only thing we've found is rubble and more rubble."

"Don't forget that broken chair leg we found."

"This is just because that Darus Flynn kicked up a fuss about it. The King probably only pays attention to him because his kid and the Prince are friends."

"I don't doubt that."

Their chuckling came to a halt when they heard movement from behind.

Before either of them could do much more than turn around, there was a flash of red and both of the Guardians had their heads severed from their bodies.

The Guardians fell and Draken stood above the gruesome scene, the curved blade of his scythe dripping with the same blood that was creating such a mess at his feet. He took a moment to make sure there were no others nearby he had to dispatch before he allowed his scythe to fall from his grip. It vanished into thin air before it could touch the ground.

Stepping around the decapitated bodies, Draken picked his way across the terrain of snow and rubble, the ruins of what had been his hideout for the past few years. He also supposed that—in a way—it had also been his home. It had been a place where he ate and slept, after all. But Draken wasn't sure he had ever really thought of it as home. He certainly didn't feel any sort of sadness one might usually feel if they were walking amongst the destroyed remains of their home. Instead, all he felt was a mild irritation that this place that had served him well over the years was no more.

"Where is it?" demanded Asmydionn's voice in his head.

"It's here," he answered back.

"If you lost the mirror because of that stunt you pulled—"

"I didn't lose it. I am not that careless."

The daemon king didn't say anything more and Draken continued searching through the wreckage of the fort to where he believed the remains of his study might be. When he came across what was unmistakably one of the brass, bear-shaped knobs that belonged to the drawers of one of the desks in the study, he slowly waved a hand through the air in front of him, as if he were wiping away dirt and grime from a window pane.

The air before him seemed to pull back, like a cloth being pulled from a grand display, to reveal the furnishings of the study, still standing and completely untouched by the surrounding wreckage. Even the snow had left them untouched.

There were the two desks, still standing across from each other. The bookcases, and, most importantly, the mirror. Still covered with its velvet cloth.

Stepping forward, he pulled the covering away from the mirror to find that it was still perfectly intact—apart from the one missing shard, of course.

"See?" Draken said with more than a touch of smugness. "It's still here and with not a scratch on it."

He was answered only with silence. Not that he had really expected much else, Asmydionn wasn't one for smugness in others. Draken imagined that had they not been separated by realms, Asmydionn might have punished him for his cheek just now.

Having confirmed that the mirror was still there, Draken turned his attention to the rest of his belongings that still remained. Specifically, the framed portrait that stood on the desk behind him.

This time, Draken felt a flood of relief when he saw it. As he picked it up and examined the pencil sketch of the round-faced, dark-haired boy and the fair-haired woman, he thought to himself that this would have been the one thing he would have been most distraught about losing—perhaps even more so than the mirror.

He felt an ache in his chest as he gazed at faces in the portrait. An ache that he always felt whenever he looked at it. An ache that had not diminished even after all these years.

"Soon, your revenge will be at hand," crooned Asmydionn's voice in his head.

"Yes," Draken murmured, still gazing at the portrait. He looked up and over at the view that this mountain overlooked, as he had done many times before from the fort's windows.

He thought about what lay beyond the mountains ahead. About the many towns and the people who were all enjoying these peaceful times, in blissful ignorance of the cost of this peace. He thought of Ember, how it was the worst of all. How it was rife with the ghosts and sins of the past.

I'm going to burn it all down, thought Draken with vicious certainty. *Everything that you tried so hard to build, Aryanna. I'm going to tear it all down and watch it burn with a smile.*

He looked back at the faces of the woman and the child.

At the faces of his wife and son.

For you

Acknowledgements

Publishing a book is an incredibly nerve-wracking venture, especially when it's your first book. But publishing your second book? That comes with a special type of nervousness. Especially when it's the next book in a series and you're terrified that it'll be a letdown compared to the first. Thankfully, I've been able to surround myself with people who have assured me that is not the case with this one, which means a big thanks is in order.

To MLStevens, Talli, Julian, Holly, and Jade, thank you for taking the time to beta-read this for me. Your encouragement and critique were invaluable and this book wouldn't be what it is today without it.

Thank you to all of my online writing buddies, especially those of you over at Queer Lodgings. Stay unhinged.

Thank you, Emily, once again for coming through with a fantastic cover design.

About the author

Rita A. Rubin is an Australian born author who currently resides in Melbourne and is living her best introvert life. When not writing, Rita can be found with her nose in a book, or PS4 console in her hands or making up ballads to sing to her dog and cat.
Follow Rita on Twitter and Instagram @ritarubin9.

www.ingramcontent.com/pod-product-compliance
Lightning Source LLC
Chambersburg PA
CBHW030512120726
47904CB00005B/1430